The
Garden
Next Door

ALSO BY JOSÉ DONOSO

The
Garden
Next Door

JOSÉ DONOSO

Translated by Hardie St. Martin

Grove Press
New York

Published by Grove Press
A division of Grove Press, Inc.
841 Broadway
New York, NY 10003-4793

Published in Canada by General Publishing Company, Inc.

Originally published in Spain by Seix Barral, S.A., Barcelona,
under the title *El jardín de al lado*

"Kooks" by David Bowie copyright © 1971 by Fleur Music/Tintoretto Music/
Moth Music. Rights for Fleur Music and Tintoretto Music controlled
and administered by Screen Gems–EMI Music, Inc. All rights reserved.
International copyright secured. Used by permission.

"East Coker" from *Four Quartets* by T. S. Eliot copyright © 1968 by
Harcourt Brace Jovanovich, Inc. Reprinted by permission of the publisher.

Library of Congress Cataloging-in-Publication Data

Donoso, José, 1924–
[Jardín de al lado. English]
The garden next door / José Donoso : translated by
Hardie St. Martin.—1st English language ed.
p.   cm.
Translation of : El jardín de al lado.
ISBN 0-8021-1238-2
I. Title.
PQ8097.D617J3713   1992
863—dc20   91-41842
                                                CIP

Manufactured in the United States of America

Designed by Irving Perkins Associates

Printed on acid-free paper

First English-language Edition 1992

1   3   5   7   9   10   8   6   4   2

For Mauricio Wacquez

". . . un instant encore, regardons
ensemble les rives familières . . ."

The
Garden
Next Door

1

SOMETIMES IT PAYS to have rich friends. I don't mean to advocate, à la F. Scott Fitzgerald, an irrational and exclusive addiction to such relationships. But sometimes the friend has always been a friend: from early childhood in school, from our teenage years spent at the beach or in the country, when the world was a Garden of Eden because it had not yet presented us with the tyrannical alternative of perhaps being loved and famous. It is therefore natural—given that over time the successful friend has known how to maintain a relationship on equal terms with someone like me, whose circumstances are so different from his—that, upon returning home at the end of a nerve-racking evening at La Cala, I would be very happy to hear Pancho Salvatierra's voice calling me from Madrid to ask me something quite normal:

"Listen, Julito, what are your plans for the summer?"

As if Gloria and I were in that class of Latin Americans who can allow themselves the luxury of making "plans." We had never doubted that we were condemned to spend our seventh European summer trapped in the hell of Sitges. It's true that from time to time one runs into deathly-pale Chileans and Argentines, fresh arrivals from Norway or Germany, who swear that in this dying Europe, Sitges is Paradise itself: where they come from no one ever even gets a glimpse at the sun, fruit tastes like sugarcane pulp, and no one gives a damn about what happens to his neighbor.

But . . . what about here? June had just arrived. Even after cognac and Valium, Gloria and I would start bickering about every little thing, in preparation for the quarrels that would grow stormier in July and August, filling us with enough resentment to last the whole year. We preferred to stick to our minuscule apartment so as not to compound the deterioration of our homelife by also becoming embroiled in the general deterioration around us: the impotence as prices rose and quality slipped; the futility of trying to pry a smile from the cashier at the greengrocer's, that old Catalan bitch; the beaches jam-packed with bodies; the vulgarity in several languages assaulting one's ears in the shops, at the tobacconist, and at newsstands that were always out of newspapers; the entire town reeking of potatoes fried in the same oil used to fry a thousand portions; and the Belgians, Germans, and Frenchmen, stuporous from a whole day lying in the sand, settling toward evening at noisy sidewalk cafés, eyes vacant, silent, looking as if they'd been squeezed into their reddened skins, shiny with foul-smelling sun cream. They were all staking their claim to use the sun and pollute the sea because they had paid for it with good foreign money.

The day Pancho Salvatierra called, I noticed that the first traces of summer decay had made their appearance in our home. The glass windows facing the terrace roof demanded cleaning; the geraniums were wilting under layers of dust; Gloria had put on a washed-out muumuu over a bikini whose components, leftovers of bikinis from other summers, didn't match—yes, no matter what she said, she had put on weight. But for once I was careful to keep this observation to myself. In view of all this, I slept a drugged, drawn-out siesta to pass the time till evening without having to face the usual dilemma at the typewriter: either the documentary-novel, rejected once before by the formidable Núria Monclús, that I was sure I could rework into a masterpiece superior to the consumerist literature—so popular these days—of false deities like García Márquez, Marcelo Chiriboga, and Carlos Fuentes, or the boring translation of *Middlemarch* I was collaborating on with Gloria, a task that seemed endless but would bring in an assured, if modest, sum.

Luckily I was spared waking up to this decision by the loud buzz of the doorbell. It was Cacho Moyano, inviting us to an Argentine barbecue—with guitar-playing—at La Cala, his run-down place just outside town. He would come by to pick us up in half an hour. I knew that the barbecue itself would be, as usual, the only reprieve from the tedium of the party, but I accepted immediately. As soon as our good savior had left, I told Gloria, "At least this means you won't have to cook."

I thought that I'd be able to get away from the others and chat with Carlos Minelbaum, which I always enjoyed. But things took another turn at the party, and I didn't get the chance—and it was poor Gloria who finally had to prepare the legendary Argentine barbecue, because the Zamora brothers, cult specialists of this sacrificial rite, showed up very late, with two well-stacked Norwegian girls who happened to pick them up.

Then when we were home again, I heard at the other end

of the telephone line—as if it were coming from another
galaxy only six hundred kilometers away—the tinkle of ice
cubes in Pancho Salvatierra's gin and tonic, the perfect
summer drink, a fine echo of cut crystal that, for the
moment at least, soothed something in me that was much
more oppressive than the mere suffocation of what prom-
ised to be an endless series of sultry nights in Sitges.

What did Gloria and I have lined up for this summer?

Pancho has a knack for asking such a thing without
wounding one's pride. He made me feel as if I were a
cosmopolite who might answer that I was going off to the
villa I'd just rented on the Emerald Coast, let's say, or that
Gloria and I had decided to spend the summer—a traveler's
tip Gloria had read in a popular women's magazine at the
beauty parlor where she goes to dye her hair—*dans le grand
vent* of a cold beach on the Île de Ré (this was reportedly
back in fashion), or on the Normandy coast, like Proust
. . . a mirage of figures swathed in white tulle, as in Lar-
tigue's photographs. For the sun is the complexion's worst
enemy, and the Mediterranean in summer is an invention
of titled German pederasts and second-class British novelists, and besides being a kind of awful soup of Nivea cream
and prophylactics, it had now lost all its glamour. Pancho
understands this line of thinking and would have relished
these incidental details, but I didn't pass them on to him;
they form a part of the atmosphere in which his talent—
unquestionable, amazing, infuriating—thrives and is pro-
ductive, in a way that's difficult to explain but is borne out
by each of his shows at the Claude Bernard Gallery in
London, Paris, Zurich, or New York, and by every spectacular commission he takes on. These always make the
front page and draw from Adriazola a vitriolic torrent of
envy that he tries to pass off as the moral censure of "a
political and ethical attitude unacceptable in an artist, who

must be, first and foremost, a voice outraged by the injustices committed against our suffering people."

On the other hand, in Pancho's world things are insubstantial, gratuitous: they're free of history, of causes, of a future, and fortunes can be unexpected as well as ephemeral. He would have shown no surprise if a writer of less than average success, and over fifty, like me, announced that he intended to spend the summer on a cruise around the Aegean islands in his own yacht. For him it would have been gauche to ask me to explain or justify my hypothetical cruise, for in his world it was essential to accept sudden rises or falls in economic and social fortunes without asking questions.

Yes, when I talk to Pancho I feel affluent, successful, like an F. Scott Fitzgerald in starched white ducks, free from the tyranny of my superego, the warm beer in my paper cup transformed into a magical gin and tonic in cut crystal—I even feel young and paunchless. And Gloria, starved for the nice things I don't say to her often enough, feels beautiful and desirable; and we must admit that Pancho's compliments are justified in her case, because he knows she won't be deceived by the flowery paper garlands he throws at his less wary girlfriends. This knack of his, this extraordinary social grace must be, I suppose, one of the many charming traits people acquire with success, because at one time Pancho lacked it. For me it was easy to answer his ingenuous question about our summer vacation with equal simplicity:

"Nothing. We don't have a peseta to our name."

"What about your novel?"

"Rejected. A fiasco."

"Sons of bitches!"

"Daughter of a bitch, you mean."

"Why daughter?"

"I'll tell you later."

Very sensitive to the undertones in the utterances of his friends, Pancho knew that at this moment of shattered nerves, Gloria and I would not turn down anything that could take us away from Sitges, the hated witness of our humiliation. Irresistible and subtle, he started to describe at length the delights of Madrid in summertime, when there wasn't a soul or an automobile around, all the houses were closed down—"the only people left in town are the concierges, who are the genuine, the real Madrid that as a novelist you'll find absorbing" was his touching, knowing comment—and you could even go to the movies without standing in line, and to restaurants without reserving a table.

"And the sales! Tell Gloria about them. Even those highway robbers at Loewe's give everything away! Why should you two stay in Sitges when you can come and spend three months, and maybe more, in my apartment?"

But he admitted that it never cools off at night in Madrid. Still, what did that matter? His whole place was air-conditioned and even had a special humidifier system for his winter garden. He acted as if he were pleading with us to make the sacrifice because we were good friends, to take care of his plants, his pug, Myshkin, and his Siamese, Irina, whose coloring matched the dog's.

"You know my apartment. I'll leave everything open, except my studio—it's such a mess. You can use all the stuff in the pantry, the tea, liquor, preserves, canned goods, all of it; I'll replace everything when I get back, because by then it would all have spoiled. And there's a Fred Astaire–Ginger Rogers series at the Cine-Club, I believe it's over on Onésimo Redondo, I never have time to go. My apartment isn't a bad place to spend three months writing."

As a matter of fact, Pancho Salvatierra's apartment right in the center of Madrid wasn't bad at all. I recalled the small winter garden, an island of fluttering, almost animal, vegetation. I recalled, and it made me feel slightly timid, that the only decoration in the marble-tiled hall was a huge fragment of an Etruscan funerary monument—the heads were gone, alas, but the classic flow of the robes and the tenderness of the man's hand interlocked with the woman's seemed a metaphor of eternal love—illumined by a lamp of Milanese design that looked like some being out of a UFO.

I remembered windows that opened on a grove of chestnuts, lindens, elms—amazing in a Madrid stripped of all its trees. "As if this were Hampstead," Pancho sometimes said. "This apartment costs me my left nut and half of the other, but it's worth it, if only for the snobbish pleasure of watching my neighbor, the Duke of Andía, sweat blood mowing the lawn on which I feast my eyes. You're not going to tell me that having a grandee of Spain as your gardener isn't the height of elegance, are you?"

Our recent history has turned me into a puritan suspicious of any pleasure, and at first I rejected the whole idea. I despised Pancho; I was angry, no doubt jealous; I felt a hatred (worthy of Adriazola) of his frivolity, of his disgraceful indifference to the world, to Chile, of his self-love, his shallowness—all of which was in puzzling and disturbing contrast to the high standards of his art. My sense of humor, almost a trademark of people like me, was lost after the Eleventh.* Why, I asked myself each time I talked to him, each time I saw his apartment or his paintings, why did Pancho have the terrible virtue of making

---

* September 11, 1973, the date of Pinochet's coup d'état against the Allende government. —TRANS.

me face the problem of the relationship between art and ethics, which I had considered solved?

But my anger at Pancho is always short-lived. As a teenager he had been a runt, so skinny that he never had a girlfriend, so awkward no matter how hard he tried, and so nearsighted before he discovered contact lenses. And in those days, so long ago, Pancho lived on an aristocratic street, but at the less elegant end of it, so that he preferred to make a detour through the better end to reach his house.

Poor Pancho! And so I would quickly forget my rage and turn everything into a joke, speaking in a parody of the gallery talk he used.

"Your apartment's nice, Pancho, but it's a little too much on the *fifties* side, too David Hicks, really. . . ."

"Of course it is, but don't tell anyone. In any case, I don't believe anybody in Madrid knows who David Hicks *is*, because Franco was around and everything was either in the Spanish tortured or National Parador style—and no one has any idea of what the *fifties* were. People would think you were talking about a new disco. That's how up-to-date everyone here is. Madrid is nothing but a suburb of Marbella now."

My imagination stirred, I went over that magnificent place in my mind, one object at a time, while Pancho continued singing its praises. He added that Begonia, his *Chinese*, would come in every morning to take care of us.

"So why do you need us there?"

"Houses take on a very strange smell when they're empty all summer. That awful Carlota de Teck made me rent her horrid Belle Époque palace on Corfu for the whole season, if I wanted to go to bed with her. And with her portrait thrown in. The portrait will be my revenge—I'll paint her just like her aunt, Queen Mary. The worst part is that I'll have to put up with her as muse-in-residence.

Otherwise I'd invite the two of you. Don't let me down, Julito, please come to Madrid. Remember whose math you used to copy in high school? You'll be able to rewrite your great novel in peace and dedicate it to 'Francisco de Salvatierra, without whose help this novel would never have been written.' "

Ignoring the aristocratic *de* he'd bestowed on his surname, I exclaimed, "But Pancho, don't you realize that would get you in hot water with Pinochet?"

"Ah, poor old Pinochet, such a good man and yet you people have given him such a bad name. What a pity he's so N.O.C.D., as London debutantes would say. But still, what can you do, you UP* followers were much worse. Why not leave him alone, now that the country's on the way up—not like when your mother had to hoard things—and there's no shortage of anything. The fact is, with all your marches and letters of protest and congresses you people have picked up a masochist syndrome, a vocation for martyrdom: 'You spent more time in prison than I did, but they tortured me more.' And they didn't torture anybody. It's all lies. It's not true, Julio—Chile was a Cuban and Soviet arsenal before the coup. Okay, okay, let it slide, let's not argue like all Chileans about this crap. Besides, after twenty years abroad I have no idea who's who in Chilean politics. Tell me, does Gloria find the Cardinal sexy? No, you don't have to get so flustered, don't shout, Julio, I was only asking because my daughter writes me that in Santiago *nobody* finds him sexy anymore. Stop screaming and see if you can talk Gloria into being an angel and agreeing to come look after the place. Tell her that the first time I lay Carlota de Teck, who everybody in the world—except in Chile, the asshole of the planet—

* Unidad Popular, the leftist coalition that elected Allende. —Trans.

knows is completely frigid, I'll whisper in her ear that she's just like Gloria, the first of so many unrequited loves of my teens, and that's the plain truth. Maybe Carlota will finally have an orgasm and lower the price of her palace. Tell me, does Gloria still have her glorious red wavy hair and her divinely Pre-Raphaelite look? I have to know, because, you know, I don't like to lie, at least not much, in affairs of the heart—people spread everything around and I might end up looking like a fool."

I put my hand over the receiver to ask Gloria—sitting out on our modest terrace, under a naked bulb blurred by a big cloud of insects, her coppery head bent over a book— if she'd like to spend the summer in Pancho Salvatierra's apartment, with air conditioning and a paid *Chinese*. She shrugged without raising her eyes from the book on palmistry she was reading: she was preparing a study on sexism in the occult sciences, a sporadic work that, she claimed, was "getting done," at least in a modest way, and that, strangely enough, she took up with renewed energy whenever her irritation at me, at the whole world, at Pinochet, Adriazola, Sitges, guitar sessions, and Argentine barbecues, spilled over. Her shrug told me that she couldn't have cared less about what we or anybody in the whole world did—obviously there was no salvation, not even evasion, everything and everyone were going to the dogs.

I took advantage of Gloria's indifference—she's usually full of opinions on every subject—to promise Pancho that we'd get to Madrid as soon as we could. I also assured him that for all her fifty-plus years, there were times—such as this very moment, with the pain inscribed on her face in the shadow of the gold dust and the crumbled wings of moths in the bottom of the lamp overhead—when Gloria was the living picture of a Pre-Raphaelite fantasy, and that even if the disastrous state of our bank account kept her away from clearance sales, with her regal bearing and her flair with clothes Gloria wouldn't let him down in front of the elegant neighbors in his building.

"What about Pato?" Pancho asked.

"Just this afternoon they told me he's in Marrakesh," I answered, remembering recent incidents at La Cala. "We won't leave him your address, because I'd just as soon have nothing to do with him till summer's over. I need peace and quiet to rewrite my novel."

Pancho let out a sigh of relief.

"So much the better: *loin des yeux, loin du coeur*. It would piss me off if that little slob came in here and put his filthy hooves on my furniture."

Pancho was beside himself with gratitude for the favor we were doing him. But, calculating as he is, a characteristic that has played no small part in the phenomenon of his success, he suggested: "Don't be foolish, Julio—sublet your apartment in Sitges, without telling your landlord. Prices skyrocket in the summer. Look, I know a gay couple without much money; they make fantastic mirrors after Italian designs, and they're dying to take up nudism this summer. I don't think they've got enough money to get them any farther than Sitges. Would you like me to talk to them? Then Gloria will have something to go spend on sales."

I passed the word on to Gloria, the family's financial whiz. The thought of getting some money out of our depressing apartment, and especially of cheating our hated Catalan landlord, with whom month after month she carried on furious shouting contests that could be heard as far as the Plaza de España in Barcelona, suddenly spurred

Gloria into action; she snatched the receiver away from me
and on the spot arranged our prompt departure to Madrid.

PERHAPS I'M ASCRIBING too much importance to Pancho
Salvatierra—who has little to do with the heart of this
story—and to that lethargic summer in Madrid, where,
nevertheless, everything took place.

Pancho has the infuriating habit of phoning at the worst
hours of night, usually when we've finally managed to fall
asleep. He makes these calls with the apparent intention of
sharing with us—Chileans like him, and therefore superior
beings, since only Chileans understand certain nuances of
the ridiculous—some bit of gossip about the Tecks or
whoever has replaced them at the moment in his personal
Almanach de Gotha. We knew, however, that this was only a
pretext; he really called to tell us that, for one reason or
another, tonight he felt old and alone and like a foreigner in
spite of his twenty successful years in Europe: with whom
except us, since only we knew them, could he talk about
his selfish brother and his vulgar sister-in-law, who were
poisoning his poor parents' old age? Besides, he wanted to
know how we were doing, and we found it touching to
hear him say that he missed us, his life was a mess, he'd
had enough of the Teck sisters, painting was a bunch of
shit, dealers were thieves, art critics didn't know the first
thing about painting, and that in this fucking life the only
thing that mattered were a few—very few, fewer each year,
because as he got older he became more picky—lifelong
friends like us. And even if we didn't see one another often,
it was a comfort knowing that we lived in the same country. Gloria and I felt the same way and would immediately
forgive him for robbing us of our sleep. We would chit-
chat or talk about personal matters for hours at a time, he,

Gloria, and I laughing, arguing, remembering; after a short while our Valium-dulled senses would clear up. And after saying goodbye to Pancho, we'd fall asleep content, happy, our arms around each other sometimes, with no need for more alcohol or tranquilizers.

On this particular night Pancho hadn't awakened us, since because of the incident with Pato's friend we had left La Cala close to eleven o'clock, and when Pancho called we hadn't yet managed to black out the lucidity of our hate.

We had shut the apartment door behind us with the feeling that we were closing the lid of a coffin. In the darkness of our narrow hallway, looking for the light switch, our fingers touched: victims of something like an electric shock, they pulled apart in a split second. Neither of us turned it on, each expecting the other to do it. Gloria seemed to be too close for comfort in the darkness we could have avoided and yet let drag on for a few seconds. I said, "Ugh! You smell of barbecued meat."

Gloria switched the light on. She looked vulnerable, drained. I saw right away that this was one of those dangerous days when—to use family slang inherited from the caretaker of my grandfather's country place—"her mind was all fucked up," and it was best not to rub her the wrong way if either of us was to survive. She preceded me down the long hallway to the rest of the house.

"How do you expect me to smell, when all I've been doing for the past seven years is cook for you and Pato?"

She went into the bathroom and bolted the door. I stood outside, listening: the once-perfect outlines of Ingres's Odalisque—gorgeous full thigh, long, caressable arch of the shoulder, long leg, long neck, and elongated eye beneath the turban around the half-turned head—were being sketched for me (beyond that door but, above all, beyond time) by the familiar rustle of her clothes slipping down the contours of her body. And then I heard her, contemporary, normal, imperfect once again, turn on the shower and step under it.

As usual, Gloria had not missed the chance to throw in my face the first thing she could think of to make me feel guilty—for instance, her answer to my simple observation in the dark hallway. And what if I were to die? I asked myself. What if the papilloma Carlos had removed two days before turned out, after the biopsy, to be something terrible, maybe carcinoma? I rapped softly on the bathroom door. Gloria didn't answer. She was humming in the shower. What was she humming? I listened carefully: *Death and the Maiden*, the last movement, the obvious, the easy one, I thought scornfully. But more important was the fact that Gloria was humming without the least concern that I might die, for no matter how much Carlos reassured me, he didn't have the result of the biopsy yet.

"Open up!" I shouted.

No. It's not true. I didn't shout. And I didn't rap on the door. I just jiggled its handle, murmuring, "Gloria, please . . ."

She went on humming. I recognized the passage where each Schubert instrument goes its own way, each rendering its specific idiom, all of them opposing one another for the moment, a brilliant homage to the central theme. I found it irritating that Gloria should have such a perfect ear, especially with her negligible training. But she was in the habit of singing, humming, or whistling the most difficult pieces with a fidelity that to me, incapable of reproducing the simplest tune, was an insult. What would Gloria have been with more musical training? Many things. Anything. Because she was a mine of natural gifts that had died for lack of structure, dried up under the ground, without enough drive to break through and sprout. And so, spurred by envy of what seemed to me a gift she didn't deserve, I banged on the door, shouting:

"Open up! Do you want me to piss in your philodendron?"

Gloria went on humming as if she couldn't hear. She knew me well enough to judge me incapable of carrying out such a threat. What's more, I was sure that Gloria knew I was not pressed but was up to something else. I yelled:

"Open up! Idiot—is it my fault that you go around with your hair smelling like a kitchen? Damn right you have to cook: you're no longer the little girl of the diplomat who used to ring the buzzer just to have someone bring him cigarettes. We all have to do things we don't like in exile. Dammit, if you don't like to do them, it's your problem, not mine. I didn't force you to come with me. When they let me out I begged you to stay in Chile. During the UP we were already floundering, but you said no, being in exile will bring us together, I'm going with you for the kid's sake, I don't want him to grow up brainwashed like his whole generation, I want something better for Pato, you said, and look at the way your little Oedipus Rex has turned out—a high school dropout who wastes his time over on Dos de Mayo Street smoking pot with whores and queers, he says he's going to be a photographer and he's doing nothing, we have no idea where he gets the money to keep going, we never know where he is, apparently he's in Marrakesh now, that's what Hernán Lagos's son said at La Cala—because of the photographer bit, I suppose, or want to suppose so I won't suppose anything worse. A nice little education we were going to give the kid here in Europe! Brainwash! Look at the way he laughs at us when he says we're like a record stuck at the UP and the Eleventh and don't know how to talk about anything except Allende and the DINA,* pure horseshit, he says, nobody my age gives a damn about that crap. . . . And me unable to re-write my novel. If Pato read it the way I want to rewrite it, he'd understand. Yes, he'd understand everything. Gloria, you came along because you wanted to. You took the hard revolutionary line even if you didn't join any party. Not me. You looked down your nose at me for being active in a moderate party, a soft liberal like your father, you accused me, 'who never did anything in Congress but take siestas in the armchairs.' So why didn't you join an extremist party? Why couldn't you do anything but talk, talk, talk, with a pisco sour always in your hand? Why did you try to push *me* into being an active revolutionary instead of be-coming one yourself? Why do you always have to live a borrowed life? I'm not young anymore, and I'm wiped out, I feel sick; the responsibility of living your life for you is killing me. Oh no: you came away with me because you were afraid to stay there and be dependent on your reac-tionary family, it was less humiliating to depend on me, because you don't respect me, don't deny it, the way you respect them. . . ."

Standing next to the bathroom door, my bladder ready to burst, listening to the shower run, I may or may not have said these things, but I'm inclined to believe I didn't. As they say happens just before death, all these accusations and justifications and protests and complaints, one after the other, flashed through my mind. Maybe I said some of them, not as clearly put but in broken phrases, outcries symptomatic of my anxious state of mind. Anyway, I must have said something, because Gloria stopped humming and turned the shower off. I glued my ear to the door

---

* Dirección de Inteligencia Nacional, the Chilean secret police. —TRANS.

again. Silence: the Odalisque dissolved in water going
down the drain. . . .

"Gloria?"

I listened. Silence. I jiggled the door handle again.

"Where's the Valium?" I asked.

Silence.

"Gloria? You haven't done something . . . silly?"

I thought of my Gillette blades. Of the cabinet full of
deadly medicines.

"No," the revitalized Odalisque answered. "We've had
enough silliness after the way you acted at La Cala! The
Valium is in my pocketbook, on the table in the hall, I
think. One, at least, would do you good."

Of course it would, but I'd had too much cognac at La
Cala, and I was only too familiar with what happened
when you mixed the two: sluggishness that lasted for
weeks, depression that kept me away from my typewriter,
revulsion at the thought of food, irritation at everyone
around me, especially Pato, whose tendency to cry easily,
when he was small, I could never stand.

I headed toward the terrace, but before I reached it the
sight of my typewriter on the dining-room table stopped
me. There it was, just like yesterday, no, like the day before
that, no, like four days ago, surrounded by a mess of
papers. And what if, to defeat Gloria and Pato (who, having spent two summers in Paris at the home of the Lagos
family, now called himself Patrick), to defeat the whole
world, including Núria Monclús, who had given me her
negative verdict during a ten-minute interview right after
getting off a plane from London and just before catching
another to New York, and after I'd sat waiting two hours
in her reception room with my manuscript in my lap, what
if I were to go to my typewriter right now and write and

write and write, day and night, night and day, consuming coffee, amphetamines, wine, cognac, and rework my novel and take it beyond all of Núria Monclús's expectations? "To *see* it," she had said.

"Yes, to see it in the mind's eye . . . there's need for a wider dimension and, especially, for the power to transcend, not just describe or analyze situations and characters, to convert them into metaphor, metaphor valid per se and not for any extraliterary light it may shed on things, not as an account of events the whole world knows, condemns, and, what's more, people are beginning to forget" was the verdict Núria Monclús used to reject my novel.

No wonder more than half of all Spanish-speaking writers, and almost all the editors, were screaming for her head. Where in the world did this Catalan mercenary, who was really only a glorified bookseller, get so much improvised wisdom? On what knowledge, on what specific authority, on what solid theory, did she ground her judgments? What did she know about Barthes, Lukacs, Lacan or Derrida or Kristeva besides prices and the number of copies their books sold? No, it was public knowledge that she was not a critic. There was a story going around—one of a good many rather sinister stories about her—that she had never read a book in her life but kept a stable of highly paid readers, and that she just mouthed their words, words like those she had used to hurt me. Nor was she an editor of the stature of Carlos Barral, for instance, whose dialogue with culture was spontaneous: Núria Monclús's modest role should have been just selling books.

But in my case, seeing me so weak, she had not only exceeded her authority but also vented her cruelty on me. What did she expect me to make my novel into? A hodgepodge of the *nouveau roman*, of deconstruction and intertextuality with pedantic quotes from authors who owed their prestige to the fact that they were obscure but seasoned with superficial "social" or "political commitment," a frivolous bait for buyers? No, no, I was something else: after the Eleventh I had spent six days in jail, and they didn't torture or even interrogate me, but this had become a reserve fund of pain that didn't need metaphor: telling the straight facts was enough. Damn Núria Monclús and the editors and readers and authors she had invented and was promoting. She couldn't play with my integrity, even if her word carried the implicit promise of turning me—she who knew everything and could do anything—into a writer as sensational as Marcelo Chiriboga or García Márquez. I left her office determined that next time I'd slap her face or riddle her with a machine gun.

How sad it was to acknowledge defeat at her hands, to feel humiliated, guilty, and vulnerable because of the hatred and terror she inspired in me. I had to fall back on the stories going around, about her avarice, her indifference, her opportunism, to appease my anger, and this only made me feel even weaker and more humiliated for having come to this with a woman who knew so many angles but who to weak persons like me showed only her bloodthirsty sadism.

More than the rejection itself, more than Núria Monclús's personality, what made me feel so strongly about all this was a subjective reaction of my injured sensibility: in other words, a product of my imagination, since, after all, stories about everyone circulated in the small world of Barcelona, where one could still get a whiff of gunpowder and sulfur left in the air after the Boom had died away. The differences among its members, some but not all of whom were respectable, was still common gossip on evenings around the corpse of the *gauche divine* in the Flash Flash café; Leopoldo Pomés officiated as high priest there, where you could watch the more or less graceful decline of the beautiful people and the talents of five years ago, and where Rosa Regás invented new collections of books everyone fought to be included in. Hard feelings. Pain at being left out. Envy. Yes, all this was the cause of my unthinking anger at Núria Monclús, who was slamming her door in my face.

And yet that wasn't what really had me scared on my way back to Sitges on the crowded train. It was something entirely different: the feeling that time was passing and my great Chilean experience was receding, made worthless as a source of inspiration by the years. I couldn't adapt my country's sufferings to the demands of literary trends sponsored by Núria Monclús or, through her, by someone who was using her, someone higher up, more powerful than she, someone behind the strange mafia of literary fashion I wasn't about to defer to. How was I to keep my six days in prison from fading and disappearing when they were the pencil strokes that traced the main features of my identity? How could I stop something so much a part of me from vanishing into thin air, something all the stronger because it was the first time I had been swept along by the forces of history to form a part of my country's destiny? Those days were my passport to success, the credentials that would rescue me from obscurity.

But of course, seven years had gone by since then, seven years full of less important and more confused experiences, empty personal experiences that had brought me nothing but humiliation: my inability to survive without the protection of the university; Patrick's totally unfounded hatred; my relations with Gloria, sometimes stirred up by resentment or compassion or memories; my permanent sense of failure, of not being *bien dans ma peau*, as Patrick— no, Pato—would say. This whole series of humiliations had overshadowed the experience whose priority I was so desperately trying to keep intact in my notes; it was like watering a plant that was drying up in spite of all my care. My heroic experience was fading, my ties with others who had gone through the same kind of thing were loosening, their heroism was becoming questionable, ridiculous, and my claim to having been part of it seemed more and more suspect. I was even horrified that my early hatred was losing its edge: it was becoming more and more difficult to put together, in some other way, this second version of my novel—more remote in time and place from the original events—so that it wouldn't lack the fire of that first explosion Núria Monclús, that money-grabbing goddess, had not appreciated.

When we had arrived in Sitges seven years before, shortly after the Eleventh, we Chileans were unchallenged heroes, the most admired witnesses of injustice, the leading figures in a vast tragedy that mattered to everyone. But other exiles soon came along, Argentinians of all stripes and colors, with conflicting ideologies, but intelligent and very well prepared for exile: the tragic Uruguayans who fled in large numbers, emptying their country; the Brazilians and the Central Americans, all of them running away like us, some of them persecuted, most going into voluntary exile because back home it was impossible to live and go on being yourself, with the ideas and feelings that made you who you were. But the years went by, and causes and hopes eventually died: you had to forget in order to survive. Our children grew up with identity problems, separated parents, broken homes, reexamined ideologies, general disillusion, dispersion, defeat, in spite of generous efforts that sometimes, for a moment only, stirred to action those who had the power to help us. Our children entered their teens speaking foreign languages or a Spanish that wasn't ours, with a Catalan or a Madrid or a Paris accent, more *banlieue* than Lycée Condorcet. They had been so young when we left Chile. Everything in us and in the world had been so effervescent! But their current lives, poverty and in some cases the trauma of drifting from one country to the next, the terrible distance, the loneliness and time that break up memories, making them scatter and grow remote, and the forgetting or rejection of the mother tongue, all this was a swarm, an aggressive cloud, that now made it hard to see clearly what had driven us here and made us stay, barely able to make ends meet in a place where we had no reason to be. It was all this—yes, let Gloria stop being an idiot and see it once and for all—that had made me give Pato's friend such a rough time.

I walked away from the typewriter and sat down under the clotheslines on the terrace, without turning on the light. From the disco on the ground floor, noise floated up to our fourth-floor walkup, the laughter of those going in, the coarse talk of those leaving: happy tourists, not hard-up Latin American political exiles on the move like us. We often hated our fellow exiles but could not do without their company—Argentine barbecues and *empanadas*, *feijoadas*, corn cakes, *anticuchos*, dishes our nostalgic tastes imitated with products so different from ours, always getting together again to go on probing our resentment. . . . How was I to narrate, from this abyss, an experience that was now so remote?

After turning on the moth-attracting light, Gloria skirted past me and took her place on the other side of the table, her water-darkened hair hanging in heavy ringlets, her book on palmistry open on the glass tabletop: she was set to go to work on her article, not on the translation that would feed us. During the exhilaration of the UP years, when our friends' marriages broke up and they looked around for more temporary passions, our solid union was almost a pathological phenomenon. They didn't know that by nursing the flame, sharing the good or the bitter years, "the pleasures and the frustrations," as people who speak our language say (those who are "on our wavelength," as kids say now), are transformed into another form of passion. Gloria and I knew that you fall in love again, at this point in your life, because you need to renew your personal history by telling it to someone who hasn't heard it before. Without the novel, Gloria would not know my complete history; as the thing that kept our union going, it remained my unresolved promise: to hurdle the obscurity of my position as professor of English at the university and create something beautiful.

"I want you to write another *Hopscotch* for me," Gloria would say, before hope had died in me; she demanded it, laughing, while I stroked the precise line that followed the naked curves of the languid Odalisque.

Every now and then, my name, Julio Méndez, would appear in the newspapers, side by side with the most brilliant names of my generation. I was swamped with local respect for my two novels and my book of short stories, a respect always circumscribed by different versions of the same commentary: "His world is too small and personal, without the great contemporary Latin American novel's ambition for the universal. We expect this very promising writer, though not one of the youngest, to fulfill what we thus far only get a glimpse of in his novels." Writer in a minor key condemned never to cross over to the major key of today's great novel.

Still, I asked myself, wasn't it possible that the impact of Núria Monclús's rejection would make me change keys? Did she know, even vaguely, anyone who had gone through six days in prison and could talk about it? With the

new strength brought out in me by my hatred for that
woman, would my six days now give me the right to make
the leap to success and salvation? In spite of the literary
mafia's superagent, would I see my name up there with the
names of Vargas Llosa, Roa Bastos, Marcelo Chiriboga,
Carlos Fuentes, and Ernesto Sábato? Yes, those were the
glorious days when no one talked about anything else
except *One Hundred Years of Solitude, Aura, Conversation in
the Cathedral*, and *La caja sin secreto*. Where were they now?
the Santiago newspapers asked. Where was Chile's Vargas
Llosa hiding? How was it possible that a country like ours
should have no one to represent it in the disparaged Boom?
And yet I was drunk on the wine of hope! The sting of
envy, the itch for revenge drove me on!

All that, including the brilliance of those names, was far
behind now. Undermined by the trend in literary taste and
the aesthetic demands of younger writers and newer politics, the Boom was definitely a thing of the past, and this
gave me a small measure of pleasure, even of peace: the
names of those whom, ten years before, I and all the
would-be writers of my time had wanted to emulate, to
imitate, to equal or surpass, had faded, and we, the rejected, were the only hope. . . . Why didn't Núria Monclús realize this?

But of course there was no peace. My wife's beautiful
hennaed head—as the breeze picked up, her wet, darkened, heavy hair became lighter, fluffed up and waved,
turning into Pancho's Pre-Raphaelite fantasy—her ugly
muumuu, the old bikini's shoulder straps that didn't cover
the marks of the sun left by this year's bikini, did away
with all illusion of peace; they were an outright insult. As
for the new bikini she saves for special occasions, she had
bought it to provoke me, spending the entire fee for her
first two articles in a feminist magazine without setting

aside a penny to pay the telephone bill, which this month was enormous because of the illness of my mother in Chile.

"I need to give myself a treat," she had said.

Buried in her book on palmistry under the vaguely golden bulb, she was taking notes, underlining, now and then marking a page with a strip of paper. She smiled a little as she did this: yes, she was enjoying herself, something I couldn't stand, because it had been ages since I'd found pleasure in anything, much less my work. Gloria, who had never pretended to be "creative," knew how to sink deep in concentration: she might deny it, she might be so neurotic that it hardly ever took place, but she was happy doing it, and I would often tell her that it was her saving grace, her means of surviving everything. On the other hand, I, mediocre and lazy, was the real creator. Didn't Gloria remember Hernán del Solar's enthusiasm for my book of short stories? Yes, she did. But she also remembered that Alone hadn't even mentioned me in *El Mercurio*. Week after painful week we had waited for his recognition, but it never came. Of course, I hadn't yet spent the six days in hell, and those opened possibilities that, as a middle-class liberal educated in good schools, I hadn't had before. Alone had been perfectly right not to single me out. But now, with my new projects, for good or bad he couldn't help doing it.

"Gloria," I said.

She didn't raise her head.

"Gloria, I can't concentrate on anything. It must be on account of that idiot Adriazola and the kid."

"That's not my problem."

I let a minute go by.

"Would you like to do some translating together?"

"I'm not wasting my time. You go ahead and translate."

I controlled my anger: "How come you're not wasting your time?"

"I'm writing my article."

I slammed her book shut.

"That shitty article of yours! So that I'll have to end up rewriting it when you no longer feel up to it? And you cry and go into a Valium stupor? You'll take up all the time I need to translate or to write my novel."

Seated under the light of the yellow bulb, Gloria stuck a pencil between her lips like a cigarette and looked me up and down.

"Forget about your novel."

"Now what do you mean by that?"

"You don't have the balls to understand an experience that's bigger than you."

I let out a horselaugh. "You're talking just like Adriazola."

"Look, Julio, you and I both know that Adriazola is an idiot, he's mediocre, an opportunist. But we've got to admit that in a sense some of the things he says are true."

"Are you out of your mind?"

"No, you are. It showed at La Cala."

I snatched the book on palmistry from her hands and hurled it over the wall of our terrace into the street. Between the roofs you could just make out a dark, pubic triangle of sea.

"ADRIAZOLA'S PALLAS CX!" I called out, upset at seeing, through La Cala's grilled fence, Adriazola's silver Citroën gleaming among the secondhand Seat 600 and Mini-Morris models whose dusty and tarnished metal could no longer reflect the Mediterranean sunset.

"Don't go picking on him," Gloria warned.

"Why didn't you tell me you had invited him?" I asked Cacho angrily.

"I didn't invite him," he explained, maneuvering the grilled door of his house so that the one intact hinge wouldn't jam and we could sidle inside. "You know Adriazola, Julito—he'll crash anything."

"We wouldn't have come," Gloria said.

"Come on, he's harmless, a windbag nobody gives a shit about. As for me, I got up very early this morning to shop for meat. You'll see, it's going to be a beautiful party."

We knew all about Cacho Moyano's "beautiful parties": couples disappearing, one after the other, into the garden and bedrooms after stuffing themselves on grilled meat and wine, everything ending up as usual in a sleepy haze of joints, alcohol, and *milonga* music stretching out into a night during which there had been nothing to say. Cacho claimed that he was the only one in Sitges who could talk the fierce Catalan owner of the best butcher shop in town into cutting meat properly, and that only his close friends the Zamora brothers, silent and single-minded as assassins, knew the secret art of preparing an authentic Argentine barbecue. Around the white house, with its arcaded porch and its faded paint, standing half-ruined on its rocky peninsula, were the remains of what at one time had tried to be a garden: one pine bent horizontal by the wind and some shrubbery squatting down to avoid it, genistas, the leftovers of a bed of succulent plants, a path only hinted at by the shards of brick lining it—all of it invaded by sand that left its stamp on everything. This was Cacho Moyano's mansion, his dream palace, the private garden of Eden he was so proud of.

But Cacho was a happy man, proud of everything he owned. Four years ago, in the Sandra, a bar on Dos de Mayo Street, he had met a lovely young German who was

traveling in a Mercedes with a ferocious Alsatian dog. She
and Cacho had slept together for a week without pretending to love each other or thinking that this would change
the course of their lives, or even their itineraries: pure
pleasure, without problems, promises, or the question of
faithfulness, as only the younger generations can do it. On
a walk outside Sitges just before she left, the German girl
saw La Cala; she bought it because it looked like it might
be fun and wasn't expensive, the idea being that she could
lend it to friends and perhaps come back another year for
another week—and she had, once. So she left Cacho the
keys, and let him do whatever he liked with the place so
long as he didn't send her any repair bills.

At night, especially in August, on Dos de Mayo Street,
when the leading attraction, backed up by the sound of
earsplitting music, was the heavy stream of flesh heated by
the sun, alcohol, and sex in any form, the Sandra was
general headquarters for Cacho Moyano and the Zamora
brothers, who owned an Afro-Hindu-folk-Western-
hippy-protest boutique. With their Afros or slicked-back
hair, whichever was in that year, dressed in Ibiza-style
white, carefully tanned by a process that started long before the season—their skin had a bronze hue, like that of a
Calabrian bandit, that was absent from the skin of sun-
lovers just passing through—and wearing amulets on their
hairy chests, the Zamoras attracted the blond dryads who
came down from the urban forests of the north in search of
rest or fun, or of their "sexual identities," as everyone now
said. Cacho and the Zamoras waited on the steps of the
Sandra to trap them, ready to drink, dance, make love, and
in general show them that Latin Americans, especially
Argentines, were the true Latin lovers of their dreams,
unlike the Spaniards, who were just common brutes.

"Public relations for the boutique," Cacho would say.

And it must have had excellent results, because other store owners in Sitges bitched that things weren't the same as before, but Cacho and the Zamoras said they had nothing to complain about. Sometimes, sick of Gloria or feeling unbearable guilt for having punished Pato, or when some especially depressing political news came to spread fear like liquid fire among Latin Americans, I'd escape to Dos de Mayo Street and sit, to put it one way, in the last row of my fifty-odd years to watch—since I hardly ever took part—the happiness of all those bodies, so unaware and, from what I could see, so free of problems. I tried to block my mind, to kill my sensitive nerve ends, to fog my vision by accepting all the stimulants that were being passed around, the electrifying music, the parade of dazed and sex-hungry young people ready to reap all the night's pleasures: lots of coffee, whiskey, hash, marijuana, kif, any more or less inoffensive grass offered by the pushers who swarmed the streets of Sitges, in addition to the empty—but always tension-free—conversation of Cacho Moyano and the Zamoras and the night's blondes. Cacho, who never read anything, would introduce me as "the great Chilean writer," not knowing that, especially in those first years, people were more impressed by my being from Chile than by my being a writer.

Cacho never failed to ask me to his parties. He would also invite Gloria, a little reluctantly perhaps, not only because he was against the presence of legally committed women at any reunion, but more because, or so it seemed to me, Gloria threatened his self-assurance with her obviously patrician origins, which could not be disguised by her poverty, her depression, her bitterness, her political commitment, or her lack of purpose, which was now a general evil. To cover up for this weakness, Cacho treated her like his one-night dolls—like a depraved French girl or an English chick who, at twenty, had already seen it all—and Gloria loved this when she was in a good mood.

"Do you realize what those idiots, the Spaniards and you Argentines too, miss because of your country's poor orientation to the sun?" I asked Carlos Minelbaum when I got to La Cala.

"What do you mean, you fucking Chilean?" he asked me, laughing.

Near the arches that looked like the leftovers of a movie set, on a pile of rocks in the sand, Minelbaum tended the fire on which the Zamora brothers would start preparing the barbecue as soon as they got there. The other guests waited, sitting around on beat-up plastic or wicker chairs under the arches or on the terrace that leaned out over the rocks and the sea. Others wandered around inside on the tile floor strewn with sand carried in by the gusts of wind that blew in through the badly fitting windows or by the feet of guests barely covered by bikinis or bathrobes or *tangas* like G-strings; they were all holding glasses of wine and calling for the barbecue or tuning their guitars with tangos or *cumbias* or *carnavalitos* or *chacareras* or *chamamés* that later on, after dinner, would drown out all attempts at conversation and were in fact a good substitute for it.

"You can't take poorly oriented countries like this one and yours seriously. You never see the sun set over the sea, as it should," I answered. "But Chile—"

"Cut out the bullshit, Julito. We're all oriented like Chile—just look at the way Videla followed in its steps."

"You're right. We've been an instructive example."

"Don't let Adriazola hear you, he'll think you're serious. Look, today he's . . . he's worse than ever, he's fit to be killed! He came in dressed up as God only knows what, wearing a Cordovan hat and a cute little poncho that doesn't even cover his belly button."

Incredible: not because I didn't know that very few things could cover Adriazola's big gut—I had seen it on the beach, sticking out, solid as industrial plastic, his tits as hairy as those on one of Diane Arbus's hermaphrodites—but because I was repelled by the look of satisfaction on his face, with its marked Indian features, its bushy eyebrows, watery eyes, and wet lips, not to mention the disorderly mess of graying hair falling back from the top of his bald skull. Showing up suddenly at Cacho Moyano's simple party dressed like a Chilean peasant was, like everything he did, his way of playing the patriot.

"A little respect for our national costume!" I protested to Minelbaum. "How would you feel if I made fun of your chiripá?

"Yes, but who can take Adriazola seriously?"

At one time, for a short while, I had taken him seriously. Now I could see him out on the terrace with a glass of wine in his hand, playing the oracle to disciples of both sexes gathered around him. Was this the man who had first definitely drawn me to Sitges?

When I left Chile after the coup—I had lost my job at the university after six days in jail, because, before they caught him, I had been accused of hiding a cousin who was a member of the MIR*—I moved with my wife and ten-year-old son to Barcelona, headquarters of the big Spanish publishing houses and especially of Núria Monclús. The rumor was going around that this arbitrary goddess was capable of making and breaking reputations, merging and founding publishing houses and literary collections, of building fortunes and breaking companies, and, worse, of shattering forever the nerves and the balls of writers or editors who were too sensitive to resist her power, so

* Guerrilla movement in Chile. —Trans.

apparent in the bearing of her head and the authority of her voice, nourished on the box of chocolates that was always on her desk, within reach of fingernails painted a bright red that made them look as if she had just sunk them into some failed writer's jugular vein. I had hoped to put my future in those hands.

My conversation with the pleasant, perfect, distant superagent had lasted ten minutes and was constantly interrupted by calls from Paris, Denmark, Tokyo, and New York, each and every one answered in the appropriate language—or so it seemed to me; I couldn't tell the difference—because one of the things said about Núria Monclús was that she had read everything and been through so many universities that she was entitled to look down on all kinds of learning. A hairnet veil held together at the back of her neck by a little velvet ribbon, a black spiderweb with little dots that barely hid the glint of her pupils, seemed to keep any emotion from disturbing a single hair of her elaborate white hairdo; it gave a look of discipline to everything about her, to her imperious bearing as she led me to the door, and even to the studied compliments and the verdict with which she was turning me away. She had let me know, without saying it, that I didn't interest her as an author for her stables, something it hadn't been difficult for me to predict when I saw her surrounded by portraits, framed manuscripts, personal mementoes, gifts, inscriptions, fetishes from all the "greats" and their families; this made my hopes come crashing down right there, even before she had passed sentence.

Enigmatic? With a flair and literary know-how so accurate that it seemed magical, as was alleged by those in her mafia? A magnificent shell that was only a cover for avarice and cruelty, as rejected writers said? (I was one of these.)

What else could I hope for, with only one good review by Hernán del Solar to my credit—at one time it had seemed such a wonderful distinction—and with one short story included in a Danish academic bilingual anthology? Núria Monclús had no time to build reputations from zero, a zero that may not have been such a zero in Chile but certainly was at the international level on which this woman, who could explode with the force of dynamite, moved. I recalled that she had eaten a chocolate during our interview but hadn't held the box out to me. When I left her office I was numb with the conviction that I'd still have to climb many more rungs before she'd make room for me in her exclusive stables, which, everyone knows, need constant renewal if you don't want to go out of business, since that's what it's all about.

I returned to the seedy hotel, near the Ramblas, where Gloria and I were staying. That night, with the light out and my wife's arms around me, we talked on and on, reaching the conclusion that, to attract the attention of that vestal virgin with eyes veiled by her wicked spiderweb, I would have to risk everything.

After all, the chances that she'd show interest in me weren't too bad. She was considered a leftist sympathizer. Chile was then in the limelight: there were statements in the press, signed manifestos, art shows, protest songs, new magazines, and the Barcelona equivalent of American "radical chic"—the *gauche divine*—that required the presence of at least one exiled Chilean at every sophisticated gathering. In my favor I had one experience none of the Boom's cosmopolites had: writing their novels in cushy self-exile, they hadn't taken part firsthand in a national tragedy as I had. Wasn't this an extraordinary trump card? After my interview with Núria Monclús, Gloria and I decided to look for a cheap, quiet place to live and, in just one year, I'd finish rewriting my novel; its eloquence and on-the-spot insights would cast its shadow over the scene of the contemporary Latin American novel, which in any case had now become repetitious, aestheticist, and pretentious.

That's when I heard about Adriazola, this extraordinary Chilean protest painter. Around this time, color reproductions of his work had appeared in magazines. He lived in Vendrell, an hour's drive down the coast from Barcelona. This man, who had been living in Europe long before the UP and the military coup, had taken over a long wall abutting the highway traveled by all the tourist traffic from France and countries to the north to the Spanish Levant and the Costa del Sol. On this wall he—along with twenty or more disciples of all nationalities, ages, and sexes, all enthusiasts of the cause of freedom—painted interminable murals representing leaders of coups as well as their victims, and as if their meaning were not clear enough, they also painted in slogans that left no room for doubt. Each week, this group—which considered artistic expression important *only* insofar as it served the community or was an instrument of protest or a message for the people, and as such considered it perishable—destroyed the previous week's mural and painted another illustrating the latest disasters and disappearances, using sketches prepared by Adriazola in his studio. He had turned his house into a gallery; snoopers soon started flocking in to buy his paintings, ceramics, sculptures, etchings, lithographs, all the things made in his workshop with the help of a growing number of followers. It was this obvious commercialism of Adriazola's messianic work and his opportunist revolutionary rhetoric that, after a week's stay in Vendrell, made me break with him in an unpleasant way and turn to my own affairs. I escaped to nearby Sitges, which seemed

peaceful and was the home of people with less extreme
political convictions.

But Sitges turned out to be quiet on the surface only. A
sweet trap as sticky as flypaper, it was in a continual state of
unrest because of the squabbles and envy of those Latin
Americans who had come to stay in a setting that was a
caricature of tranquillity, to seek a respite from their com-
plicated lives and have time to think and lick the wounds
that had made them leave their countries. The long arm of
Adriazola's fame did not reach into Sitges. He himself was
careful not to appear too often on its streets or in its
sidewalk cafés; he knew that, among the exiles, there were
serious people, Chileans with an L on their passport, Argentinian and Uruguayan former guerrillas who had
risked their lives in covert operations—like Dr. Minelbaum; Adriazola would have given his right arm to win
Carlos's respect—and he was afraid that his profit-making
protest art would be unmasked.

On Sunday mornings, Las Gaviotas, a quiet sidewalk
café facing the sea, where almost all the steady customers
were friends or at least knew one another and the waiters
and street musicians often greeted us by name, was the
place where everybody met on mellow fall or sunny winter
days, when no one else remained but native Catalans and
the residents, mainly Nordic models of both sexes—
essential material for television commercials filmed in Barcelona, since Spaniards consider this kind of look more
commercial than the native variety—and art gallery
owners, antique dealers, free-lance journalists, owners of
restaurants that stayed open in winter with their cozy
fireplaces burning pointlessly, painters, writers, transla-
tors, actresses, and others more or less connected with the
arts who made up the standing population of the resort

because their work required that they live cheaply and near Barcelona.

On his way to the city one Sunday morning, Adriazola dropped in at Las Gaviotas. I introduced him to Cacho Moyano, with whom I was having my usual Campari. Like all the people I introduced to him, Cacho took Adriazola for an intellectual celebrity worthy of respect not only because he was endorsed by me, Cacho's "serious" friend, but especially because, by coincidence, that Sunday the magazine section of *La Vanguardia* had shown Adriazola in Vendrell, hair disheveled, surrounded by his disciples, painting his *Mural of Desolation*. From then on Adriazola made cunning attempts to worm his way into the various circles in Sitges, starting with those he knew were too naive to keep him out. This explained his presence at La Cala that evening.

I saw him wave and then shout at me to come over, without moving his huge bulk out of the armchair from which he was holding court, near the railing above the rocks hit by the surf.

"Go on," said Carlos, while Gloria and Ana María Minelbaum set up the grill and put on the meat, because the Zamoras hadn't showed up and people couldn't wait anymore. "He knows I've wanted no part of him ever since I told him to his face that his act is a disgrace to the entire left. And if you don't go over, he'll say you're a fascist. I believe he's already going around saying it because you refused to be his disciple."

In spite of what Carlos Minelbaum had said, when I went over to Adriazola I found him quite relaxed, little inclined to be dogmatic. The twilight had faded, but night had not yet covered the peacock blue of the sky; the sea was black, and everything on earth had turned into dark shapes, grotesque masks exaggerated by La Cala's poor lighting. Bothered by the humidity and the heat, the Chilean painter had shed his folkloristic clothing. The strings of his *tanga* had disappeared under the rolls of his enormous stomach, making him look practically naked: a deceitful, garrulous Buddha with a glass of wine in his hand.

"*Compañero*," the painter said, after greeting me with something like a salute, "this boy wants to talk to you. He's a countryman of ours."

A kid stood up in the middle of the group around Adriazola. He looked no more than fourteen and was dressed in blue jeans and a white polo shirt. He said hello with a smile (luminous even in the dark), his hair gold curls like those of an *angelo musicante*, and asked if I was really Patrick's father. Then he introduced himself as the son of Berta Sánchez and Hernán Lagos, painters who were lifelong friends of ours and who had been living in Paris since the coup; Pato had often visited them, and it is there that he had changed his name to Patrick. This young boy, whose name I was straining to remember, was blinking in an odd way, as if the poor light of the bulbs hidden in the false beams under the arches hurt his very pale eyes, and I noticed that he talked Chilean Spanish with a very strong French accent.

I asked after his parents, but I remembered that our very irregular correspondence had brought us news of their separation and Hernán's return to Chile. The boy denied this; they never stopped talking about going back, and they could do so, because they didn't have an L stamped on their passport. They were sick of each other, he said shamelessly, and fought constantly. Besides, they felt out of place in Europe, anonymous, lost, unmotivated, so it was logical that they'd want to return.

Adriazola immediatcly launched into the subject of return as treachery to the cause, concluding that all those intellectuals who had stayed in the country after the coup were also traitors, because their presence legitimized the regime. Gloria, who was serving pieces of barbecued meat onto our plates, was making signs for me to stop arguing with Adriazola, but I questioned the point that, with political activism fading into the background now, kept coming up in all the conversations of Latin Americans in forced or in "voluntary" exile: should those of us who had the choice go back or not? Adriazola was especially rabid on this point: those who returned were fascists and that was that. The poor kid, whose name I had made up my mind to ask Gloria, declared that he wouldn't go back whether his parents did or not.

"Why?" I asked him, attempting the sort of a dialogue I could no longer have with Pato.

He thought it over for a second while we chewed on the delicious meat. The guitars were catching fire on the arcaded porch, and a raspy voice—I recognized it as Carlos Minelbaum's—was trying to sing what, ignorant as I was about folk singing, I took to be a *vidala*. The boy explained that he didn't want to, wouldn't go back. That's exactly why he was on his way to meet Patrick in Marrakesh, where Patrick seemed to be very happy. But, turning to Adriazola with a kind of violence hidden behind the fragments of his broken diction, he said he wasn't refusing to go back to Chile for the reasons laid down by the painter.

"Then why?" Adriazola challenged him, setting a plate full of meat on the little ledge of knees his drooping belly left free.

Somewhat sheepish in this circle of listeners but driven by a kind of extraordinary conviction, the *angelo musicante* stammered that he was fed up; he couldn't understand the discussions, always harping on the same subject day after day, that took place among his parents and their friends:

Chicho, Tencha, Altamirano, Volodia, Lonquén, Payita, Letelier, Guardia Vieja were all ciphers of a code that made no emotional sense to him. What's more, who in his generation remembered those legendary names after having spent half of their lives in Europe? But what annoyed him most, he said, was that his parents should use him as a pretext for going back to Chile, insisting that they wished to return because they didn't want him to forget his roots or to lose interest in everything Chilean—but he had already done so, so why hadn't they thought of going back before, when he was smaller, since there had been nothing to stop them?—didn't want him to feel a stranger to his own language, to his family, his traditions, his saints, and his martyrs, or to talk with such little respect for all that, and, what's more, with that awful French accent. It was all lies, empty words, a big show, the boy explained with passion: his parents were going back to Chile because they couldn't take it anymore, they were old and out of touch, besides having failed as painters in the European world, which hadn't given them the place they felt was theirs. Why hadn't they been honest with him? It's all he was asking of them so he wouldn't have to feel guilty for wanting to live his own life and not the one they were trying to force on him.

"Of course, your parents are right in that sense," Adriazola said.

"In what sense?" I asked, set to attack.

"Well, in the sense of losing roots. The main duty of all of us Chilean artists and intellectuals in exile is to preserve not only the flame of our patriotism, but also our rancor, our open veins—"

"But really, Adriazola, you and I are not exiles," I said. "You and I could go back anytime we wanted to; we don't have the L on our passports, we're not on any blacklist—"

"You're quite wrong, Julio. It's true that I don't have the damn L and am not, strictly speaking, an exile. But the government would never accept my return. It would stop me from entering the country because of my activity in revolutionary protest abroad. I must be on all the black-lists. I'm recognized everywhere as a great enemy of the regime, and that's why I suffer exile."

"Have some more meat, Adriazola," Gloria said, depositing a large chunk on his plate. "How is Berta, son? This boy looks so much like Berta. . . ."

But, dismissing attempts at small talk, Adriazola continued his variations on the theme of roots. Sitting before him and Patrick's friend, I saw him swell up with his antifascist and anti-imperialist handbook rhetoric. I also saw the clear eyes of my son's friend turn glassy with restrained tears, or maybe simply with boredom, until he couldn't stand it anymore and broke in:

"My roots are in Paris."

"Paris?" Adriazola roared as if personally offended.

"I left Chile seven years ago. I'm sixteen, a year younger than Patrick. I've grown up and gone to school in France, living like French boys my age. There are kids from Chile who aren't like me and are interested in what's happening there. I guess it's because they sense more honesty in their parents' attitudes. But not me. Anyway, Chile has gone out of fashion—"

Adriazola sat up in his throne, livid. Snatching the huge chunk of meat from his plate, he hurled it at the boy's face. He jumped to his feet with a speed I'd never suspected him capable of, lunging at the *angelo musicante* to slap him but failing, not because the kid shielded his face with his help-less arms but because we had all come to his defense; some were swearing at Adriazola, and others, the ideologues, were shouting at the kid that what he had said was the limit, it meant forgetting our dead, the martyrs of all of America, for something as frivolous as fashion.

This general indignation was over quickly, lasting for as long as it took the *angelo musicante* to wipe off the blood that the meat had left on his face. Right after that, the group dispersed into the night, into the house or to join the chorus on the porch that faced the sea, singing what seemed to me a zamba from the Salta region in Argentina. The boy remained behind, alone but for Gloria, who kissed his forehead almost on the sly, and gave him a message for Patrick. He whispered something in her ear before going off into the night that the waves were rocking to sleep.

An hour later, while Minelbaum sang to the guitar, Gloria came over and asked me quietly if I remembered the name of Hernán and Berta's son. I didn't, and neither did she. She kept looking at her watch every two or three minutes. I noticed, and asked her softly—she was scrunched down against me as if she were afraid—what was wrong. Was she cold? Would she like to have someone drive us home? Because the Adriazola incident had left me emotionally drained as well. No, the trouble, she whispered so as not to disturb the singer, was that the boy had told her he was going for a swim down by the rocks; that had been an hour ago. She had begged him not to, not on such a dark night; the sea down by La Cala's cove was dangerous at night, even for those familiar with it, and treacherous at all times. He had been gone exactly fifty-seven minutes. She had just walked around the garden, and on the sand she had found a bundle of clothes, his jeans, polo shirt, and Adidas shoes. If his clothes were there, it meant that he hadn't sneaked back to Sitges without saying goodbye to anyone, as she had at first supposed.

Why couldn't I remember the name of Hernán and

Berta's son, so we could go into the garden and call him without causing panic? An odd name, French, she thought. He had been almost a baby when she had known him in Chile, and she hadn't seen him since. I had no idea what his name was. Indignant, I saw the boy's vanishing act as typical thoughtlessness, like something Pato would do, and I whispered to Gloria that the best thing was not to take any notice; kids did this kind of thing to get attention, but they could take care of themselves.

Still, Gloria went out again. She came back and whispered that the pile of clothes was still there. The sea, she went on, looked calm from above but was roaring against the rocks down below, and she couldn't help feeling scared. She leaned her head on my shoulder and put her arm under mine to grip my hand.

"What are the lovebirds whispering about?" Minelbaum asked, breaking off his *chacarera*, because he always lost his sense of humor when anyone interrupted his music.

"Nothing, nothing," we said, laughing to keep from looking nervous.

Gloria's neighbor, a California divorcée into batik, asked her if we were talking about the cute kid with the strange expression in his light blue eyes. Minelbaum was trying to get the guitars started again, but Gloria couldn't keep herself from explaining to her neighbor what was going on. In a few minutes everyone was talking about the boy; Minelbaum and his accompanists put down their guitars, and even Cacho Moyano untangled himself from the blonde he had been exploring. He rose to his feet and asked:

"What boy?"

"Didn't you see him?"

"Who brought him?"

"I don't know how he got here."

It didn't matter, anyway, people always dragged other

people to his house, it wasn't important. Wasn't it Adriazola who had brought him? Where was Adriazola?

"He's on the back steps with two disciples, improvising a protest mural to leave you with a souvenir of his historic visit to La Cala. No, the kid isn't with him."

Yes, the sea was dangerous at this hour, Cacho said. It was always dangerous—he himself seldom went down to swim, and even then only in spots he knew well, and always in the daytime—and the boy had been gone an hour. People looked for flashlights or improvised lanterns with candles shielded from the wind in paper bags, and we all went out to the garden, the terrace, the rocks. Even Adriazola interrupted planning his revolutionary mural and, along with his assistants, joined in the search.

"What's the kid's name?" he asked me.

We can't remember, a strange name, Gloria and I answered.

"Aren't you friends of his parents?"

"Yes, but we don't remember the names of all the kids."

"Isn't he your son's friend?"

"Yes."

"Then I think it's odd that you don't know."

"Well, okay, Adriazola," I answered, feeling unreasonably guilty. "We can't all be as perfect as you."

Then the yoo-hoos, the hey-theres, the hellos started up among the younger people who had gone down to the rocks with their lights, scrambling down the cliff to the sea, searching all the ledges, exploring inlets and caves, calling out to the nameless boy who'd got himself lost or maybe killed; shouting up to us who had stayed above, worried and silent, unable to help, that they couldn't see him, couldn't locate him, he was lost, and the sea was rough and dangerous tonight, and pitch-black. Why go on looking? What more could be done?

From the terrace above we could see the reddish sky over toward Sitges, with its festive summer lights: international jazz or horror film festival? The sea, a heavy black sheet of iron, whispered enigmas that grew more ominous by the minute: the searchers' lights flickered, were lost, went out, reappeared among the rocks. Some of the women, clustered together on the terrace, were starting to shiver. They were brought shawls and jackets, but then they started to whimper. And when the lights fluttering among the rocks seemed to disappear, an Englishwoman suddenly started screaming hysterically, aggressively, terrified, at me:

"It's your fault, your bloody fault, you bloody idiot, your fault, you frightened the poor dearie, you idiot . . ."

And she was screaming and crying while the other women, especially those who had tried to calm her down at first, also started to cry, while Gloria tried to placate them as well as me by calling down to those below holding the eerie lights and asking, over and over, whether they had seen anything. But they had wandered off, way off, too far to do any good, it seemed to me, and couldn't hear poor Gloria, who, I realized, was also quietly crying.

Much later they began to return, discouraged—by then the women and Adriazola were asleep in their chairs from drinking too much wine and cognac to steady their nerves—and with terror in their eyes, doing their best to keep their voices from breaking; they had found nothing, not a single footprint, not a track, and it wasn't worth going on with the search in this darkness. We decided the best thing was to go into Sitges, report it, and get help from the qualified authorities; after all, we were all involved, in one way or another, in the disappearance of this boy without a name, and we needed ropes and ladders and more lights, and maybe even a motor launch, and especially people who knew what to do. One group would stay in the house, just in case he happened to return. . . .

We headed for the cars, which were parked outside the iron fence under the shelter of a stand of pines. Cacho was the first to leave, taking off at top speed with Carlos. I was about to get into Adriazola's car, but when I opened the door the light inside went on and we saw the *angelo musicante* sleeping stark naked, curled up like a fetus and sucking his thumb like a baby.

"The little fucker's here," I yelled.

Everyone rushed over to surround Adriazola's car. I shook the boy savagely. Opening his innocent blue eyes, he asked:

"*Où est-ce que je suis?*"

Furious at those clear blue eyes, I slapped him, splitting his lip; a thin thread of blood started to spurt from it and soon dissolved in his tears. I was unmoved.

Everyone, including Adriazola, protested against my violent reaction, Gloria most of all, though she scolded him with the anguished irritation she usually reserved for Pato. Everybody railed at the little bastard who had put us through two hours of panic, driving us to the brink of our inner abysses. Those who had stayed in the house came out. When they saw him, the women alternately kissed and swore at him for what he had put them through and for ruining Cacho Moyano's beautiful party. And Cacho would be back with the police any minute now.

"*Pas des flics . . . !*" the boy muttered.

Not to please him but to let the police know that they were no longer needed, more cars headed for Sitges. Everybody started leaving: the important thing now was to get away from the abyss quickly, to escape far from the tragedy that might have been, in which each and every one of us would have shared the villain's role. The boy's—I was still trying to remember his name but wouldn't ask him for it, because that would have been too humiliating—blue eyes had dried. Someone brought his jeans, his polo shirt, his Adidas shoes. He covered his white body, childish and almost feminine, with the speed only children have getting dressed. Then his fingers felt the blood on his split lip. Looking scared at the red stain on his fingertips, he turned to me.

"C'est donc vrai ce que Patrick m'a raconté à propos de vous."

What had Pato said to him? That I became furious when he cried and that then he'd cry more, making me even angrier? And when he got older he'd retort rudely that hadn't he at least the right to cry. And as he irrevocably hardened, a hardening I'd never intended to produce, he would shout at me and accuse me of being a big bully, a dictator. Yes, these are the things that boys like them, lighting up joint after joint, would whisper about, always blaming their parents for their own failings.

Those who still hung around in the light of the car watched us, as if expecting another act, another scandalous scene in which we, not they, would unmask ourselves. After my stupid outburst of fury, Adriazola of course was not going to miss the opportunity to offer the kid his house in Vendrell, explaining that there he'd find an atmosphere of work, of friendliness among young people with ideals, and would meet his wife, who was a mother to all his disciples. Unfortunately, tonight she had been the victim of one of her frequent headaches and had been unable to come to Cacho Moyano's.

"I don't like young people with ideals," the boy answered.

"Well, it won't be that bad. Anyway, let's put this discussion off till later," Adriazola broke in. "But tell me, who do you want to go with, this man who hit you or me?"

The kid pointed to Adriazola, who quickly let him into his car and took off with his prey, a triumphant silver streak headed for Vendrell. Gloria got into the backseat of the last car left; it belonged to someone we didn't know. He was taking us, we felt, because he had no other choice; he couldn't very well leave us stranded under the clump of pines.

A little farther on, Gloria whispered that Adriazola was a pig. But neither of us felt like talking, and we didn't go into this observation of hers. We drove the rest of the way in silence. Near Sitges, I heard Gloria, in the backseat, sniveling.

2

STAVES OF LIGHT: octaves, arpeggios, quavers. Under the sheet of my dream or behind the silk folds of my still-closed eyelids? No. Outside. On the resplendent staves, the shadows of the horse chestnut's leaves transcribe complex scales sparked off by the summer morning air surrounding me with a wild frenzy of birdsong and the rustle of branches. My mind clears and I know I'm in the center of Madrid. Irina, the cat, comes back after a night of lust, perhaps, in the Duke's garden: Pancho gave us instructions to leave a small window in the servant's bathroom open "to let her go out and do her thing."

Yes, it's Irina. Even the soft beige velvety measured tread of her paws makes this proud old parquet floor creak. In a moment, just as back in another place and another time, its wooden vocabulary will announce the steps of someone bringing me breakfast. I have the feeling that, as over there in that other time, through the staves of the shutters a green luminosity is sinking this bedroom— someone else's, but made mine by a night's sleep—into an undersea silence where my consciousness can still float for a little while with nothing to brush against it, because there are a few minutes left before Pato's footsteps will make the parquet creak in its unmistakable way: before leaving for school, he'll come in to kiss my forehead and ask for money for the bus—no, the minibus—and an ice cream. "In my trousers," I'd answer him each morning, just as my father used to answer me: I'd be awakened by the eloquence of the wooden floors of another time, lost so many years ago in the silence of Mediterranean tile floors.

I recognize the steps of my wife, who is bringing breakfast to me in bed. She comes in, preceded by Myshkin, who leaps onto the bed and settles down at my feet, as if I were a recumbent statue on a tomb doomed never to rise again, simply a figure on the alabaster slab, a metaphor that commemorates but doesn't replace the person whose poor bones it hides. But I'm not alabaster, I'm alive and I can smell the scent of the Lapsang souchong coming closer. No, it's Earl Grey. Or Darjeeling? Last night we went over the many-colored row of different teas in the well-stocked pantry Pancho left us. Myshkin and Irina play at my feet for a minute and then curl up together, mingling the soft tones of their fur.

Gloria sets the tray down. She hasn't brought me breakfast in bed in so many years! Another dimension I've missed since leaving Chile; then, not even our tremendous arguments could destroy this small ceremony so much a part of our union. It's true that back over there all the floors creak; as well as a characteristic voice, everyone has a characteristic sound, his or her own tread on wood, a personal signature that follows one around, as inseparable as a shadow. But I've noticed that here in Spain people's identities seem incomplete, because the sound of their footsteps is missing on floors that grumpy housemaids rub and polish to give them a strong scent; they sweep the floors with blond *curahuilla* brooms that spread tiny purple motes, which sometimes crackle when you step on them. With a reassuring gesture, Gloria lifts her lovely mature arms, which take on a greenish tint from the light outside, and opens the blinds—here and now they're blinds, not shutters as back over there so long ago—and brings into view a profusion of luminous green.

"Look . . ."

Gloria finishes drawing the curtains, and I get out of bed to look: yes, a garden. Elms, horse chestnuts, lindens, a thrush—or its equivalent in these latitudes; I don't intend to learn its name because I'm too old to add it to my personal mythology—hopping on the not very well kept grass: the Duke is lazy. The swords of the irises march solemnly alongside the wall, almost hidden by the foliage. Flowerets I can't identify bloom in the shade of the branches—flowering rushes? cinerarias? no, those bloom at the beginning of spring, and we're already in early June—much like the shade of branches in a garden in another hemisphere: a garden quite different from this small aristocratic park, because back over there it was the shade of avocado and orange and magnolia trees; and yet the shade is the same as the other, hemming in the silence of the house where my mother is now dying. Why doesn't she die, once and for all, poor thing, and stop suffering, she's so old, and the doctors can't diagnose the illness that's killing her, while outside spring with its flowering rushes has given way to summer with its plum trees and summer has died to let autumn with its dry leaves burning in heaps on this garden's paths come in before winter (cold and rainy back over there), when everything green must die.

"Rome . . ." I murmur, admitting that for me all roads lead to the same place.

"Yes," Gloria whispers next to me, and puts her arm around my waist. "The house on Rome Street, right? . . ."

In the unbroken silence of the deserted garden we see from our bedroom window, each plant, each flower, each path, each bench is sure of its meaning and its place and especially of its endurance. How much longer will it be before the house on Rome Street is sold, when my mother dies, and in its place an ugly tall building goes up, there for eternity? Not very long. My father, who lacked the ambition to rise above the little his family had always been, is calling her from the grave, because he feels cold and alone, and she'll follow him, thinking she can relieve her husband's last discomfort. When that house is gone I'll have nowhere to go back to. Or nothing to go back for. You dream of returning to your country, an abstraction that's real not just because you were born there but because the dream of returning involves a particular window opening on a garden, a tapestry of greens crisscrossed by private histories that illuminate our ties to people and places. All this can be distorted in grand ideological pronouncements, if you're Adriazola. But underground groups met in Carlos Minelbaum's house in Santa Fe; they prepared direct action and pamphlets; and in Sitges now, every time the doorbell rings, Ana María trembles, scared that they're coming "to get her"; yes, Minelbaum can't go back to anything in his country, because there's a death sentence hanging over his head. By the Mediterranean now, he's building other windows and another garden, where maybe he'll grow old like my father, sitting on a low bench under that tree I can see from here, reliving his passions to keep homesickness from destroying him.

"Shall we go and look out the other windows?" Gloria suggests.

"Let's go."

From the other bedroom the garden looks as thick as a
forest. From the kitchen windows we can see clusters of
different flowers. In the living room, two bare symmetrical windows that overlook square patches of forest scenery,
like tapestries, and between them, exactly the same size, a
painting depicting the white curtains found throughout
the apartment; in it I recognize Pancho Salvatierra's gift for
reproducing a false reality. And the huge dining-room
window reveals the triumphant grandness of the swimming pool—you can also see one end of it from our
bedroom—surrounded by an immaculate lawn and the
terrace of the ornate town mansion (it looks nothing like
my parents' unpretentious home), decorated with classical
urns and fragments of columns and capitals and equipped
with comfortable wicker chairs. All this is organized
around a cypress as magnificent as the one at the monas-
tery of Santo Domingo de Silos: a tree so European it's
impossible to imagine it among my country's flora. Looking at the cypress, I remember how, wanting one like it,
when I was eighteen I planted a cypress in the garden of
our house on Rome Street, but a few years later we had to
ask the gardener to cut it down because it had grown
without any shape, sparse, scraggly, a vegetable that in its
brief history had nothing in common with the European
elegance of this symbol, compact and black, that contem-
plates the arrogance of its perfect shape in the swimming
pool's blue eye.

The Duke of what, what had Pancho told me? He had
explained that he was one of the richest men in Spain, but
now, in the twilight of a life privileged with little but the
mundane, he sometimes whiled away the time watering the
lawn, pruning the rosebushes, mowing the grass, climbing up in something like a tractor that was a joke because it
looked like a wagon on a children's train: a world where all

that counted was pleasure, pure and simple. I don't have access to that world, perhaps because of my temperament, or perhaps because the whirlwind of our lives swept us off to other things, but I can watch it from a distance: it's as enigmatic as a cat with its eyes closed, resting but not asleep. I belong to a generation of puritans reduced to servitude by superegos as inflexible as sergeants who can't even feel homesick for East Egg, like Gatsby. But there's still the terrible sadness of not having the moral right to feel homesick for East Egg. The small portion of the garden next door seen from my bedroom will be mine until the unthinkable moment of the demise of Rome, when Mother dies. The wall I glimpse beyond the quivering lacework of linden leaves, the wall brushed by the row of irises, will vanish. I turn my back to the pool.

"Are you ready to go out?" I ask Gloria.

"Yes," she answers, very excited. "I'm going to the Prado. Do you want to come along?"

"I don't know . . . I don't think so," I say. "I'm still bushed from the long trip on that weird train. You women have such energy! Like Anita Ekberg climbing the steps of the Vatican with poor Mastroianni in tow, panting hard. . . . No, I'm not playing Mastroianni today. I'm going to stay here and rest."

"Well then, I'll go be Anita Ekberg. We'll do it another day. We have plenty of time, and even if they've stolen three hundred and fifty paintings from the museum, I don't think they carried off the Bosch or the Velázquez or the Goya or the Zurbarán paintings. Get some rest, darling. Katy invited me to lunch."

"Who's Katy?"

"She's Ana María Minelbaum's cousin from Uruguay. Remember how much we liked her when she was in Sitges? You don't mind, do you? I left you a few Cordon

Bleu delicacies, straight out of their cans. Do you want me
to call you at lunch?"

"I don't know . . . no. What for? I want to have a good
siesta. And after that I'll organize my papers and my dictionaries and set up my typewriter."

"Where?"

"In the dining room, I think. I like the white marble-top
table, it's large and cool. I don't think we'll be giving any
fancy dinners like Pancho. We can eat on the small table in
the pantry."

"Sure . . . bye . . . Get some rest."

BUT I DON'T put my papers in order. I avoid even going
into the other bedroom, where we put our suitcases, mine
with more books than clothes.

"Heavier than madam's," Beltrán the doorman remarked, as he helped bring them up, with a smile that
dazzled us with perfectly fantastic teeth. "Mr. de Salvatierra asked me to take good care of you. He was good
enough to explain that you were childhood friends. There's
nothing like those friendships! In my village, a group of us
get together every year. . . ."

Gloria had spent the morning hanging up her clothes.
How much trouble would it have been to have done the
same with mine? As a matter of fact, she has never done it,
and now, after twenty-odd—how many?—years of marriage, I'm becoming resigned to her not packing my bags
or hanging up my clothes. Why am I thinking about this
now that I'm alone in this apartment, so large and silent,
appointed with iridescent, mother-of-pearl, opalescent,
ivory, and crystal objects, not many, but all quite incredible. "Maybe you'll find the place too *dépouillé*," Pancho
had warned us, remembering Gloria's eclectic taste, which

was nothing more than a brave effort to hide poverty. I plan to enjoy myself here.

I leave everything as it is and go around inspecting the windows of the apartment—the "flat," I correct myself. I pause a few minutes at each window, studying what I can see from each. I pass up those without a view of the neighbor's garden. I also pass up the one facing the clusters of flowers alongside the wall, and the one from which I can barely make out a smaller house in the back part of the park. I even give up the two spectacular symmetrical living-room windows with the false curtains between them.

I go back to our bedroom window, because it's my favorite. I'm glad to see that before going out, Gloria, so unlike her, has made the white king-size bed we slept in last night. She has even put away my things: prompted, I believe, by the beauty of the place and the absence of anything tawdry, since a vulgar disorderliness of despair haunts our odious daily life. And me? If I recover my ability to feel pleasure, and renounce my passive citizenship in the provinces of personal failure, which is only an extension of the failure of everything we gambled on, will I then be free to write another or even the same novel, brilliant because it analyzes cruelty and singles out injustices without overlooking the pleasures of beauty? No, I may take my papers out of the suitcase right now, but the vision of Núria Monclús with the spiderweb hiding her eyes and the fiery sword in her bloodstained hand would come between me and the pleasure.

I draw the curtains. For a split second the sun shining through the leaves stirring in the wind blinds me: under the avocado tree in the garden next door my father, an invalid now, snaps his fingers to make the dog come and lie at his feet, or maybe he's trying to call me, because from his grave he can see me hiding here behind the curtains. In his last desperate letter my brother begs me to go and close my dying mother's eyes, there's so little life left in her, and she keeps asking for me, for Gloria, for Patricio. . . . Are they well? she asks, worried. Why don't they come to close my eyes? Don't they know that this burning clarity is blinding me like an overwhelming light I can see from my bed but will stop seeing when they move me into the coffin?

How can I travel to Chile, Papa? Don't you know our situation has forced me to choose a life outside that tiny, isolated, protective womb Chile still is, in spite of the dangers we all know, because it's protective, compared to the cruelty of this immense world outside, where they've forced us to be born all over again? To spare her, my brother, Sebastian, never tells Mother, whenever she asks after us, that sometimes I don't even have the money to give my son for an ice cream cone. Pato's footsteps on the parquet floor. He fishes in my pockets. He can't find the small change that was part of my professor's salary at one time. Mother doesn't know, Sebastian, don't tell her, that I've asked you for an advance on our inheritance—which won't amount to much—to be able to survive a month, two months, six months.

From my window I can see my father's hand shaking as he tries to say no, to emphasize. Stop making up stories, he says, that's not why you don't come to close your mother's eyes, questions of money can always be skirted. The thing is, I don't want to face the shameful sight of the National Congress closed down now—how could you know that, Papa, I interrupt, when you died in the last year of the UP, when Congress still existed?—the Congress at which I represented the region where our family was rooted, and at which I stood for a civilized liberalism that was perhaps unjust, but at least intelligent. I must be honest, Julio, I was a very undistinguished representative, seldom attending debates and committee meetings, yawning on the benches while the speakers offered explanations they didn't have to give, because everybody knew that mostly all they had to do was round up the field hands on family estates and take them to vote for the owner's candidate. . . . Later I'd get together around a card table with other representatives as indifferent as I. That's why you don't come.

The old man believes in nothing, neither in what is nor in what isn't. But my mother is in agony in a world that no sinister short circuit in her unconscious will allow her to accept as it is, and, always passionate and extreme in her loves and her hates, she loses weight and is now like a sparrow, wounded by the simple contact with the sheets on which she lies. She has not seen this summer. Nor the previous summers. From the window next to her bed, she can't see the plum tree she sat under while she waited for them to take her away. She doesn't see these shadows, the green, the branches. What is such a little girl doing alone in such a large garden? She's carrying a yellow plastic hen. The drawn-back curtains aren't enough. I open the window. Together with the chemical blast of hot summer air from the center of Madrid I hear the roll of traffic, a few streets away, going around this microclimate of green in which such a small girl can appear and disappear, playing under the branches of such a big garden. She's singing:

> "*Guten morgen,*
> *Margarete . . .*"

"Why are you singing in German?" my mother asks her granddaughter Andrea, who was brought up by her maternal German grandmother till the poor foreigner returned to Hamburg, her native city. She preferred to die there, in a home for the aged, and not here, in this strange country, with its avocado and araucaria trees, where she had lived for sixty years but had never learned to speak the language without an accent.

"Why is this child, who I imagine is the Duke of Andía's granddaughter, singing in German?"

It's an unhurried question, not urgent like my father's; it requires no answer, because I know that this little girl hugging her yellow plastic hen and singing in German is now a grown-up woman sitting at my mother's deathbed. Mother's glance is penetrating: maybe she guesses that my reasons for not returning to Chile are all pretexts connected to her dying. I close the window to keep the little girl and my father, who sits her on his knees, from finding out that I'm not going to Chile because of something else, something much less noble, less justifiable: terror that my mother's agony will stretch out for a month, six months, a year, two years. It's already been so long! I'm afraid I wouldn't be able to take leave of her, to sell the house, to dispose of the furniture. I'm afraid that day after day her death would be predicted for the next day, and I'd have to wait, and would eventually be trapped in Chile, far from my partner in a marriage that sometimes seems as mediocre as all other marriages, but whose strength I can't deny, far from my son, who thinks I'm a tyrant because I'm not the father he wants me to be, far from the "white walls and the upright cypresses" of Europe (the Duke's cypress is a deluxe edition), far from the irrational hope stirred by the proximity to the Barcelona publishing houses that invented the Latin American novelists, or maybe it's the other way around, maybe Núria Monclús invented them all; far away, immersed in the immediate, failing to see beyond local events, local tastes, local demands; devoured by the stifling familiarity of everything, because the signs that distinguish me are written all over me, and back over there they won't let identity be synonymous with mask, one of so many masks that I'm free to change here and would not be able to change as I please there, where I would be spotted immediately because of my clothes, my vocabulary, my accent, my behavior, and my preferences, no, there I wouldn't be able to choose who or what I want to be, as I can here in Europe, where, Mama, I have to pay for the luxury of being free with the coin of not belonging, with the terrifying yet wonderful solitude, with no one interested in sticking a label on me, a stranger everywhere, at Argentine barbecues, at parties where they serve Chilean corn cakes or Peruvian *anticuchos* or Valencian paellas, even if I'm invited to all of them. That's why, because I'm scared of your end, Mama, that's why I'm not going back to close your eyes.

WE SAID GOODBYE to Carlos and Ana María Minelbaum in Las Gaviotas on the Sunday morning before the Monday on which we took the slow train to Madrid. Before the women, who had stopped to buy some dessert, caught up with us, Carlos and I talked for a long while under one of the umbrellas outside the sidewalk café, crowded with people hungry for the sun at this time of year, people nobody knows and whom we didn't care to know, because in a week they'd be on their way back to Nottingham, Düsseldorf, or The Hague.

My cancer, of course, was not cancer but papilloma, as he had diagnosed. After all, Carlos explained with the same feeling that makes his voice break so attractively when he sings, I was a writer, a man who lived by the imagination and should never doubt it, even if they had so vilely rejected my novel. Proof of this fantasy life so deep inside me was that it is automatic for me to turn my violent aggression against myself, to punish myself for what I considered failures, and so every so often I invent these simulated deaths. My mother's approaching death. Patrick's potential death, simply because he was absent. My own death at the hands of Núria Monclús. And political death as well—even if I objected that I had lukewarm feelings about this death. All of it somatized in various forms of death. I expanded on this theme—perhaps Carlos's most appealing trait is his capacity for intimacy, his deep concentration in the other person, asking and listening and, in turn, confiding things he's sure will interest the friend—and I explained that, terrified by the insomnia that projected exaggerated shadows of our failures over a landscape of ghosts, instead of falling asleep naturally at night or accepting our wakefulness, Gloria and I committed nightly symbolic suicide with Rohipnol. I'd sleep all night, sealed in a dreamless sleep, black and stifling. I'd wake up in a bad mood, as if I'd mislaid a part of myself during the night. But, jumpy and depressed after her menopause, Gloria would wake up every two hours, even with medication, and get up each time to take a long swallow of cool white wine in summer, and a tart red in winter. But I drank during the day for courage to face my typewriter, or to kill my unbearable lucidity, sometimes my hate, always my insecurity; but since all this only succeeded in aggravating my anxiety, I'd take Valium until I ended up in a stupor in front of the television set.

"That's bad," commented Carlos. I shrugged.

The sun was beating down on the sea, thick with bathers, drying up the palm trees and frying the oiled bodies of the tourists all around us. He and Ana María were that institution, so pleasantly middle-class, we call "our best friends"; with them we went to concerts, to the movies, out to dinner, and shared problems. In Madrid we would miss this closeness. Talking to him under the green sunshade, I thought that Carlos would not have been in front of me now, drinking his whiskey, if one night a grateful patient, in spite of close ties with the Argentine reactionaries, hadn't warned him that they were coming after him the next day. That same night, Carlos had crossed the border with his wife and children. That's why he considers nostalgia a sterile occupation and leaves himself open to the present and the future.

I told him that on the afternoon following the barbecue, Pato's friend had come to my place with his head completely shaved, saying that one night and a morning had been enough to make him sick of Adriazola, his wife, and his disciples; he had shaved his head in protest, because long hair was the court uniform at Adriazola's. The boy had hitchhiked from Vendrell to Sitges and—he didn't know how—had lost all his money. Would we please lend him some to go join Patrick in Marrakesh? I had said no.

"Why?" Carlos asked me.

"I don't know," I answered. "In the first place, because we don't have it."

I didn't say that if I'd had it, I'd have given it to him, because I'm a coward. What's more, the *angelo musicante* looked so frail without his long hair. But I would have liked to give him the money, more than anything, to make that boy love me. Patrick doesn't love me and says he doesn't want anything to do with me because I'm a big bully; yes, I'd have given money to this one so that my son would stop considering me a tyrant, shielding himself— when I wouldn't let him go out—behind the earsplitting music of the record player he had bought with money only God knows where he got. When he came home with the machine I punished him by keeping him in the house for three days, but couldn't get him to confess how he had obtained it; he retreated, as he always did in similar cases, into an ugly silence that would persist for many weeks.

"But I was right not to give the kid money," I told Carlos. "I was able to prove it that same evening."

Anyway, when I refused him the money, Bijou—that's what he called himself, I finally found out; God knows what his Lagos relatives, who were so *vieux Chili*, would have said!—started to talk about Rimbaud, unnerving me by saying that he *was* Rimbaud, though he'd never written anything. Rimbaud! I'd thought I'd recognized the evil blond filth, the perverted defiance in those clear eyes, the dirty uneven teeth of the character in *Coin de table*! I went on telling Carlos that my biggest concern was that the previous day, June 2, had been my mother's birthday, she was dying but still lucid, and that if I'd called her up, if I'd had the money to do it, I would have heard her voice for the last time—I also told him, laughing a little nervously, that Bijou had tried to offer himself to Gloria and me, as Rimbaud had done with the Verlaine-Mathilde marriage.

"Quite a nice kid," Carlos observed.

"Why do you say that?"

"So what happened?"

"Nothing."

"Why?"

"Because Verlaine was a little over thirty and I'm over the half-century hump; and frankly my batteries are a bit low. What I have at home is enough and sometimes too much for me, and I don't have any extra libido for experiments. Besides, at that moment my mother was the problem."

"I've heard you complain about a lack of spark in your

relationship with Gloria. Wouldn't it have been interesting for you two . . . ?"

I brushed off this suggestion, so strangely perverse coming from Carlos Minelbaum, or at least so liberal that I chalked it up to our difference in age—Carlos is fifteen years younger than I and comes from a less conventional background—and went on with my story. While eating whatever Gloria had been able to find in the house, Bijou had heard us wearily arguing about the chances of borrowing money from someone to call Chile. He had stopped us, and after draining his whole glass of white wine at one gulp, he rose to his feet and asked:

"Don't you know?"

"What?"

"That you can phone anywhere free?"

"How?"

"What world are you living in? Come with me."

A little annoyed, I followed that young boy whose shaved head and high cheekbones made him look like an Egyptian mask. He led me silently through the Sitges night to Dos de Mayo Street, he a little ahead and I trailing behind. He went into Tommy's Bar, largely a homosexual bar, as I knew, which made me think it best to wait for Bijou at the door. Inside he was greeted by Catalan accents, affectionate words in German, English, French, or of approval and admiration from Castilians, Colombians, Cubans, Chileans, Argentines. A noisy, laughing, polyglot group soon formed around Bijou, who, without accepting the drinks offered him at the bar, asked for and listened to advice until a much older boy—a professional model who went around surrounded by admiring men and women—looked very serious and gave Bijou some directions. Bijou listened carefully, thanked him, said goodbye, and left with a wave of the hand. When he joined me outside, he said: "Follow me."

In Las Gaviotas I confessed to Carlos that I had felt uncomfortable following Hernán and Berta's son to what in my world was called "a den of iniquity," and that deep down, despite my purely mental liberal attitude, I still clung to the old opinions; my sinking feeling as I waited outside Tommy's Bar confirmed this. Everything had made me disagreeably certain what the relationship between Patrick and Bijou was. Why did he want to join Patrick in Marrakesh? Why did Patrick, who never wrote letters, not even to his dying grandmother, who was always anxious for news, write to Bijou quite often and tear up or burn the answers he received? Patrick was hardly ever so secretive, not even when he turned against us or asked us not to invade his privacy. . . . What made them so close? I wanted to ask him and make him feel that I'd understand everything. But I didn't dare speak.

Anyway, working our way through the maze of Sitges's most solitary streets, we reached the other side of the railroad tracks (Bijou, of course, had us cross them at an unauthorized place), and came to a different, working-class Sitges, new, not at all touristy, with small bars patronized by workers from Murcia, auto mehanics' shops that were closed at this hour, old men and women sitting on straw chairs in the doorways of apartment buildings even more modest than mine but that must have seemed to them, coming as they did from the country and a life of hunger, a step toward heaven. Others, leaning on ground-floor windowsills, looked into apartments where the TV was still going strong. The minute the programs were over, people would troop home to bed and the streets would suddenly empty: all this made it "very much like a hick town," Bijou observed.

At one street corner he stopped before a lighted telephone booth. Inside, a girl was talking and laughing. I
made out an Argentine or Uruguayan accent. Bijou asked
me to write down Chile's country code and the number I
wanted to call. I did it on the back of a scrap of paper I
found in my pocket, covered with notes on the people in
Sitges I intended to use in my novel. He said that the girl's
conversation would drag on for some time and it would be
wiser to move to the nearest doorway. We hung back
quietly in the shadows for a while. Bijou's fingers played
with my paper. These silences make me uncomfortable,
since I belong to a generation that feels it must fill everything with words, and to pass the time, I asked him why he
called himself Bijou, such an ambiguous name.

"That's what I like about it," he said. "When I was
younger and disobeyed my parents, right or wrong,
they'd get angry, just like you with Patrick, and they'd say,
'Look at the *alhajita*, the little jewel, that we're stuck with.'
Then, as their anger got to be a habit, they started calling
me *alhaja* or *alhajita*, and would use that name to introduce
me to the friends who came to the house to talk about the
MAPU,★ which they both belonged to. "This is our *alhaja*," they'd say. So then I started introducing myself as
Alhaja to the groups of friends, twelve, thirteen, fourteen
years old, who got together at street corners in the *quartier*
to smoke our first marijuana. And then my friends told me
that Alhaja sounded like an Algerian or Moroccan name
and that Algerians and Moroccans were inferior races, like
blacks and Chinese and Jews. I didn't want my French
friends to get me mixed up with these or with Latin Americans, especially Mexicans, who look so Chinese. . . .
That's why I call myself Bijou, not Bijou Lagos, which

★ Breakaway left wing of Chile's Christian Democratic Party. —TRANS.

sounds too Latin American, just plain Bijou, and that, you
know, is the French word for *alhaja* . . ."

"Yes, I know."

How could I ask him why he hated those he called the
"inferior races" without making him look down on me?
Before I could find a way to phrase this question, I saw
Bijou tense up, his eyes riveted on the booth.

"Come on, uncle, she's ready to hang up," he said.
While the girl in the phone booth was saying goodbye,
Bijou read the phrases on the paper, observing: "It's the
same thing all Chileans write about, torture, persons who
disappear, the silly things in communist politics—"

"Not communist."

"This gal will never quit talking. Well, let her carry on.
It's a pleasure robbing ITT, especially for leftist Chileans
like you, right, uncle?"

His calling me uncle touched me, it was so Chilean, so
childish, no doubt dating back to memories of evenings in
the Lagoses' home in Santiago during the UP, when I was
an "uncle" to Bijou—what was his real name?—and Hernán was "uncle" to Patrick, but with Bijou's next words
this emotion was replaced by another:

"She'd better hurry—the cops may show up."

"The police?" I panicked at what for Chileans of my
generation, especially for the son of a legislator, who may
have been only a vote in Congress, but a legislator after all,
called up feelings of deep guilt.

"Naturally, the police," Carlos Minelbaum explained,
drinking the last of his whiskey, whose ice was melting
fast, because the sun had slipped in over the edge of the
green umbrella. "Don't you know about rigged telephones
that allow you to talk to any part of the world for as long as
you want, without a single coin? There are experts at
rigging phones. I believe some insert a piece of wire, others

put in a coin tied to a string and then pull it back out . . . I think it can be done a thousand different ways. Word gets around to the kids about where there's a telephone they can use to call home, usually to beg for money, to listen to their mother's voice, to promise the girlfriend that they'll come back, to tell the wife or the son that they're missed but that they'll have to get along on their own for a while, to ask about terrorism and political violence, to explain that they're sick . . . and so on. At first the police weren't wise to this phenomenon, so common in all the capitals of Europe and no doubt born of the despair of the Latin Americans in exile. Anyway, as soon as word gets around that a certain phone booth has been rigged, groups of boys and girls form, sometimes waiting for hours or entire nights, sitting on the ground, standing in line, smoking grass, eating sandwiches, yes, waiting patiently, without complaining about the endless calls to Buenos Aires, Bogotá, Montevideo, or Santiago, because they know that they themselves will also talk nonstop to every corner of the world. This went on until, at least here in Sitges, the police found out and made a raid and arrested a large group of them. Now, they tell me, you have to be more careful. The telephone company checks the booths almost every day. That's why you have to get the right tip, the right booth that day, before people crowd around and it gets hot and the police turn up. You should use them if you're worried about your mother."

From now on, since I had just learned about it, I was afraid that I would also join the circle of petty criminals, I told Carlos, accepting Bijou's theory that stealing from ITT was not really a crime: disobeying the law and petty crime are two different concepts. I went on telling Carlos the story. When the Argentinian girl finished talking, she explained that all you had to do was insert a twenty-five-

peseta coin, which I gave Bijou, and dial the number: it
was a fantastic telephone, fixed up real well, she hoped it
would last, she said, and she left.

I squeezed into the narrow booth with the kid: his delicate physique fitted in disturbingly close to mine, as Bijou
too was aware, even though his mind seemed to be very
much on what he was doing. Something was wrong. Instead of working its magic in the telephone's mysterious
gut, the coin he put into the slot was rejected.

"*Merde! C'est cette conne qui l'a abîmé . . .*" Bijou was saying, passionately engaged in what he was doing, furiously
banging on the phone and repeating the same useless pro-
cedure with the coin over and over again. I would not hear
my mother's dying voice tonight. Instead there was this
thin, calculating, wised-up body almost touching mine and
waiting, I realized, for me to move a fraction of an inch
closer. I was not about to do it.

"Suddenly I understood," I told Carlos, "that for me
Bijou's attraction was not quite sexual but something else,
a desire to take his body over, to *be* him, to take over his
moral codes and his appetites; my hunger to get into
Bijou's skin was a desire that my pain would become
another pain, other pains I didn't know or had forgotten.
At least not my tyrannical code or the pains that had been
tearing me apart."

"Of course," Carlos answered. "But maybe the other
thing also."

"A part of it, maybe, but not in the first place."

"Maybe. Or maybe you're rationalizing."

"Maybe."

After one more bang the magic instrument kept the
coin. Forgetting all about me, Bijou concentrated on what
he was doing as if his life depended on it. He dialed the
number I had written on the paper, holding it in front of

him. Peering between the Celac and Fanta ads that covered the glass sides of the booth to see if anyone who looked dangerous was coming, at last Bijou smiled at me. He held the receiver to my ear without giving it to me yet. He said, *"Ça va,"* and proudly explained: "Satellite. Here, take it, uncle, but I'd better stay in the booth with you, because if the cops come by and see me waiting, they may get suspicious. You look respectable."

"And did you talk?" Carlos asked me.

"Yes," I answered, smiling like a kid confessing some prank. "I talked for at least an hour and a half."

"I'm glad."

"I heard my mother's voice. It sounded small, but not because of the distance, which the satellite eliminates."

"What did they tell you?"

"Everything's the same, just as it was a year ago."

The nearness of Bijou's body in the very narrow phone booth didn't bother me, but I felt that, like all boys his age, he'd laugh at the emotional intensity I'd no doubt show when I talked to my family, so I thanked him and begged him to leave. He got out of the booth. Closing the door, he waved goodbye and disappeared, indifferent to everything, into the Sitges night.

"Did they tell you the results of the latest tests?"

"Just as contradictory as the previous ones. And she still won't eat; her mouth, her tongue, her gums, her throat, her esophagus are all ulcered. She has very little life left, Sebastian told me, and she has to be fed with catheters. . . ."

After a moment of silence, Carlos Minelbaum said:

"You know she's going to die, don't you?"

"Yes."

"Anorexia nervosa. But it's strange. They generally don't last this long. Besides, it mostly affects young people."

There, in front of a sea that was too calm and the anemic palm trees that postcard manufacturers have to touch up to make attractive, and speaking in a loud voice so that Carlos would hear me, I explained that my mother, still holding on in spite of everything, had told me last night that she didn't intend to die before we got home. She wanted to see me, Patito, "my darling boy," and Gloria. She would wait for us. She also said that above the branches, recently stripped by winter, of the old plum tree in the garden, from her bed she could see the entire Cordillera covered with snow down to its base. It's snowed a lot this winter, she said, the whole mountain is white, the kids go up there to ski on weekends, and the railroad and the road to Mendoza have been closed off, but that didn't matter now, she went on from her sickbed in a house surrounded by a frozen garden, because nowadays airplanes fly over lightning and snowstorms and I would get there any day now, she was sure of it, with Gloria and Pato—oh my God, how could I make Pato write, even a postcard, to his grandmother who thought about him so desperately?—they'd come with me to close her eyes together with the rest of her grandchildren, as it should be, and she'd die in the bed she'd slept in all her life, in spite of that savage Allende, who had ruined us all and was still doing it—she believes Allende is still in power, Carlos, she has forgotten all about the coup. She has suppressed Pinochet in her mind, she has made him and Allende one and the same person, because she imagines that Allende is still the cause of all our disasters—and we ought to go see her as soon as possible, because my father would speak up in Congress so that Allende wouldn't stop us from coming into the country, congressmen had a lot of influence, and that was only right, even those in the opposition like my father, who was so highly respected, and that was good, because it showed that our country accepted conflict as the motor of politics: essentially, despite that savage Allende, the rules of the game were still in force."

"Is that what your mother told you on the phone last night?" Carlos asked me, surprised.

"Yes—my mother is quite a politician, like all Chilean women. She may not have used those exact words, but that's what she tried to say, in her own way."

"And what did your brother have to say?"

"That it's my duty to go and see her."

"What a strange woman!" Carlos murmured. "I'd like to have known her. Keep me informed on how she is. . . . She really hangs on to life."

"When I hung up," I went on, "my eyes were full of tears, but I was comforted knowing that, repeating my petty crime, I'd talk to her again tomorrow. Anyhow, I was glad I'd sent Bijou off so he wouldn't see me in this state."

I confessed to Carlos that I hadn't gone straight home. Unable to stand the tension of waiting, Gloria would have taken a glass of cognac and a Valium to wipe out the world—Bijou as houseguest, my mother, whom she adored, dying, the endemic shortage of money, the feeling of being used and abused, the sense of futility, of defeat—and then she'd wake up the next morning to a big cup of black coffee and feel at least passably strong enough to start her day. So I headed down Dos de Mayo Street to the Sandra bar, where Cacho Moyano welcomed me at his table, set up, at this time of year, under an awning outside on the street itself, where even in this month, and with a transient population, Cacho steadily greeted a good many people who kissed or hugged him, or offered him a drink, or patted his head, or covered his eyes asking *Guess who?* in English: a very young skinny English girl who looked like a depraved little thing, bold and demanding Frenchwomen with tinted carroty hair, tanned young guys as happy-go-lucky as he, who walked in and out of other bars and went on down the street, people, I thought, even farther away than the satellite over the wintery garden circumscribed by the white Cordillera my mother could see from her bed. I ordered a whiskey, all set to forget everything and enjoy the movie that was this crowded, hot street where all symbols of identity were scrambled. Suddenly the movie settled on a single frame: across the street, Tommy's Bar, where my eyes zoomed in on Bijou's shaved head. David Bowie was singing "Kooks," and the music, together with music from other night spots and the chatter and laughter all around us, was deafening. It was impossible to hear others or make yourself heard. I leaned across our tiny table to yell at Cacho:

"Look, the kid who disappeared in La Cala."

"Is *that* the one?"

"Yes."

"I didn't know. Are you interested in him?"

I told him that little boys weren't my weakness.

"He was cuter before, with his long blond hair," Cacho thought out loud. "But if you want him, you can have him. Three thousand pesetas."

I jumped.

"Do you know him?" Cacho asked, seeing my reaction, afraid that he had said the wrong thing.

"It looks like you're the one who knows him," I said.

"He's been making the rounds of the bars for almost a week now."

"A week? It can't be!"

"You know him, then."

"He's a friend of Patrick's, and the son of Chilean friends of mine."

David Bowie's voice was getting louder, generalizing:

> *"If you stay*
> *you won't be sorry*
> *'cause we believe in you . . .*
> *Soon you'll grow*
> *so take a chance*
> *with a couple of kooks . . ."*

"Is he . . . ?" I began.

"A male whore?"

I nodded.

"Well, he's not queer. Sometimes he goes off with some old faggot who pays him, but then, as if to clean himself, he comes back to pick up some gal in the bars, always younger than himself, lost kids, see, that suddenly show up around here, thirteen or fourteen years old. He takes them to a bingo parlor or the discos and afterward to bed, I guess."

I took a swig of whiskey that emptied my glass and ordered another, sinking back into my armchair to shade my no doubt haggard face from the light.

"What's wrong, Julito?"

I didn't dare ask him what I wanted to, the thing whose answer I knew but still needed someone to disprove or definitely confirm so that I'd at least know it wasn't a ridiculous senile dread.

"Tell me . . ." I started to ask and stopped to listen to David Bowie:

> *"We've got*
> *a lot of things*
> *to keep you warm and dry*
> *and a funny old crib*
> *on which the paint won't dry . . ."*

Cacho Moyano had shifted his chair so that he was next to me with his head in the shadows, watching the freeze-frame of Bijou in the bar across from us, clearer now that the crowd heading for the discos was starting to thin out.

Cacho whispered in my ear, "I know what you want to know."

"What?"

"Patrick."

"Yes. Is he . . . ?"

"He's not a queer. I'll put my hand in the fire."

I let out a sigh of relief that in a way relaxed me, leaving only hatred for myself, easy enough to manage, for this fear of homosexuality felt by people of my class and generation. I thought I had gone past that. But, I told myself, of course this had to do with my son, and if that had been the case, perhaps I could have helped him . . . but no, not me. Only a kook can help another kook.

Cacho was saying, "This kid is a pervert, capable of anything; he knows very well what he's up to and what's useful to him. Patrick, no—he's a nut, a nice thoughtless kid who may wander off, but he's not a queer."

"And . . . what about the rest?"

"What?"

"Marijuana?"

"Julito, you're old enough, you know here on Dos de Mayo it's like drinking Coca-Cola. Do you want a puff?"

I inhaled the grass, hoping it would pick me up a little.

"And . . . and the rest?"

Cacho rose to his feet slowly, greeting someone a way off. His mind was somewhere else, looking for other people. Our conversation had been too long to hold his attention. But he said to me with emphasis:

"Don't ask me any more, Julito. Patrick is a crazy kid, but he's not bad, see. . . . I've got to leave now with that Australian girl I said hello to; she's waiting for me. Take it easy. Drink your whiskey and go home to bed. *Ciao!*"

"Then," I finished telling Carlos, who was rising to his feet to welcome Gloria and Ana María to our table, "I got up to leave. And listen . . . when I asked for my bill they told me it had been paid, a kid with a shaved head, who was no longer in the bar across the way, had taken care of it."

I GET DRESSED and go down to buy bread—like a true Chilean, without it I feel as if I haven't eaten anything— which Gloria had forgotten, and some bottles of beer. But I go down mostly to keep our promise to Pancho that we'd walk Myshkin around the block twice a day. It's so typical of Gloria's selfishness, going to the Prado today, our first day in Madrid—as if we didn't have months for it—and leaving the important things undone.

I run into Beltrán, the concierge, who is watering the rosebushes in the entryway. He puts down the hose and, wiping his hands on a white handkerchief so different from the Kleenex I use, comes over to say hello. Myshkin jumps up and down around him with the familiarity of an old and possibly amusing friendship.

Talkative, like a good Madrid concierge who knows all the ins and outs of the small world around him and nothing else, outspoken but not nosy or rude, he tells me that this morning he's had the pleasure of greeting my wife, very good-looking, of course, and elegant, as they say South American women are. I don't feel much like going out. Would it be right to ask Beltrán, on our first day in Pancho's apartment, to go buy the things I need and take his friend Myshkin for a walk? But seeing his white linen handkerchief that matches so well his gray uniform and its silver buttons—real silver?—I don't dare. Nor am I ready to sample the "local color" of the concierges that Paco had

forced on me with his preliminary remarks about Madrid
in summer. I let Myshkin pull me toward an irresistibly
odorous ash tree at the edge of the sidewalk.

Beltrán follows me, telling the dog, "You've already
taken a walk once this morning, so that's it, home you go.
You don't have another walk coming till this evening."
And turning to me: "These dogs have such a flat nose that
the heat tires them out and they have a hard time breathing,
like Pekinese dogs. But the pug is a better breed, more
select. Not many people own them. The Duchess owned
some. . . ."

"The Duchess of . . . our neighbor?"

"No, the Duchess of Windsor. But they were black."

"Who walked him this morning?"

He answers that my wife did, very early. I'm ashamed I
judged her unfairly: yes, when she's happy, as she seems to
be here in Madrid, she does all her chores without a word
and, what's more, with elegance, for instance like taking
Myshkin out this morning. This may be the first sign of a
long spell of peace. But the dog keeps pulling on his leash,
he wants to smell the next tree, and the next, and he pees
again and again to mark his territory once more. I follow
slowly.

"Nice neighborhood," I comment to the concierge.

"The best in Madrid."

"Good houses," I observe, as we move along. "It's a
shame they're almost all hidden by such high walls."

"People have to defend themselves."

"Of course," I answer without asking him to explain
against whom.

"Only a better class of people live here," he says. "Ours
is the only apartment building around here, only three
floors, two apartments on each. All the families are away
on vacation now. The building is empty, except for you.

There are generally few people in this neighborhood at this time of year."

"There's such a pretty view from Mr. Salvatierra's apartment!" I say. "Especially remembering that we're in the heart of Madrid. This is so quiet it doesn't seem real, there are elms and horse chestnuts, and ash trees on the sidewalks, and the street has paving stones, it's like living in a small town. We never seem to hear the traffic over on Serrano and Velázquez streets."

"Ah!" Beltrán sighed, puffing up contentedly. "Mr. de Salvatierra's apartment has one of the most beautiful views in Madrid, because almost all its windows face the Duke of Andía's park. It's glorious, one of the few left now, not like in General Franco's time, when all better-class people lived in their palaces. . . ."

Myshkin gives a strong tug and makes a dash for a tree some distance off, and I do my best to leave Beltrán behind. I'm not about to complicate my stay in Madrid with Franco-sympathizing concierges, who anyway are almost all retired members of the Guardia Civil, spies and informers who had Madrid in their grip during the dictatorship. And so I make up my mind that even if Gloria brought Myshkin out this morning to go around the block and Beltrán has told me about it, I'll take him for another walk.

The houses in this part of Madrid, all of them surrounded by gardens or small parks, are walled in like impenetrable bunkers and defended, I imagine, by alarm systems and fierce dogs, as if the people lived here in paranoid terror of being what they are—exposed to the threat of robbery, murder, kidnapping, terrorism, political violence—and their gardens are hidden by walls that are sometimes peeling, over which thick ivy creepers hang or the branches of flowering trees lean out. I notice something

very curious on some of the walls: they're covered with
what my son's generation calls *pintadas*: DOWN WITH THE
KING, A FREE AND UNITED SPAIN, CARILLO MURDERER,
MONARCHY YES JUAN CARLOS NO, LONG LIVE FRANCO,
and the fascist emblem of the rightist Falange, revived and
threatening, omnipresent. Yes, in Madrid the political cli-
mate is much more disturbing than in peaceful Sitges. Or
is it peculiar to the small world of this neighborhood
accessible only to people who appear in the popular magazine *Hola*, which my wife devours in the beauty parlor
because she's ashamed to buy it? This is like a small walled
feudal city inside another city, a bulwark with a paranoid
heart, whose only sign of aggressiveness, at the moment,
is to allow its elegant walls, shaded by collaborationist
vines, to keep the fascist slogans: LONG LIVE BLAS PIÑAR,
LONG LIVE FUERZA NUEVA, REDS-MURDERERS, and even
KING JUAN CARLOS MURDERER.

As I approach my building from the street at the other
end of the block, I see Beltrán, who has obviously been
lying in wait, coming to meet me. He takes Myshkin's
leash and lets him loose, saying, "Mr. de Salvatierra always
lets him off the leash here, because Myshkin, who knows
all the trees and has pissed on all of them, goes straight
home to wait for him."

We walk under the huge peeling wall that hides the
Duke of Andía's villa. I mention how badly kept up it is, in
contrast to the perfection inside. He answers, with what I
feel is a kind of superior air, that it's better to keep the wall
that way so as not to tempt thieves and especially terrorists
trained by the Reds, who threaten the peace of decent
people. Seeing this wall, who would ever guess, he asks,
that one of the richest men in Spain, one of the most noble,
a true national glory, lives here? He's married to a French-
woman, very elegant, like all Frenchwomen. The mansion

is closed now, because they go away for the summer. People don't like her very much, or her children, whom Beltrán has watched grow up. But they married well—an expression I haven't heard since the Chile of my childhood, in my grandmother's time—to their mother's great joy.

If I'll notice, he informs me, there are really two houses in the garden next door: the mansion, with the swimming pool, the lawn, and the cypresses on the street side, and then at the back of the garden, hidden by the trees—especially horse chestnuts that are so thick with leaves at this time of year—another house, also very pretty but smaller. That part of the garden was run-down for a long time, because no matter how much her ladyship the Duchess begged them to move into it, none of her sons wanted to live near their mother.

He, Beltrán—we're at the door of the building; as he talks he takes a pair of shears and trims the hedge here and there—explains that he's taking the liberty of telling me this because they say that her ladyship is very strict with her sons and daughters-in-law but is all charm with the help: all her servants adore her and side with her against her uncooperative sons. A year ago, however, her youngest son—married to an Austrian baroness with a name nobody could pronounce . . . photographs of the wedding had appeared in *Hola* . . . Beltrán and his wife clip everything out and paste it in a scrapbook, where they save everything published about the people they know, or whose servants are his and his wife's friends—well, her youngest son finally agreed to move into the house in back. Her ladyship had the long-neglected pavilion restored and the garden replanted. And now the son, the count of something or other, Beltrán can't remember now, and his wife, who is not Spanish but dotes on their two children, live happily in the pavilion at the back of the park. Beltrán thinks the small girl, the little blonde, is an "angel":

> *Guten morgen,*
> *Margarete . . .*

The Baroness's Austrian origin unveils the mystery of the German children's song on the lips of a Spanish grandee's granddaughter. I take leave of Beltrán, explaining that I have much work to do, putting off his offer to show me his scrapbook, which contains, in a special place of honor of course, clippings on an exhibition of Mr. de Salvatierra's attended by none other than Mr. de Areilza, Count of Motrico.

"Perhaps some other day," I tell Beltrán as I leave him, noticing a tiny Spanish flag in his lapel and thinking of how Gloria would laugh at my flirtation with the fascist world: LONG LIVE BLAS PIÑAR, LONG LIVE FUERZA NUEVA, UCD IS RED. Are Beltrán and his concierge friends in the neighborhood told to paint those irritating slogans on the walls of this quiet part of town?

When I take off Myshkin's collar and let him run in search of his close friend Irina, I tell myself that some other day I'll take a walk in other Madrid neighborhoods and look for slogans with equally strong but opposite sentiments. I gulp down whatever food I find, standing next to the refrigerator, whose door I leave open while I eat and drink a glass of wine. Then I go to the bedroom, so white, spacious, neat, and quiet, with its huge open window. I stand next to it, almost among the curtains, to watch the garden next door.

What was an empty stage when I left, before the performance started, is now invaded by the characters of the drama, whose plot I may never learn. They move about the set acting very naturally. There are two now, a boy and a girl playing with the yellow plastic hen under the elms; the nasty, bigger boy is trying to snatch the toy away from his sister, making her cry. A gardener kneeling next to a flower bed along the wall is planting mastic shrubs, of course, at the beginning of June, zinnias, salvias, dahlias, campanulas that I will see in bloom, I say to myself, with sudden joy, at summer's end. A servant girl in uniform comes in along the path with her shopping in a huge package, from which something I recognize as a bundle of leeks is sticking out. Suddenly a very slender and very blond young woman appears, a woman with shortish hair, its ends combed inward in a hairdo they called a "debutante bob" when I was young. She goes up to the servant, asks her something, pulls the leeks out of the package, looks them over; madam approves of their quality, and the servant smiles and disappears, while the "doting mother" goes over to her children, who are both crying now. She breaks up their fight gently, comforts them, hefts the girl up in one arm and holds out her other hand to the boy; she promises them something and takes them toward the house, floating off in an atmosphere of sunlight and green and violet shadows, down the flagstone path bordered by patches of marigolds.

They must have gone to lunch, I say to myself, coming out of my hiding place among the curtains from where I've watched this scene, so *gemütlich*, in which the blond "doting mother" leaves behind the aura of her slender presence and her smooth, supple hair.

Then I lower the blinds very slowly to blot out the extra

brightness. Anyway, it's too hot outside—one can never be sure of this in a new place—maybe it's just that the walk with the dog has drained me so that I give up all thought of work. I'll take a siesta. At this time of day in summer all of Madrid—but for my wife trotting around in museums, or confiding her frustrations to some new friend over a bowl of gazpacho in a dive—is having a siesta. But why, I wonder as I flop into bed, haven't these rich people, so young and full of fun, why haven't they gone away to vacation at one of their many estates, farms, or beach houses? Is it chic now to spend the summer in Madrid when you have a garden like the one next door, a luxury that very few people can boast of these days? Or is it possible that the husband of the girl with the blond hair that swings like a gold bell in the sun does something as extravagant as work, for instance, or is he mixed up in one of the political factions of the moment? I'd better ask the concierge another day, when I take Myshkin for his walk, without letting him see my interest, which I don't really have anyway. Curiosity? I guess so. But it won't last very long. I put on the black night mask my wife wears to blot out everything when she wants to sleep, even if I don't need it in this bedroom sealed off by blinds, window-panes, and curtains. I curl up on my side to sleep.

Before I drop off, however, a steady noise I can't identify breaks the silence of the bedroom and comes in through all the elements I thought were cushioning me from the outside world. All of a sudden I feel like emptying my bladder, an urge I must obey right away. And when I come back to bed, lying on my back on top of the bedspread, I listen carefully to that steady, fresh, soothing murmur, like a running stream: so, I've had to visit the bathroom because of the sound of water rushing into the Duke's swimming pool. As soon as I identify that sound, I drop to the very depths of sleep.

THE PHONE ON the night table wakes me up: Gloria. I asked her not to call me. How did I make out on my first day of work in Madrid, she wants to know. Very well, very well, I tell her. She asks me what I've done, she's interested, but I know that when she insists so much it's only so that after listening to me for a few minutes, she can start on her own "thing," as Pato would say, and tell me what she wanted to tell me about herself in the first place. That's why I answer that I'd rather not tell her anything yet: I assure her that I'm relaxed and contented. I lay down for a minute after lunch, I say, and dozed off listening to the stream of water filling the Duke's swimming pool. . . . It's better to mention it in case my voice sounds sleepy. She asks if I would mind very much if she didn't come home for dinner: she realizes it's our first day in Madrid and we should spend it together, but in Katy Verini she has discovered a human being who's even more extraordinary than she at first seemed to us when we met her in Sitges, and she'd like to go with her to see *Les Enfants du paradis* at the Cine-Club, after a light snack. Was I tempted to go with them? Wasn't I always complaining in Sitges that there were never any good movies?

I answer no, not today. I may want to work or rest. . . . I know I shouldn't work so hard the first day, but it's best to get going even if later I have to tear everything up . . . it's always good for limbering up. Gloria tries to make me share the excitement she felt in front of Rembrandt's *Lucretia* at the Prado, she mentions the mother-of-pearl tones of the nautilus reflected on her skin and in the gold in her hair— Gold in her hair? A gold bell? No, not a bell, and I don't think it's a Rembrandt but a Titian. Gloria will never learn to be accurate. But I tell her that since she'll be coming home pretty early we'll have time to talk this evening, yes, because tonight I want to read Styron's *Sophie's Choice*, I found a deluxe edition on a table in the living room; and that way I'll get up early the next morning, fresh and full of energy for work. I'll just have a snack. She's not to worry. She should go ahead and enjoy herself. Later, she can tell me all about *Lucretia* and about her Uruguayan friend, and we'll talk, once again, about *Les Enfants du paradis*, which we never grow tired of.

I don't heat up any food; I eat ham and a tin of something on the small table in the pantry, because I realize that, lulled by the stream of water, I've slept so long that when Gloria called she couldn't imagine she'd be waking me up. Solitude and silence are luxuries only the rich can afford: in Sitges the walls are almost as thin as paper, and the television of the apartment on the other side of the street, the shouts of passersby, and the dreadful music from the disco invade us. Gloria always turns on the radio to hear the news and find out what's going on in the world, she says, but most of all to cut herself off from aggressive reality, so aggressive that it is the time of day when she starts to drink: her blood pressure is low, she says, or has gone down after coffee and she has tried to bring it up with a little *agua del Carmen*, but later to start cooking she needs a glass of wine, and another, and another, in good spirits at first, either because she feels cold, or because she argued with me, or because she can't bear Patricio's not talking to me, and then her good spirits are followed by an awkwardness you can hardly detect, she drops things, puts too much salt in the pea soup or forgets it altogether, she hits her leg on a stool, and everything seems to get in her way and she can't judge distances, and she repeats things over and over until Pato blows up and howls for her to stop repeating herself, that she's drunk, she's an alcoholic, she's stammering, she's lurching like a sailboat . . . But no, Gloria's not an alcoholic, even if I've also accused her of it. I drink too, and I lurch and stammer and everything becomes pleasantly hazy, we drink a bottle of ordinary wine together while she cooks and we listen to the news or argue because she hates to cook, it's only human for her to hate it, I understand and I drink wine with her.

Why aren't there people "who have a drink," only alcoholics? How much do we drink in comparison with Americans? Hemingway, F. Scott Fizgerald: their novels all take place in bars, with people who are much more drunk than Gloria and I have ever been in our lives, but the stigma of being alcoholics doesn't hang over their heads, as Pato, in his very modern way, accuses us of being. I know we're not. What's bad about it is that sometimes we don't stop, but not often. We're both responsible for this failure; I didn't drag her into it, I still have hope and so has she, but sometimes everything looks black, as if everything went on behind the night mask, and then the wine makes us believe the other one is to blame for our unhappiness: the failure is only partly ours, because no one can identify himself or herself, in an absolute and personal way, with the failure of our plans in general.

After eating I go into the bedroom where our bags are: I take out my papers and carry them along with my typewriter to the dining room. I put everything at the near end of the white marble-top table: blank Greyhound paper, the heaviest kind, five hundred brand-new sheets . . . my rejected manuscript . . . several rough drafts to check back on. In front of a second chair I set down the translation and some dictionaries: yes, let Gloria see that if I'm going to

work, so can she. And between our two places, the Casares
dictionary that we'll share. What time is it? Ten-thirty.
Gloria and Katy Verini are just going into the movie. How
time stretches out in the orderly silence of Pancho Salvatierra's place! I'll be able to work well here. Oh, I mustn't
forget my notebook! I sit down at the head of the table.

I push the typewriter away from the chair. I'm not going
to use it yet. I set the rejected version in front of me,
because I intend to read it *da capo*, like someone reading a
stranger's work for the first time, and really "see it"—
Núria Monclús's words—then jot down suggestions in my
notebook. The manuscript has blue plastic covers: a false
binding, a make-believe edition, I tell myself. But I don't
open it, because the white curtain in front of me, beyond
the other end of the table, bothers me. I get up, open it, and
return to my seat.

When I open the blue plastic cover of my rejected novel,
I discover that what bothers me most in the room are the
huge blinds cutting me off hermetically from the outside,
sealing me in. I take a slug of cognac and lift my arms to
slowly raise the blinds, which open gradually, unfolding
their marvelously articulated vertebrae: between their slits
I see the light in the garden next door. Before opening
them farther, I turn out all the lights in Pancho's dining
room, in case anyone outside should lift his eyes up to this
floor and discover me living in a house they had assumed
was completely empty. Only after turning out the lights
do I finish opening the blinds slowly, to keep from making
any noise, and they roll up into their invisible casing like a
two-dimensional mollusk into its shell.

"Magic spell" is an unpopular term, I know, but I have
to use it: suddenly the radiant magic spell of the world
outside subdues and replaces my poor reality. Through the
lacework of some black leaves in the foreground I can see

the swimming pool lighted from within: it's aquamarine, and spotlights hidden in the shrubbery light up the mansion's facade, the full height of the cypress that looks as flat as stage scenery, the black-and-white-striped canopy, the fragments of classical ruins, the wicker chairs, and the dining room's marvelous great French windows facing the terrace and now wide open: inside, around the table with flickering candelabras—are there really people for whom *dîner aux chandelles* is a regular custom?—I watch six persons in bathing suits moving around. No one is serving them: they leave their seats informally, fetch things, no doubt exquisite, from the buffet, and eat standing up, talking, drinking, laughing, changing groups.

Now they're coming out to the terrace next to the swimming pool! There are three girls—I recognize one of them, the blondest one, with barely a gentle hint of breasts and hips, she's the "doting mother" who soothed her children this morning and examined the leeks, but I can't imagine why she's acting as hostess in her in-laws' house, closed now that they're away; that's how young people are, I say to myself—and three boys; the girls are in very brief bikinis covered by long scarves tied at the waist or the neck, and the boys are in swimming trunks. They're bringing out drinks, a plate with dessert, or a coffee cup, and they chat and laugh a little. They're happy. All of them, the men and women, with bodies trimmed down to strictly essential form, without excess, as if built by Brancusi. Sexual plenitude is direct, expressed less with insinuations and teasing than with a kind of elasticity and freedom of movement that seem to put them in instant touch with everything around them and with one another: they make up a rhythmic frieze of stylized bodies in which no feminine or masculine attributes are missing. Before my eyes this frieze is in the process of being composed; little gestures join the figures together: someone handing someone else a glass, or stroking the back of a neck, or taking off a robe and dropping it on a chaise.

She's there: the gold bell, the most Brancusiesque, the most golden and polished of all of them, with long movements that have nothing indolent about them, with her rib cage and the natural softness of her pelvis revealed by the skimpy bikini, transformed into an immaculate object of luxury that seems to have no connection with the *Hausfrau* who examined the bundle of leeks this morning. She appears to have regular features. Her smile reveals teeth that flash as do other objects shining on that stage, glasses, silverware, the swimming pool's surface where the steady stream makes the light from the spotlights glitter, a thread of gold around one wrist, the candles still lighted in the dining room. How old is the blonde with the golden bell? Twenty-six . . . twenty-eight . . . twenty-nine? No, not twenty-nine. . . . When a journalist asked Myrna Loy— why do I remember these stupid things, where do I read them?—what a woman's best age was, the actress answered: "The ten marvelous years between twenty-nine and thirty." This blond woman with such economical lines, who is swaying and holding her arms high to encourage the others to dance, is not twenty-nine, she's still far from entering the maturity that's in her future, not her present or her past, she's dancing and the others dance with her to the beat of music I can't hear. . . . The movements of today's strange dances, strange mostly because there's nothing particularly sensual about them, or because their sensuality is ciphered in a code I don't know how to break and that therefore excludes me.

They make up a bas-relief of stylized gestures: *L'Après-midi d'un faune*? They dance by the glow of the spotlights, almost lackadaisically, reflected in the water, switching partners with the music never seeming to stop or change, without tension or effort under the striped awning, presided over by the authoritative presence of the cypress tree. Now they're dancing what Pato calls "a slow one," the almost-naked couples with their arms around each other, slim naked body against slim naked body. The blond hostess dances with a dark well-built boy—the Spanish cliché of the "handsome brute"—with a splendid neck, at least it's all I see, revealed by the short hair in fashion now. That intimacy . . . the parted shoulder blades whose line and gleaming skin barely oscillate to the music's beat, and the sureness with which he leads his partner: I sense the danger of his attraction, and I'd like to slip into his body, to be him, to wrap my arms around the slenderness of the girl, whose head rests on his shoulder, covering it with gold; yes, to be him and change my codes and problems, like this burning in my stomach brought on by the Courvoisier I'm not accustomed to, yes, to rub out my tracks and fly in search of another superego or, better yet, none at all, in search of pleasure only.

Ah, the splendor . . . the old heart-rending nostalgia for impossible times and bodies! The Gatsby–F. Scott Fitzgerald part of a world out of my reach, the party I wasn't invited to and can only dream about. . . . Ah, the childish fantasy, the terror at being left out! Left out? Impossible? What about my novel, that fierce weapon, to start forcing the breach? Núria Monclús, Vargas Llosa, Roa Bastos, Fuentes, Chiriboga, Cortázar . . . do they have access? No. This is a closed circuit, with its own language and values, an underworld with its slang and symbols that can't be substituted for those in my own underworld with its different stars. I long to pass through to the other side of the looking glass they live in, where perhaps the air is so thick it stops you from breathing.

The "handsome brute," the dark guy, so slim and strong, is he her husband?

The couples break up, chat, drink, and then form again in a new configuration, their arms around different partners, as if body contact were not part of a bigger involvement in an exclusive and binding passion. Slowly, in perfect harmony, they spin, shift about, while the light glittering on the water rejects the reflections of the couples to show off its own brilliance. Are there fragrances, sounds, that the glass window and the fragile latticework of the leaves in the foreground cut off from me? Those six beings are a mystery to me on all except the visual plane: I want to be them, not me. I open the window to look for fragrances and melodies: then, as if I had burst in on them, the undecipherable but moving eurhythmic figures in *L'Après-midi d'un faune* in its modern version suddenly change; they turn into caricatures, comic poses, and movements exaggerated to draw laughter, not harmony and body contact, in any of its forms:

> *"Stop,*
> *you're going too far,*
> *Stop,*
> *you're drivin' too fast,*
> *Stop,*
> *you're breakin' my heart . . ."*

I recognize the Glenn Miller song we used to dance to in my time. To this group of young people it is "nostalgic"— but it isn't, because it breaks no hearts and turns instead into a ridiculous yet moving parody of itself. I close the window and, humiliated, I shut out the fragrance of the water falling on the leaves, the jumble of sounds with which they are making fun, with their gestures, of my nostalgia, my reality.

When the "slow one" ends, four of the six sit down to drink on the cushioned wicker sofa. The blond Baroness and another girl, a little rounder, with tousled henna hair like my wife's, dance apart and at the same time together, interweaving different yet coherent movements with excited bodies that exhibit the pride of being what they are, and the pleasure of their rhythms and of their skin: the two female bodies acknowledge and accept the sexuality that gives them contact without touching: their fine arms, their tossing hair, lowered eyelids, the gallop of the tanned thighs, the arch of their necks, eyes, teeth, gold, crystal, skins that give off a glow, changing to the beat of the clapping hands of those who've remained seated. The clapping excites them, frenzied now at the edge of the pool, so frenzied that the string of the hostess's bikini top snaps, to the hilarious amusement of all the others, and exposes her small white breasts vibrating on the gold of her skin. The top has dropped to the ground, but she keeps on dancing, her nipples almost touching the more generous coppery breasts of the other dancer, who, to keep up with her, strips off her top and then her bottom, exposing her tuft of pubic hair: the hostess imitates her, everyone joins the dance, men and women shedding their skimpy swimming suits, dancing apart, frenzied, naked, until the well-built dark guy trips and falls into the pool, pulling the blonde with him, followed by the others, who also plunge into the water naked: I didn't hear the music or their voices, but I hear their bodies thrashing in the water.

And yet this familiarity between the six bodies, the three couples—how many are really "couples," I wonder—is not just the familiarity of bodies that delight one another: sure, they're friends, but the language of familiarity, when you're these youngsters' age and your body and your skin are tense and hungry, is very different, let's say, from the familiarity between us and the Minelbaums; we'd feel ridiculous letting ourselves go like them, not only ridiculous because of our age but also because our urgencies are of another kind. Sublimation? No, let's not pretend: I feel a sad emptiness opening inside me when I grow aware of the hopeless separation of my body and my world from the easy vigor of those bodies that go on swimming, splashing one another, laughing or floating in bunches with their arms around each other.

When they come out of the water they dance on the terrace again, for a short while, naked, changing partners. Soon the hostess gathers them around her, whispering, and boys and girls disappear together, arm in arm, in the direction of the house at the back of the garden. I make a wild dash for my bedroom: I can make them out in the darkness of the path, boys and girls, their silhouettes joined confusedly now; I make out the gleam of a watch, a glass in someone's hand, pointing out to me their course toward another, greater intimacy. Behind them is the turquoise brightness of the swimming pool, the terrace littered with bathrobes and bikinis, the unruffled cypress, and the Duke's dining room, where the candles in the silver candelabras still glitter over the banquet's leftovers.

I notice that I'm tightly gripping the glass of cognac in my hand as I return to the dining room; I also have been drinking for some time. I take a long, burning swig and bring the blinds down, but without looking because it hurts too much, and then I close the curtains. It hurts. Hurts. I go back to my typewriter. I look at it with disgust:

a placebo. A substitute for the pent-up feelings that I can't sublimate and that make me stretch out stiffly in my chair, like someone embalmed, facing my worthless work, my head all mixed up, my heart broken.

WHEN I HEAR her at the door, I open the rejected novel and pick up my pencil: "At dawn on September 11, the sky over Santiago was clear, as it generally is at this time of year in that part of Chile." False, weak, worthless. No, the dark one is not her husband. . . . Which of the others . . . ? What am I doing trying to recapture an experience that's absolutely pointless to me now?

"Julio?" I hear Gloria calling as she comes in.

"Here," I answer, sucking on my pencil.

Gloria comes over on tiptoe, almost without making the parquet creak, as if she were entering a tabernacle that she suspects is not empty: she does her best not to profane it.

She says, "Don't let me disturb you, love. I'm going to bed. Keep on working, I'll tell you everything tomorrow, it was quite interesting. . . ."

"I'm dead tired. I've worked so much."

"Is this cognac good?"

"Exquisite. Try it."

Kissing me, she smells my breath without meaning to.

"How much have you had?"

"Not much."

"That's a lie."

"Why are you accusing me if you don't know?"

"I myself filled the decanter with Courvoisier this morning, since Pancho said we could drink all we wanted, because he had hundreds of bottles of it."

"So then why shouldn't I drink?"

"You don't get any work done when you drink."

"Well, sometimes . . ."

"Have you worked?"

"Don't you dare question me."

I stand up suddenly. She's ugly, old. The corrupt Odalisque, creased, hysterical, full of anxiety, neurotic, guilty
of leaving me all alone on our first day in Madrid, without
her languor, her repose, a stranger to all pleasure, her body
without the economy I love so much in Brancusi, and now
also without Ingres's eloquent sureness of line. I go into the
bedroom and swallow a Valium.

"Ten milligrams of Valium after all that cognac?"

"If you don't shut up, I'll take another ten milligrams
and let's see what happens."

"You can do as you please."

"Why do you have to make me feel guilty for everything
I do or don't do?"

She stares at me quietly for a minute, a blank expression
in her eyes, her face empty.

She says, "I'm going to sleep in the other room."

But first I hear her pouring herself a glass of cognac. She
shuts her door: through the crack underneath I can tell
when she turns off the light.

I remain alone in the huge white bedroom, now dark,
listening to the stream flowing into the pool. No, not
alone: a cat, not one from Madrid, never stops purring in
my ear all night, like another instrument joining the water
in a duet:

> . . . *wait without hope*
> *For hope would be hope for the wrong thing; wait without love*
> *For love would be love for the wrong thing; there is yet faith*
> *But the faith and the love and the hope are all in the waiting.*
> *Wait without thought, for you are not yet ready for thought:*
> *So the darkness shall be light, and the stillness the dancing.*

Whisper of running streams, and winter lightning.
The wild thyme unseen and the wild strawberry,
The laughter in the garden, echoed ecstasy
Not lost, but requiring, pointing to the agony
Of death and birth.

3

HOW CAN EVERYTHING in the garden be the same, as if nothing happened on that marvelous night, and these were not the same shadows shivering and prowling around the house in the opposite hemisphere from where my mother is dying, sometimes lucid, always in pain?

After the six figures disappeared arm in arm between the foliage on their way to the pavilion, I believed that everything would change, or at least that the protagonists—I watch them at their daily tasks, receiving a visit by a girl-friend, on the way to work or to play squash or go shopping on Serrano Street—would be definitely marked. But no: the girl with the bell of polished gold is the "doting mother" praised by Beltrán, busy with her children, giving the gardener orders, dressed in clothes that usually show the wear and tear of two or three seasons; and her husband—not the "handsome brute" I assigned her that night but a less striking boy wearing glasses, with slightly wavy hair, neither long nor short—comes home after what I suppose is a working day, and plays with his dogs and his children, who leap up and down around him like me with my father when I was small. His wife serves tea on a tray on the lawn, under the chestnut tree that is opposite my bedroom window. It's hot outside: but the pollution, driven away from this microclimate by its privilege of trees, lets through the famous opal of the Madrid skies, blue but never primary, sometimes partly sifting through, frequently decorated with a cluster of clouds that dissolve and allow the gold to spill out around the couple lying on the grass and having tea, sheltered from the heat that gives a purple tint to the underside of the leaves, beneath the branches tossing to close or open up in the recently minted light and reveal the tête-à-tête of the young couple who still show so much trust in the virtue of pleasure.

On the other hand, I'm protected by Pancho's artificial comforts: air conditioning, the coolness of mirrors and marbles, double-glass windows that shut out all noise. Several days ago I finished rereading my novel, and the experience left me unfit for everything except spying— when Gloria isn't watching me, because she watches and asks me a lot of questions, pretending to show interest in my work—on how, day after day, a coherence different from all those I know gradually evolves in the garden next door. I've read my almost five hundred pages, removing myself, tearing myself away, untying myself from them as Núria Monclús suggested: veiled, behind the spiderweb of her arrogance, haughty with emphasis and without any shade of doubt, she suggested that it might be interesting for me to . . . well . . . try to "see it," a phrase no doubt put in her mouth by her phantom readers.

And I "saw" my luxuriant, sentimental, self-indulgent, boring novel. At first I took notes with a disinterest that didn't quite exclude hope. But I'm by nature an enthusiastic reader, especially of the contemporary novel, a subject I teach, or, rather, used to teach: so, as I got further into my thick manuscript I grew sure that the passion that should have breathed life into it was not convincing as literature nor valid as experience. From here, far away in place and time, the "good ones" are no longer quite as good as we believed at first, when some, not me, risked or lost their lives for it. As for the "bad ones"—I tremble at my profanation as I ask myself this question that may be a betrayal—were or are they quite as bad? In the prison camp, during the hour when we were allowed to walk around in the compound at dusk, behind the wooden walls of the latrine or hidden by the shadows in a corner, sometimes I heard the whispers of persons afraid of being recognized but whose voices could only be those of the guards themselves, with their fierce-looking machine guns. Those voices said:

"Not all of us are bad . . . we're afraid too . . . tell it to the others . . . we're not all bad . . ."

When I hate her because she's ugly or sloppily dressed or she salted the tomato soup too much or won't come out of her maddening stupor to sew a button on one of my shirts, I think that Gloria still needs to simplify everything to nurse the hatred she spreads around in gossip or secrets she now tells to Katy Verini, who has her under her thumb and comes around almost every day. From my work table I hear them talking for hours, sitting on one of Pancho's sofas, drinks in hand, Katy muffled up to her nose in shawls and scarves because she claims that she freezes in this igloo, the beige cat curled up in Gloria's lap, the beige dog rolled up in the would-be rags of Katy's lap:

"*Orecchini di veluto*, small nose like an upholstery button . . . look at all the extra skin you have, spoiled dog, we could make three normal dogs with those rolls of yours," Katy says, kissing Myshkin's smoke-colored snout. Then she turns to me, laughing till her face, a dark-skinned apple, like a mulatto's, protected by her defensive bangs, fills with malicious dimples: "And you, precious, are an old anarchist, with a fascist streak, like all anarchists. Look at Nietzsche. . . ."

"Your disillusion didn't go through the illusion that struggle gives rise to, Julio. Your 'humanist moderation' is nothing but gutless conformism," Gloria accuses me, tortured, unsmiling, a victim of Katy's stories about Uruguay's political ills told from a strongly Marxist point of view.

" 'Right' is the man who holds power," I answer, stripped of anger by exhaustion and repetition. "I wasn't born to be a hero, or even to be right, and this may make me look limited and conformist, but what can I do? That's the way I am. After everything I've been through, it's very hard finding out that I'm more interested in romantic pieces for the piano or Laurence Sterne's novels than in being right in any field whatsoever. Let me tell you, these conclusions about myself don't make me proud, and I don't deny that there's some resentment left in me, and maybe even the ability to channel it. Everything deteriorates and loses meaning, and I no longer have the strength to transform anything into theory or action that would compensate and explain it all."

Gloria and I have agreed to take the subway this Sunday and get off at the Latina stop, where Katy is waiting to lead us through the labyrinth of the Rastro's summer flea market, whose secrets she insists she knows in detail; to forget, at least this morning, my duty of taking stock and organizing debatable truths in the pages of my novel, which is lying on the dining-room table in a disorderly mess. I think of a general reorganization, without much feeling like it, while Gloria goes to put on makeup.

"I'll put on my face in a minute," she says, "and we'll leave."

As if it were easy. She doesn't have to confront a novel's cruel mirror that shows even the tiniest crow's-feet; yes, she can allow herself the luxury of "putting on her face," any face she feels like, a different one each day if she wants to, with rouge and other kinds of crayons, in imitation of the models in the magazines, as I saw her and Katy doing one afternoon, convulsed with laughter, playing in front of the mirror like two young girls. But I have to see my immutable face every day: mirror, mirror, on the wall, who's the fairest of them all . . . No, the mirror on the wall always answers that my thinking is confused, my sentiments weak, and that my stiff style is only good for exposition: my novel, in short, is lousy. Why not burn it, then?

"Burn it if you like," Gloria answers, listening to my discouraged words as we walk to the Rubén Darío subway station.

"Yes. I'm going to burn it."

Once seated in the subway car, Gloria tells me, "No. You'd better not burn it."

"Why are you contradicting yourself?"

"It would stay locked up inside of you, rotting and poisoning you. Good or bad, you're condemned to finish and publish it if you want to rid yourself of it."

"How do you know?"

"Ah . . . !" Gloria sighed, the irritating little gleam in her eyes somehow conveying both her confidence and my naiveté. "If you only knew how many unwritten novels are sealed up inside me, like cats in a sack, gone wild, fighting and tearing one another apart!"

"Cut out the nonsense! Are you trying to make me believe that you're a frustrated writer?"

The train is delayed at Chueca, and she takes a deep breath.

"Well, who knows? It may just be a classic case of penis envy."

"Well, it's normal if you aren't doing anything."

"I suppose so."

I will not accept the life Gloria condemns me to: she anchors me to my old longing for the Parnassian privilege of "being a writer," a fixation I've had since I don't know when in my neurotic adolescence, to fight in my fantasy my older brother Sebastian's demands, who now insists— no, he begs—that I go back to close my mother's eyes.

Why go on bowing down to that old tyranny at my age? Why not accept failure once and for all? I have nothing to say. Nothing to teach. I can't create beauty, but I know how to appreciate it. How can I have the guts to defend a position of "moderate humanism" if all this ideal comes down to is that I prefer to spend the afternoon with a good drink in my hand, watching stupid movies on television? To accept that I'm something I never planned to be: per- haps an excellent translator—*Middlemarch* has just been lying there since Katy showed up—certainly a good pro- fessor of literature. Not to go on being a slave to my desire to evoke a poetic universe governed by its own resplendent laws, like the one—in spite of all the unbearable commer- cial lies—García Márquez, Carlos Fuentes, Marcelo Chi- riboga, and Julio Cortázar are sometimes able to create. To surrender: the sweetness of accepted failure.

"Shall we have one of those awful fried squid sand- wiches at the Rastro? They ooze oil, deadly for the liver, but they're so delicious!"

I nod as the train pulls out of the stop with a jolt violent as an earthquake. At what time will I be able to go back to my window, to my luminous garden with its avocados, araucarias, and the old plum tree sheltering the wicker armchair where she waited for them when they came for her? A cool garden despite the sun falling like hot lead on the chestnuts, and very quiet because someone is dying in the house hemmed in by branches that add their whispers to the silence. I want to return, to be there when the girl with hair heavy as a gold bell appears, passing from the shadows into the light to exhibit herself like a dazzling contradiction of death. We leave the station, and I hope that Gloria's plans with Katy will leave me the afternoon to be alone by the window.

I ask Gloria, "What is there for dinner this evening?"

The answer is of no interest. Nor did I know the reason for the question. It's an old phrase, soft and polished from so much use and manipulation, an echo of phrases that were always the same. What do you have for dinner this evening? What is there to eat this evening? What have you got for our dinner this evening, Rosa? What have we for dinner? Never a fried squid sandwich; she almost died of disgust when I suggested that she'd have to try one in Spain, or would have died of disgust, because in the end she never came to visit us as she had planned at first, she wanted to see Pato, she'd write to us when she could still write, but she never made the trip, because later on she'd never even go out of the garden, where she was visited by the women in town who hadn't turned their backs on her at the time of the Allende affair, as well as by others who had, but whom she forgave because they were brought by a new hunger mixed with fear now, which was only another kind of hunger; she would never leave her garden, and then her house, and then her bedroom, and now her bed: sometimes her head is clear and she recognizes them all briefly before partial death comes to haunt her, converting her into a wreck separated from death only by the bubbles in the catheters and serum bottles used to feed her.

"What is there for dinner this evening?"

On the day of the coup, she hid my cousin Sergio—how can I refuse to take in the son of my sister Marta, even if he's one of the MIR's insane criminals?—in her cellar, crammed with packages of sugar, flour, rice, tea, coffee, pasta she had managed to hoard: food so that there'll be no shortage in the house, even if that outlaw Allende means to starve us to death, she would say. Eat, eat anything you want, I have plenty of everything. And Gloria, Pato, and I, who could barely get along on my university salary, moved into my mother's house, overflowing with the shadows of servants she'd had all her life and with the kind of abundance that neither we nor anybody else had enjoyed in years. Those women who hadn't given her the cold shoulder would stand in line for hours with her money— "There are chickens at the Unicop, hurry, they're almost out of them . . . the Almac has some sugar"—and her women would rush from one place to the other and she'd give them something for their long wait in line. The rest she stored in sacks and boxes in the cellar, and she had hidden Sergio among them. The home of the liberal congressman's widow was very respectable, and nobody, Sergio knew, would suspect this bulwark of traditional institutions that we were identified with, that my father had defended with his little-noticed and modest vote. They won't come to look for me here, Sergio thought.

But they did, one afternoon when my mother was in bed with the first fevers: hurry, hurry, before they come in, let Sergio come upstairs and get under my bed, they'll search the cellar but they'll never dare look under my bed. They left without finding him, backing out the door of the widow of a congressman and a gentleman. That night

Sergio jumped over the back wall that separated us from an empty house waiting to be torn down. Two days later he fell with a bullet in his shoulder as he fled cross-country over the hills of Olmué; he was one of many who, guilty or not, died in the massacre we must never forget. Later they came back and took away my mother, who received them, sitting in her white wicker armchair under the plum tree, and they also took me. They kept her under arrest for five hours. They didn't grill her. Nor did they feed her. It was when they announced to her that they would give her something to eat before setting her free, so she'd recover her strength, that she automatically came out with the phrase she used with the cook every day, without awareness—perhaps?—that she was now face to face with the authorities:

"What's for dinner this evening?"

They blindfolded her—respectfully, she admitted, because of course they know who I am—and left her in the middle of the night in a quiet neighborhood, from where, with almost all her strength gone, she took a taxi home: a shattered home, because they had also taken me in, Gloria was waiting, calling influential relatives, mobilizing Sebastian, who knew everybody, into action; at the end of six days, he got them to release me without interrogating me. Upon arriving at my mother's house, I also asked:

"What's for dinner this evening?"

"Leave," she had said to us then; that's when her mind definitely started to fail. "This country isn't a republic anymore. Congress is shut down. Leave while you can. What good is a country without Congress? I have to stay. What would I do abroad? At my age, how can I live away from my home, my garden, without the cook I've had all my life, and without Maestro Almeda?"

Maestro Almeda, her right hand at grafting tree peonies

that won prizes at the flower shows—before politics did away with all human activities, reducing everything to it—had died a toothless, crippled alcoholic in President Frei's day. At the time my mother said this, I didn't catch her error. It was only on the plane on our way to Spain, ten days after the university let me go and fifteen days after my release, flying over the Cordillera of the Andes, that I suddenly said to Gloria, who wouldn't stop crying, "But Maestro Almeda died five years ago!"

"What are you talking about?"

"Nothing."

"What's for dinner this evening, Dad?" Pato asked me.

I don't want to see my mother again. She's dead: the narrow gate at the airport, where she said goodbye, framed her like a coffin. This image serves as an excuse to stay away: she's dead. So there's no reason to go back. Nor anywhere to go back to, because the garden with the whispering leaves no longer exists, nor does the affirmation of life the gold bell stands for . . . it glitters, it dances, but I don't hear it ringing. What's for dinner tonight? We could still laugh, in the teeth of terror itself, at what was going on around us, when we found out that this question was the only exchange between my mother and those who had arrested her. Just like mother, Sebastian said; so did I, and Sebastian's sons said it, laughing, it was just like Grandma to think of food before anything else.

It was right before the coup, when the program of the left started to collapse under its own weight and the weight of other things, and my father died because he saw what was coming; that's when my mother, who had never eaten much, started to reject her food, at the same time she rejected Pinochet, or Allende: it's the same thing, child, she would say, they're both madmen and scoundrels. Later, when she discovered that "the stores were well stocked" and you didn't have to stand in line or beg, she heaped blessings on the new leader, in spite of the way he stepped all over everyone—and her and me—and even though he was keeping Pato, her favorite, and Gloria far away from her and kept Congress closed. But as time went on, the women of the town—in rags, terrified, with dead husbands and sons who had disappeared—started coming to her door again; this was simply another face of the hunger she couldn't tolerate and the fear that was only an even more terrible version of hunger. She'd give them something, Sebastian wrote, but what could she do, she couldn't bring anyone back to life, much less the communists and the MIR activists, and she couldn't feed them all even if their husbands were out of work, because they've closed down the factory, señorita, and they killed my Facundo, sure he was one of the Altamirano socialists, who were the worst, what could she do when she couldn't feed them all: she forgot the Eleventh, she put Pinochet's name out of her mind, and thanks to the new madness that erased dates and differences between the ideologies that separated one man from the other, she let Allende's faults— which she had been very much aware of, because there had been no flour for the *pantrucas*—drag on in her mind so she could blame him for these other deaths and hungers. As a measure of security and a certain amount of prosperity, which she hardly understood, had started to establish itself in her circle, my mother gradually began to eat less and less, or almost nothing, to lose weight, in solidarity with her women, to refuse all food in disgust, and now she has stopped eating altogether; they say her mouth and her esophagus are ulcered, they nourish her with catheters, they extract her saliva with plastic tubes so that it won't hurt when she swallows, she has a lost look in her eyes, she weighs nothing at all, her mind wanders, especially when she talks against that savage Allende, who sent part of her family into exile; may little Pato not be deprived of anything, the poor child must be starving to death in those foreign countries, and Gloria, so nice and so intelligent, but she's not really the best housewife in the world, and who knows how she manages to keep from going hungry, my God. Her voice is a hoarse whisper now: she's the one—not Pato, nor Gloria, nor I, nor her women—who is starving to death at home, a ruin that's vanishing, the leaf trembling in the garden . . . it's lifeless now, the branches of the trees are dried up, the lawn is scorched by freezing weather, the ground hard with frost . . . but no, the avocado, the araucaria, the orange, and the magnolia trees haven't lost their leaves, they shiver, still green, even if everything around them is dying.

KATY VERINI HAS a sloppy look that transcends plain neglect. Sometimes I think I won't be able to put up with her any longer: everything she wears is dirty, shabby, old; even things she has just bought or been given look wrinkled right away. She combs her hair with a kind of tic, with little tugs here and there, to cover her face as much as possible, to defend and hide herself and let her unpleasant eyes take in everything without being noticed. I imagine her use of ragged clothes as a style, *la femme pauvre* of ten or fifteen years ago, a throwback, long gone out of fashion, to the days of the hippies, when she was young and in her heyday as muse of Montevideo. She's almost forty now. Even her abuse of marijuana dates to that time. On the other hand, we get drunk or take Valium or Tranxilium or Librium. They—she too—smoke: they go around with their heads even more mixed up than ours, always laughing on the edge of the abyss. And yet Katy is attractive:

sitting on the sofa with her legs stretched out, talking to
Gloria, her head foggy with pot smoke, with her waistline
looking so fragile, there's something weightless, dusky,
warm about her, and there's always that laugh of hers
showing a carefree acceptance of her own madness. Her
frame of reference is similar to ours, and that makes it easy
to get along with her.

Her last husband was a painter of passable reputation
who stayed in Montevideo on good terms with the government. But when they closed down *Marcha*, she came
away with her grown sons—she had her first when she was
fifteen—who are now professionals living in Paris, where
she visits them from time to time, and then returns furious
because they're so *square*. One is a professor of philosophy
in Nanterre, and the other, the girl, is married to an intoler-
able young executive in some industry or other: naturally
neither one has much tolerance for a charming hippy
mother who rightly prefers to live a comfortable distance
away. They help her with money, only small amounts, of
course, because they're young and have their own families
to support and are not millionaires: Katy never has a penny
to her name. She lives among Latin Americans who do
batik and tapestry and hook rugs and make "objects" and
jewelry; they sing tangos and *chacareras* and zambas in
places where you eat meat grilled the Argentinian way;
they write good poems that a few people read, printed
with money collected from friends who sell stones or sea-
shells spread out on the ground at the Rastro flea market
. . . but, Katy complains, handicraft is dying out now. . . .

"When we first arrived we worked hard to make lovely
things, jewelry that girls and boys wore around their necks
and that looked good, but now it's all crap, two little wires
and a stone and that's it. And imagine, there are those who
buy them, I don't see why. . . ."

Downhill from the Plaza del Cascorro, the flea market is a jam-packed sea of humanity; an army of young people, unarmed, lost, selling anything and everything to buy hash or some food for the family, selling secondhand books and flowers made of paper or cloth, manipulating marionettes, dancing—the bearded guitarist plays Buxtehude while his companion passes the hat around to an audience that has no idea who Buxtehude is; there are knife fights between Argentinians and Spaniards because one has spread his goods a few inches into the other's space; pickpockets, wallets that can't be found, children who get lost, and older kids sunning themselves and smoking pot on the steps at one in the afternoon without giving a damn; a strong smell of garlic and sweat; bracelets, keyrings, lace, horrid little figurines made of pebbles glued together or of plaited straw, plastic things so cheap they seem about to melt in the heat, Indian or Moroccan goods bought and resold at almost the same price, Japanese things some friend left behind as part payment for his lodging before moving on to Ibiza or Altea or Sweden for a summer job to earn enough money to last the rest of the year; sluggishness, body smells, shiny naked torsos covered with sweat, all characteristic of nonconformist young people we thought went out after May '68, and yet it is a fashion that still lingers, nobody knows how or why. The drifters in Madrid make up a subculture that's identical to what you'd find anywhere else; it's no longer an ideology, only a mannerism, I explain to Katy, they are the children of ex-hippies like her who were absorbed into the establishment; nobody's children, the offspring of a dozen frustrated revolutions, on the run from defeats or triumphs, depending on how you look at it. Survival is the game: an army of the young who turn to petty crime when they can't get ahead with either a stroke of good luck or backbreaking work.

Do these stupid asses think they're the first ones to come to Europe to fuck around? Katy asks. Well, I was fourteen when I ran away from home to Paris with a guy, and I stayed and did all kinds of crazy things before these kids, who think they're inventing everything, were even born; don't anybody give me that crap, I would tell the gal who was psychoanalyzing me then, because now I'm under treatment with a sharp guy, and I'm better off, I get along better with men than women, you're an exception, Gloria, you're the victim of a system, but you're not satisfied with this victim role, you should go into therapy, Gloria, yes, I know it's expensive, I can do it because the Argentines don't charge for Argentinian exiles who can't pay, and the same must go for the Chileans, I'm sure; and you too, Julito, so that you can finish that fucking novel of yours. Anyway, Gloria, I hate those damn drifters because they think they invented it all, when we had to fight for it and handed it to them on a silver platter, look at that blond kid, Julio, look at him, he has the face of a wicked angel, he thinks he's a lost soul when all he's done is take up with that broad he has his arm around, to make her paint faces on those little stones they're selling. . . .

I've already spotted him, from far off, the focal point toward which the tide of bodies is dragging me: the *angelo musicante* with his halo restored, squatting next to a dirty cloth covered with a display of stone figurines, his arm around a girl, also blond but sad-looking and alarmingly young. They're talking to the owner of the spread laid out next to theirs, who is giving them a drag on his joint; as we've been swept along to the place where Bijou is crouching next to his girlfriend, I can't resist the thrust of the smelly crowd driving me toward him, because I want to be him, I want to don his rags and his Rimbaudian dirt, and feel "good inside my skin"—as he'd say, translating from the French—here in this world that has meaning for him but is chaos to me, because I know that the world of failure is the only one that makes any sense to me, but this child hasn't failed, since he's breaking away from his parents' failure, turning his back on them when they ask him to share their world of political defeat, just as Pato rejects the same invitation from me when I tell him: "These are the years that we've had to live through, and you've got to put up with it, dammit, what can we do?"

Gloria also sees him. She looks at me, tries to head in another direction, but the slow, hot, compact mass of T-shirts and shoulders and jeans and tits and rear ends and potbellies and sweat sweeps us toward the *angelo musicante*. The moment he sees us he jumps to his feet and abandons his girlfriend, who remains in her stupor. He hurls himself in our direction as if we were what he most wanted in the whole world, yelling, like a true Chilean:

"Uncle! Aunt Gloria!"

Uncle Julio! Aunt Gloria! The familiar, Chilean womb where "we all know one another" amid this huge crowd without ties or names, of rejected or insignificant origins, in which contact is made through the occasional transaction of impersonal sex . . . I'll give you pleasure if you give me pleasure, a simple exchange of services as long as there's no obligation for either party: compulsive, obsessive, self-defensive, don't try to fuck up my head; the communists or the fascists, it makes no difference which, fucked up that one's head, his father fucked up his head so he'd go back, or some old whore fucked up his head so he'd move in with her, or a drug dealer to get him hooked and make him push for him in Torremolinos, or a friend so he'd join some Christian sect or other: fear of having or desire to have their heads fucked up.

Laughing, Bijou falls into our arms—deeply moved?—

as if he'd finally found his long-lost family. He kisses us, stares at us, asks questions, then answers them, letting himself be pushed along with us by the multitude, far from the girlfriend he has deserted without an explanation. As if we were united by something more than the memory of a moment of violence! While Bijou talks to Katy, Gloria whispers to me: the little shit, he has no right to do this after all he made us go through; I thought he was in Marrakesh. She asks him for news of Pato. He answers that he hasn't the vaguest idea where he is or what he's doing . . . apparently he's taking photographs, that's what someone told him, but he can't figure out what photos Pato could be taking in Marrakesh that he couldn't take here. As for himself, some guy gave him a ride to Madrid and he's been staying on because it seems that all of Paris—*le tout Paris*—is here in Madrid, at the Rastro this summer, one of the hottest he's ever spent in his life, and he doesn't feel like going on to Marrakesh. . . .

THE FOUR OF us walk between the peddlers' spreads without buying anything, because there's nothing to buy anymore at the Rastro, only junk that you could find anywhere. I can't figure out why all these people come here; maybe it's like a huge club where people from all over meet and lose one another (Bijou's little girlfriend . . . when, where will he find her again? Another Sunday, at some other Rastro, maybe) and come together again and separate and fight and make up and thieve or give things to one another and eat whatever they can, pass on important news that you can be sure is not what appears in the newspapers that they don't read but that make us freeze with terror: and we, the aging drifters, don't lift a finger against the new terrors.

"No, *che* . . ." Katy contradicts me in the middle of the crowd that's so noisy I can barely hear her even though she's just two bodies in front of me. "That's a cliché, a topic, as they say here. Not everyone's a drifter, right, Bijou?"

Bijou is up ahead: I note that Katy's question is only a ruse to get him to come back. He waits for us, letting the sticky mass of people slip by him until we catch up. Then Katy goes on:

"For instance, there are people here who are very serious about politics, and at any moment the Rastro could go up like a tinderbox, even if it doesn't seem that way and all this looks like a great big festival. We all help one another, we look after one another's children, lend each other money, take each other's hand-me-down clothes and furniture. Like what I'm wearing now, I don't even remember the name of the Bolivian woman who gave it to me. So don't think they're all fools—there are university graduates, lawyers, architects, writers . . ."

I notice that in the presence of Bijou, Katy has changed her opinion of the Rastro: her desire to please him has blunted her sharp tongue. We come to the entrance of the Piquer Galleries, the huge courtyard filled with the antique stores that gave the flea market its name but are now owned by important dealers with bigger stores on Calle del Prado who keep these small shops mostly to trap rich and unwary tourists. Inside the courtyard the crowd is smaller, the people different, older, better dressed, wandering around looking for a wall sconce, a knob for an antique cupboard, a cornice for an Isabella II mirror.

"What do I care about writers?" I snap at Katy. "As far as I'm concerned, being a writer means nothing."

"But you're not saying you're not a writer, are you?"

"No, but all the same I couldn't care less."

We look in a shop window with a display of moth-eaten servant uniforms, another with a pile of old junk; in another is an opaline piece that Katy gets excited about, knowing there's no chance of buying it, since we can't afford that kind of extravagance. As we move on it dawns on me that Bijou, with his perceptive X-ray mind, is the only one in our group who has seen that my answer to Katy was a big put-on; in my mind a writer is endowed with a superior aura. For her own self-defense and security, Gloria has grown used to accepting my lies about myself as the truth. Katy takes care to present an image of herself—not a physical image; she's no fool and knows her limitations there—as free and affable, what she calls "a sharp chick." She knows it's the right net to cast for Bijou, because it's almost shamefully obvious now that that is what she's after.

We stop in front of the window of a shop specializing in antique silver: pheasants, baskets, fruit, a caravel, roosters, candelabras, everything of excellent quality and so expensive that only people like those who live in the house next to Pancho's can buy them. I'm aware of Bijou's odor of sweat at my side, his corrupt Rimbaudian presence: bad teeth, fingernails bitten down like Katy's. In the mirror of the shop window I see his halo of blond hair superimposed on the costly silver objects inside, and next to it our own poor, ragged, vulgar reflections under the punishing sun.

I can also see, beyond our reflections and the window display, a third dimension: the interior of the shop, a dark cavern, cool and deep, where three or four people belonging to a race alien to that of the street browse, pick up some silver object in their sensitive hands, examine it, chat with the dealer, smile, and then put it back on the natural-wood table. All of a sudden my eyes zoom past Rimbaud's reflection, leaving it behind, in the window, to rest my gaze on

someone I recognize at the back of the shop: Núria Monclús is holding a silver owl in her fingers, like Pallas Ath-
ena, and talking to a friend about it as if she were
explaining that it was her symbol. Without saying anything to Gloria, I try to get away, terrified, ashamed of
myself, of my friends, of my wife. But at this stage things
in my life are never complete unless I share them with her.
I'm about to let her in on it when suddenly my eyes stray
from Núria Monclús to the figure of her male companion,
whom with a shock I can't help but recognize: Marcelo
Chiriboga, the most insultingly famous member of the
dubious Boom. His novel *La caja sin secreto* is like the Bible
or *Don Quixote*, its editions running into millions of copies
in every language, including Armenian, Russian, and Japanese; he's a public figure who's almost pop, like a politician or a movie star, but to my taste and Gloria's the
literary quality of his work makes him stand almost alone
above the whole crew of pretentious Latin American novelists of his generation: he's part of and has been the center of
the Boom, yet his case was not a publishing stunt engi-
neered by the literary mafia but the result of simple and
exciting worldwide acclamation. Small, skinny, as well
made as one of those Renaissance silver figurines Núria
Monclús and he are examining, with his aristocratic bearing and his well-groomed graying hair he's as easy to spot
as a matinee idol: *La caja sin secreto* has done more to make
Ecuador known than all the other books and documen-
taries put together. Surrounded by the patina of dark wal-
nut on which the silver objects are displayed, this idol—
because, I have to confess, he is an idol of mine and Gloria's: we're always quoting him, we've read every last word
written by or about him—this writer who is delicate and
strong at the same time, who is on close terms with the
Pope, Brigitte Bardot, Fidel Castro, Caroline of Monaco,

García Márquez, and whose statements on politics or films or fashion always stir up a storm, is only a few feet away from me. Katy and Bijou are whispering and laughing about something that has to do with a pair of silver fighting cocks displayed in the window. I whisper in Gloria's ear:

"Look who's inside."

She looks.

"Marcelo Chiriboga," she says, her admiration making her profane his name.

"That's not the half of it. Do you see who he's with?"

"A very important-looking woman."

"Núria Monclús."

"Núria Monclús?" she repeats, a new image of wonder on her face superimposed over the first one.

"Let's leave," I tell her.

Gloria stays put. She stands up to her full height, which is considerable, fluffs up her hair, slides her tongue over her lips to make them shine—girding up for battle, I see—and all this performed automatically, in less than a second. She grips my arm and pulls me toward the entrance to the store, telling our friends, "Listen, we're going in here for a second. Do you want to wait for us, or shall we meet up somewhere in a couple of minutes?"

Katy, who has a way of sensing when something is up, how and between whom feelings suddenly become tense, can't help noticing it this time. Taking a step backward and assuming a haughty pose that's a parody of my wife's, she says, "We're also going in. We're not bums."

But the minute Gloria drags me across the threshold, like a child, I sense that something terrible is about to happen. Without changing his posture or breaking off his conversation with his distinguished clients, out of the corner of his eye the antiques dealer watches the disreputable-looking scarecrows who have just come in, while Marcelo Chiriboga and Núria Monclús listen to him go on and on about the silver owl: he presses a feather on its left wing and the head pops backward, uncovering a tiny greenish crystal vial inside.

"For poison," the dealer explains.

"Cyanide?" asks Núria Monclús.

"Perhaps I could find some use for it," Chiriboga suggests, smiling at Núria.

"Yes, cyanide," Núria agrees. "But I don't think they used that kind of poison during the Renaissance as much as they do now. . . ."

The dealer, who has missed the exchange, goes on praising his merchandise, explaining that at the time in the Tuscan courts they often inserted a vial like this one—which was discovered in a Roman burial mound—inside a jewel: a truly unique piece, the dealer adds, because it is a complete set. Núria Monclús closes the owl's head and, without taking her hand off it, sets it down on the table.

"Don't you have an owl with the antidote?"

"Against what, madam?"

"Against cyanide, of course," Chiriboga says.

Núria Monclús's lips curl even further into a smile. "I thought that we were looking for something that will make you disappear when the time comes, Marcelo. Cyanide should do the trick. . . ."

"You *know* I'll need an antidote against poison when my new book finally comes out. They'll write that after *Caja* I have nothing left to say. But how are we going to get out of here and avoid the mob that almost tore me apart on the way in?"

"With the cyanide," Núria Monclús says.

Gloria and I listened to this conversation, our backs to the speakers, frozen in our tracks by emotion. It's humiliating to admire a colleague so much. It's the sign of failure. It's like begging to be allowed to listen to him the way one listens to a god—hidden by one's anonymity as well as one's back. But my anonymity is not complete: if I turn around I can greet the goddess of wisdom and war, the protectress of this Ulysses. My anonymity would not be complete, then, though more necessary because my humility would be all I'd have to show.

Katy primps her disordered hair and admires herself in the mirror. Bijou walks around, looking at objects he doesn't care for but guesses to be expensive, the whole situation not affecting him because he expects nothing from this hiatus in his life. Gloria, who pretends to be examining the candlestick she is holding in her hand, pulls me closer to the little trio discussing the merits of other Renaissance poisons relative to bearded darnel. With the small candlestick in her hand, discreet, casual, Gloria turns it over, pointing at the mark on its base, and interrupts the conversation:

"Excuse me—is this by Adam?"

"No, miss, unfortunately it's not. A Spanish imitation of that style from, well, around 1855. Very pretty, of course, and it's a pair. . . ."

Núria Monclús is wearing the same dress she had on when I saw her last, except that it's dark blue now, as are the little veil that blurs her hair and her eyes and the little matching ribbon. She's one of those women who know themselves so well and are so opposed to trying out anything different that no matter what the occasion or the season they always wear the same clothes. She's about to recognize me, to say hello, to introduce me to the great Marcelo Chiriboga—but a fraction of a second before she starts to make a movement in this direction Katy recognizes the great writer in the mirror and, moving in on him, shrieks: "I just *can't believe* it! Marcelo Chiriboga!"

I listen, petrified, almost deaf with horror, to Katy's childish, stupid, humiliating awe. The sound of her chatter and her little nervous laugh seems horrible to me, as does her insistence like that of a hysterical lapdog that jumps up and down around its master, tugging at his trousers to make him notice it, drooling over him shamelessly. She touches Chiriboga, giggles, asks him questions—Gloria and I looking on in disgust, each of us holding an identical candlestick, unable to vanish the way we desperately want to—and finally hands him a piece of paper for his autograph. She calls Bijou over so she can introduce him to the writer: "Come on, *che*, it's Marcelo Chiriboga! How wonderful! What luck! It just can't be! Bijou, it's Marcelo Chiriboga—"

"And who is Marcelo Chiriboga?" Bijou asks, staring at him.

The devil in me rejoices at Bijou's ignorance: bearded darnel, not cyanide. I know very well the meaning of the double-entendre in the conversation those two carried on in front of the antiques dealer: *All admirers are potential enemies*, Cyril Connolly says.

Katy manages to hold them both in conversation for a minute, then notices Gloria and me, two dazzled acolytes carrying our candles and waiting for the moment to join the procession. She unceremoniously tugs at one of my sleeves to pull me closer to Chiriboga, and then she introduces me to him—she, not Núria Monclús!—as "the great Chilean novelist." She lets her tongue run on without letting anyone else get a word in, assuring him that I'm the best Chilean novelist of my generation, my work isn't very well known abroad but deserves to be, that in my new novel I take in all the suffering in Chile's prisons, but I haven't been translated . . .

At this point Núria Monclús, who in the meantime hasn't bothered to acknowledge Katy's existence, greets me with a friendly, easy smile that includes Gloria, too. "That's not quite true. Julio Méndez is starting to become more renowned. Marcelo, you remember his short story, it appears next to one of yours in that anthology translated into Danish and published by Det Schonbergske Verlag four years ago?"

"I believe so . . . of course, very interesting . . . naturally it's difficult to remember so many anthologies," Marcelo Chiriboga says, looking at his watch somewhat nervously. Then, to Núria: "It's getting late. Don't you think it's time to . . ."

"You mentioned there's a door here to an alley," Núria says to the dealer.

"This way."

Before saying goodbye with just the right dose of cordiality and disappearing down the secret passage reserved for the very few, Núria says to me, "Julio, I expect to see the new version of the novel as soon as you finish it."

I agree, confused, caught between the poison and the incense, while, warmly shaking my hand, Latin America's novelist says to Núria, "And don't forget to send me a copy as soon as it comes out, I'm very interested in everything about Chile. . . ."

And with the dealer they abandon the store through the secret door, leaving the place terribly empty despite the presence of two fierce-looking clerks who suddenly materialize out of nowhere—terribly empty and terribly hopeless because, for a moment, I had hope. Caught in the magic spell, none of us four moves a step or says a word.

Then Gloria and I put the candlesticks down where we found them. One of the clerks comes over.

"Would you like to see anything else?"

And the four of us go out, once more, to wander around under the cruel sun.

WE HAD A late lunch in a bar, numerous glasses of red wine, many indigestible fried squid sandwiches, leaning on the counter, standing on a floor littered with greasy paper napkins and cigarette butts, while the regular customers were leaving for their siestas.

We've already said all there was to say about our meeting with Marcelo Chiriboga and Núria Monclús. With the first glasses of wine, I let my admiration show, but gradually the wine turns sour and I start to explain that despite its reputation, Chiriboga's work is lifeless; that it's really an invention of that financial wizard Núria Monclús; that its quality is weighed down by its shortcomings; that it was invented by Núria to fill her already well-lined coffers; that she's a money-hungry, avaricious Catalan, a Jewish shark, a Fagin in skirts, and Latin American novelists are used by her the way Fagin used his little boys. She's well known for the haughty manner with which she tours the aisles of the Frankfurt Book Fair; her signature is enough for entire series, translated from the Spanish, to be brought out by Suhrkamp, by Gollancz, by Feltrinelli, by Farrar, Straus & Giroux, by Spanish and Latin American publishing houses that she has by the throat, yes, yes, by the throat. Of the two, I explain, Núria, and not Chiriboga, is the one who really counts. Chiriboga is just an imitator of Vargas Vila, an opportunist like all the rest—Gloria, who knows my admiration for him, can't bear my bitterness and my envy;

this evening we'll get drunk, there'll be a fight, and we'll sleep in separate beds—and now young writers are following in their footsteps, using everything, including the Cuban revolution and the Chilean tragedy, in their climb. But the publishers no longer fool the young, who don't even know Chiriboga's work or his name. Bijou is a good example.

"But I do know him. I've read everything he's written."

"And do you like him?" Gloria asks.

"Very much."

"Why did you deny it, then?"

"Because I knew that denying it was the only way to make him remember me."

"He's Núria's lover."

"It doesn't matter. He'll remember me; he'll forget you, Katy, and you, Uncle Julio. I can't stand people like him. I like to beat them at their own game."

"And did you beat him?"

"Sure I did. A small victory, but I won it."

I've had too much wine, as has Katy, for whom everything's a steady downward spiral over which she has no control. I say that we'll take the subway right here, on this corner; it will leave us near home. Katy interjects, "I'm going with you people. It's great to take a siesta in Pancho's apartment, it's so cool. I roast in mine. Are you coming, Bijou?"

Gloria and I feel too wiped out by our humiliation to say no, and they follow us. On the way Katy gives Bijou an intimate rundown of her mixed-up life: in Montevideo, after an all-male orgy in his apartment, which was also his consulting room, her lover's body was discovered, his throat slit with one of his own scalpels. But the story isn't of much interest to Bijou, who has his skinny freckled arm around Katy's shoulders as she talks a blue streak. He interrupts her to tell the story of his name, of his annoyance at being called Alhaja, of how some people then assumed he belonged to an inferior race or class.

Naturally he doesn't belong to an inferior race or class: you can see it at first glance even if he disguises himself as a *voyou*, as Rimbaud. The Lagos family, people of good breeding, are blonds "with corn-colored hair," as they say in our country, and with an air of owning the world. This is confirmed by Beltrán's glances at him—in jeans, white T-shirt, and Adidas shoes, Bijou could be the son of any "upper-class" family in this neighborhood—and in the obsequious smile he gives him, which Bijou returns with upper-class deference. On the other hand, Beltrán detests Katy: he says she looks like a communist. When she visits, he always rings us on the intercom to let us know she's coming up, as if she were dangerous. Though I explain to Beltrán that she's the way she is because she's an artist—a very doubtful notion, even to Beltrán, who says he knows all of Don Pancho de Salvatierra's artist friends; they are in all the magazines and are nothing like her—he just doesn't like her. But Bijou, on the other hand, is different: in spite of his grime, his wicked air, he has the allure of a young gentleman, as Beltrán would say; he has lived too long in this neighborhood not to know that the sons of dukes dress like Bijou when they want to, but the allure, ah, the *allure*—if Beltrán only knew that word!—is something you can't buy. No doubt Beltrán recognizes this phenomenon for which he doesn't have a word. That accounts for the smile, explains Gloria, who has an eye for these things and has had less to drink than I.

Bijou loves Pancho's apartment, all white, even the fur rugs and the decor. And the two bare windows with the painting of the drapes hanging between them. When he sees them from the other side of the room, he stops for a second, looking at them quietly while we wait for his reaction. There is a sudden outburst of laughter, a delightful surprised laugh: somehow he and Pancho are on the same wavelength.

"It's funny," he comments, still laughing.

Is that, I think fleetingly, the secret of Pancho's success? This ability to evoke pleasure as the first, immediate, subliminal reaction to his compelling and seductive art? To have a point of view so original that it verges on the comic . . . I'm thinking of Dalí, de Chirico, Magritte, who are also compelling, immediate, and amusing. Is that what I'm dying to possess, what Marcelo Chiriboga undoubtedly has and I don't? Is that why Núria Monclús doesn't take me on, because I don't have that spontaneity and humor that's like a spark and makes immediate contact with an audience, that Bijou admires, that Pancho and Chiriboga have but I don't? I envy it. That's why I can't help hating the author of *La caja sin secreto*, which I admire, and which even an ignorant snot-nosed kid like Bijou has read. I gulp down a glass of wine.

"I'm going to take my siesta."

I shut myself in the bedroom. A little later I feel Gloria flop into bed beside me. She cuddles up to me and whispers:

"Listen . . ."

"What?"

"Katy has gone for a siesta in the other room. With Bijou."

"So what?"

"Isn't it horrible?"

"Why is it so horrible?"

"I don't know . . . he's just a little kid."

"Some kid! This one knows all the tricks. Did you notice

the way he knifed Marcelo Chiriboga in the back? I wish
I'd had the balls to do it."

"But Katy . . . well, I don't know, she's a grandmother,
she's got sons twice Bijou's age."

"So what?"

"Doesn't it make you feel . . . I don't know . . . something?"

"No. Go to sleep."

"Okay."

I feel Gloria put a timid hand on the sweat that's cooled
off on my naked shoulder.

"Don't . . ." I tell her sleepily.

I feel her take her hand away. Now I can fall asleep.

SHE IS THE Countess of Pinell de Bray, for the Duke has
passed the title of count on to the youngest of his four
sons, but I haven't been able to get out of Beltrán the first
name of the little Countess with the golden bell of hair.
Medieval names, Hermenegilda, Elisenda, Ursula, Ber-
engaria, come to mind, but I'm sure that even if she had
the most heraldic of names, friends probably call her
Mimí, Coté, Lela, I don't know, some pet name the
bourgeoisie considers elegant right now; and she'll have
christened her own daughter with a fashionable name:
Natalia, María José, Andrea, Sandra. Since she's Austrian
she can do it easily, because what's fashionable in her
country will be exotic for me, here from this Chilean-
Madrilenian exile's window.

I'm in love with the little Countess. I walk Myshkin
frequently to get more information out of Beltrán. It's
odd, but ever since Katy's visits started that source seems
to have dried up; Beltrán no longer asks me to share the

delights of his scrapbook, and I'm sorry about this. Sometimes when, from my window, I see the Countess dressed to go out, I put collar and leash on Myshkin and rush downstairs, hoping to run into her and look at her close-up, but it never happens. But she's never on foot: she gets behind the wheel in the armored garage that Beltrán's counterpart opens with a special device. She's more protected than she would be in a Gothic castle on a rugged mountaintop in the Alps, where I imagine she was born. She is not a common creature; you can't follow her in the street, look at her legs, watch her gait, examine her skin and the color of her eyes when you pass her on a corner and catch her eye. Well, yes: her eyes are blue. I believe Beltrán told me that, before Katy created this distance between us. But what kind of blue? What specific blue? There are so many blues, aquamarine, sapphire, sky-blue, violet, periwinkle, sea-blue. Naturally a concierge like Beltrán would only deal in generalities. Blue is blue, nothing else, but that's like saying nothing, for the nuance, along with the expression, is what counts. What makes one fall in love.

What's the color of the Countess's eyes? In my mind, this is how I settle it: since I don't know her name, in my fantasy she is the "little Countess," without the intimacy that a feminine name would provide; and as in a classic marble head, her eyes are blank. But with a difference: instead of the emptiness of blank stone they are two windows opening to the sky, where clouds drift past or children play on their tricycles or, when my love hurts most, those almond sockets let me see surf breaking on cliffsides and, beyond them, the horizon of the whole world.

I watch her heading for her mother-in-law's pool, a child in each hand; she wears a brown one-piece swimming suit that makes her silhouette longer and more elegant than her bikini does; burned by the sun, all tan but for her golden

hair, today she is lovelier than ever. I move into the dining
room: through the window I see several couples with
many children splashing in the water or having cool
drinks. She laughs, talks, kisses, passes drinks, watches
out for her own and the other children bathing, chats with
the men, the women, but especially with one man I recognize immediately as the "handsome brute" I saw the first
night around the swimming pool. He looks at her from
under dark eyebrows, and she returns his look with eyes I
don't recognize! The grown-ups come out of the water and
leave the children playing in the care of a servant with the
water jet whose steady sound has become part of my
waking hours as well as my sleep. They swim, float on
rubber rafts. The guests wander around the huge garden
with drinks in hand, admiring the flower beds, where the
first zinnias are beginning to bloom, the chestnut tree, the
myrtle and the arborvitae bushes, the linden trees. And
she, in what bright tunic has she wrapped her body after
her bath? In something flashy, daring, multicolored, with
gold dots that my imagination sees as something invented
by Klimt. Born a baroness in the Austrian Alps, the
Countess has chosen a tunic that reminds me of Klimt in
which to stroll around her garden with the "handsome
brute." Pretending to admire the trees and the flowers,
they walk over to the chestnut tree. The sun is deflected on
the metal threads of her hair and glints on her long tunic.
Abruptly, as if by agreement, they slip away for a minute,
and, hidden behind the bush that's right under my window, the naked man takes the woman in the tunic into his
arms and she gives herself up to his body in an embrace as
sexual as that of Klimt's couple, in which all you see is the
heads wrapped in a riot of colors and of gold, but which
the woman's closed eyes say is the pleasure of total abandon. Then, right under my bedroom window, between

arborvitae and myrtles and the wall that separates the two properties, she opens her eyes for a second and I see that they're—how marvelous!—not blue, open to the infinite sky with drifting birds and clouds, but yellow, gold, like her hair, like the tunic she quickly unwrapped for her lover. They return to the lawn; as if nothing had happened, they talk about the light, the garden. In the second when she saw me spying on them from this window—because yes, yes, she did see me, she acknowledges me, she knows I exist, that I spy on her, watch her, love her—her golden eyes were clear.

I haven't worked in days. As if shaking hands with Marcelo Chiriboga and Núria Monclús paralyzed rather than stimulated me. I'm in no mood to write a political novel that speaks of hope for a return to a parliamentary democracy like my father's—it's what Chiriboga and Adriazola must expect of me—but more in the mood for sad verses addressed to a medieval chatelaine. I go down to the street with Myshkin, hoping to run into Beltrán, hoping he'll clear up some things, but all I get is his endless song and dance against the Reds and President Suárez, and the old story about how things aren't the way they were in General Franco's time: he believes you can set back the clock and undo everything.

I give myself up to the pleasures of love without a second thought, because Gloria goes out almost every day to the movies, to museums, to see friends who sing or write, to make tapestries on behalf of Argentine exiles—why not those from Chile or Uruguay?—or to have lunch with Katy and her friends. At her age, she lives in a world made up mostly of female friends: fleetingly I think of some "handsome brute" who might cross her path, but Gloria is now the same age as my mother when I published my first book, older than my mother was when I received my first degree from the university, so I think no more about it and return to the garden next door.

For several days after the Klimt incident, I watch her sunbathe in a swimsuit on a sunny spot in front of my bedroom window, near the myrtles where the event took place, as if she were showing herself off for my pleasure and thus buying my complicity. She generally basks in the sun with her eyes closed. But sometimes she opens them and I can make out the golden orbs, those daily reminders of my Klimt sexual fantasy. I can't hide the fact that as I watch her, I mentally run my hand over those slim, long thighs burnished by the sun. Then, for several days in a row, I see her sun herself with her shoulder straps pulled down to blot out the white marks on her shoulders, and later I see her lower her top a little more each day—oh how I sigh, behind the curtains, for her to lower it all the way!— so that gradually she displays one more finger of the milk-white breasts baking in the sun. Does she mean to expose them completely? Perhaps my hands are too big to hold them. But my hands are not clumsy, not at all. They pass sensations on to my typewriter that this innocent creature of luxury knows nothing about. Does she really intend to turn her whole body golden and give it to the "handsome brute" like the precious, solid, shining smoothness of a gold ingot?

Then one night, when Gloria has not yet returned from an evening with Katy, I see her come out into the garden very late with her husband. He's wearing a dinner jacket and she a very tight white strapless evening gown with a slit down the front showing her legs up to the knee, the perfect imperfect worldly partner on the way to meet her lover, with whom she turns her husband into the traditional cuckold. When she disappears, the darkened garden remains animated by her little white flame that reveals, as much as decency allows, the skin she has been turning to gold in the sun for days, a thin flame dancing among the bushes before it disappears.

When Gloria comes home she finds me at the window, looking for the little flame that is nowhere to be seen.

"What are you doing?" she asks me, a little surprised.

"Nothing," I say, drinking down my cognac and lowering the blinds so that she won't see anything.

"Shall we have something to eat?"

"Anything."

"Okay, I'll go fix something."

While I shut myself in the bathroom for a minute, she opens some cans and sets the table in the kitchen. In front of me she puts a plate with Russian salad, ham, and hard-boiled eggs. Enough. And a bottle of wine. She talks— obsessively, I think; yes, she has been talking almost obsessively about it since Bijou showed up—about Katy's freedom in separating sex from the commitment of love: oh, how she envies that, she says, because she herself was educated by nuns, of course, and, given the social class and the generation she was born in, she could never do the same, and I'm the only one she knows sexually.

"*Mala cueva . . .*"

"Why are you so cruel?"

"If I'm not enough for you, why don't you go have sex with other men like your friend Katy?"

"The years have passed . . ."

"For some tastes you'd still do."

"Thanks for the compliment!"

"What did you expect?"

"What's more, you'd be wildly jealous."

"Don't use that lie to cover up your fear: I couldn't care less."

"Don't say that too often. I'm quite capable of . . . Look

at Katy, she's screwing Bijou like crazy, and he's twenty-five years younger than her. Maybe I can find someone who's not quite that green. . . ."

"Go ahead. You'd take a big load off me, your sexual frustration disguised as faithfulness. We're old enough to know that no one satisfies anyone else completely, except for short spells, and much less when they've been together for well over twenty years."

"What would you say if I hooked up with a friend of Bijou's? He introduced him to me today and he stuck to me like glue. He's twenty-nine."

"I'd die laughing. Did he ask your age?"

"Yes."

"And what did you tell him?"

"It was in a loft near the Plaza Conde de Barajas, in the Madrid of the Austrias. There were a lot of people. It was dark. . . ."

"And what did you tell him?" I ask, drying the dishes.

"The ideal age for a woman: the ten marvelous years between twenty-nine and thirty."

"How original!"

"But he laughed."

"At you, I bet."

"Have you ever looked at your big gut?"

"Sure."

"Well, then, you can take what Bijou's friend said any way you like. It's all the same to me."

We're in the bedroom. We've switched off all the lights in the apartment except the reading lamps on our night tables. While I undress, I inspect the whiteness of my slight paunch with disgust and, holding up my slipping trousers with one hand, go over to close the curtains so the golden woman won't see me, even though the blinds are down already. I tell Gloria that I know that a couple over fifty, married for twenty-five years, no longer feel the sexual drive that, well . . . that a new adventure can provide . . .

"You don't have to come up with excuses," Gloria answers, undressing on the other side of the bed. "Let me tell you that nothing could excite me less than the body of a middle-class and middle-aged intellectual."

I ignore her wounding though realistic remark and say that we must admit that there may be exceptions, but at our age there are more important things, like the family—Pato? my mother dying in another garden? Sebastian and his kids?—and especially all the years we've shared. Besides, in my case there's the well-known phenomenon of sublimation, which burns up a lot of fuel, leaving me more indifferent than before, perhaps, but what can I do.

"Don't give me any stories about sublimation. Chiriboga may sublimate. But you, don't you even dream of it."

I'm not paying attention, because I've climbed into bed and opened *Sophie's Choice*, arranging the light so it will fall right on the book and she won't see, even if she looks at me, that I'm not reading but thinking about the little flame dancing in the garden below our window. Out of the corner of my eye I watch Gloria slipping off her stockings . . . those stockings that mask her no longer perfect flesh, false skin she's shedding to expose the reality I refuse to accept. She puts on her nightdress and gets into bed. She ties a strip of black cloth over her eyes and without saying good night turns her back to me. But curled up with her back to me, she says:

"I don't sublimate anything."

"Bitch," I answer. "I can't carry the weight of that responsibility on my shoulders too."

"You can't say I make you feel that."

"That's all we'd need to complete the happy family picture."

I can't read. Our story is so old, my bond with that body curled up to sleep—I think of Bijou hunched up like a fetus in the backseat of Adriazola's car at La Cala—is much too long, and my heart and my life have become much too confused with hers. Perhaps this strange unsatisfactory relationship of ours, this involvement that is sometimes pleasant, sometimes harmonious, often openly hostile, perhaps this compassion I am feeling now, perhaps our capacity—acquired over the years as if by rote—to emerge unharmed from our hatred, sometimes mutual and fierce, yes, in a couple our age maybe all this is love, even passion. I set *Sophie's Choice* down. No, I admit to myself but not to her, I wouldn't have liked it if the twenty-nine-year-old boy she met in the loft this evening had taken her to bed: but they'd have to kill me before I'd admit it to her. Yes, I was clumsy, it's difficult not to be when your world is going under. Yes, clumsy when I said "tough shit" to her, *"mala cueva,"* that terrible Chilean expression that suggests the unpardonable, the pure and simple end. I remove my glasses and turn out my light. I place one hand on Gloria's hip. I feel—with pleasure and pride—this body pulsating, flourishing, alive under my hand, my hand, the only one beneath which it has ever in its whole life dared to pulsate naked. I put my arms around her from behind, kissing her around the ear to undo with my lips and my teeth the easy knot in the black kerchief. I whisper:

"Forgive me, my love. . . ."

She turns toward me, then puts her arms around me and kisses me. We embrace and kiss, even though I have a slight paunch and her skin no longer has the vivid luster that was almost a texture you could touch. . . . She has lost the perfection of the continuous, undulating line that was once the luxury of her now no longer lustrous skin. We make love as we have become used to, now and then, sad year after sad year. I think of the little Countess, the white flame, and Klimt and the "doting mother" and of how she and her husband have tea under the trees, but she has another life, apart from all that, in which, as in all passion, imagination reigns, a life that only I know about. How am I, with my caresses over the often-traveled roads of pleasure on my wife's body, to evoke that other body? And is my wife evoking the body of that twenty-nine-year-old boy when she runs her hands over the well-known, dull roads of pleasure on mine, which is nothing special either?

"Very attractive," Katy once told Gloria when she asked how I looked to her. "But I confess that he'll be much more attractive when he gets them to publish his novel."

The secret of my relationship with Gloria is probably that she has found me attractive all these years, even if I haven't published my novel, even if at the Rastro Núria Monclús and Marcelo Chiriboga looked at me as if I were only a fly among the unpleasant mass of people they had had the good luck to avoid. But what I told her before we made love is important and true: at our age, actually at any age, but especially now, we have to sublimate. She always claims, and with good reason, that it's the fault of her frivolous parents, who never prepared her for anything, and now she's only a well-to-do Chilean girl who's no longer well-to-do or young; no one ever thought of providing her with the culture or the instruments to help her live in the modern world. "If you'd been a boy I would have sent you to study economics at Harvard or at the London School of Economics," her father used to tell her. "But since you're a girl, why should you study anything?" Her mother took her out of the convent school, where she was in her third year and at the top of her class, and sent her to an exclusive school, where every morning she studied good taste in clothes, how to sit, how to stand and walk, religion, and the most useless cuisine, but they never taught her how to sew a button or peel a potato. She remembers the sinister Carrera School with a passionate hatred that's equal only to the resentment she still feels for her parents, who followed up their worldly hopes for their daughters with humiliating economic ruin—around the time Pato was born—that deprived her of the fortune for which she had been brought up: yes, one of so many errors in life that change the future of people, even of "people like us." If I only had that money, she sometimes sighs, then I'd feel that I could help you a little, stand behind you and behind Pato; with a fantastic education I'd feel justified, I'd be on firm ground! But she's not on firm ground. *Mala cueva.* Gloria knows how to serve tea elegantly, on the rare occasions when this duty comes up; she can make anything look tasteful, even if we're poor; she knows— uselessly, because she has never had to face this kind of thing—that only the upstairs maids wear black, never the downstairs help. And the literature and art they taught her at that damn Carrera School was so conventional that the first thing she did when she came home was forget everything and start all over from scratch, da capo; helped, it's true, by some of the diplomatic posts her father briefly occupied in Europe. "I have a lot of museums behind me, but what good is that?" How can I sublimate? With a boutique, like so many of her Chilean girlfriends? Ceramics? Weaving, like Katy? No, Katy is committed to revolutions, to her children, and identifies herself with a hippy style that is questionable but makes her fit in somewhere and not drift like Gloria, who often can't even unpack a suitcase and whom I had to rescue one afternoon in Sitges, when I found her all alone by the sea crying and screaming like a madwoman.

After making love, I forget about *Sophie's Choice*. She is also lying there awake, naked, her back to me. She's reading, relaxed now: her long, lovely back, the controlled fullness of her warm buttocks, the half-turned head erect, the long legs: Ingres's Odalisque, yes, I called her that, the first time we made love on our wedding night, because until then, Gloria had been as much a virgin as the purest nun. Looking at her now, I say to myself, Ingres knew how to draw like no one else: the subtlest modulation of a line, a variation of its thickness, its density, making it more pronounced or almost eliminating it, was enough for him to suggest realistically the mass and the weight, the satin texture, the sensuality and the warmth of his model's marvelous flesh: the Odalisque, indolent and beautiful, the elongated eye in the half-turned head, the turban of the many-colored towel on her head, while she avidly read *Ulysses*, strictly forbidden then; it would have made the spinsters who taught her literature at the Carrera School go into a dead faint. Now Ingres's hand is not quite firm, and Gloria reads Marguerite Yourcenar: the proportions are still perfect, the masses correct, but the satinized, modulated line that was pure poetry, suggesting curves and inviting one to penetrate the admired animal, is missing now. She sets the book aside and kisses me. She puts out the light. The sleeping Odalisque: imperfect now, but still the Odalisque.

Is the Countess's age also "those marvelous ten years between twenty-nine and thirty"? No: she hasn't reached the ideal age yet, it's still in her future, not her past, she still looks forward to her plenitude, it's not yet a memory . . . don't let her ever reach it or look forward to it, let her avoid it, reject it: her figure is not yet ripe, and if I could bite into her flesh, I'm sure I'd find that it tasted sourish, down below the sweet part, like a fruit that's still a little green.

Next morning Beltrán rushes out, quite excited after not talking to me for such a long time, to say that last evening the Count and the Countess of Pinell de Bray had been to a dinner at Liria Palace given by the new Duke of Alba in honor of their majesties King Juan Carlos and Queen Sofía.

Dressed in white. While I'd been trying to bring the Odalisque back to life. I don't want to hear any more from Beltrán and instead let Myshkin pull me to his favorite tree, a long way off. So the gold of her skin, worked on by the sun for so many days, had an aristocratic rather than passionate motive. But then, of course, one doesn't preclude the other.

4

NOW THAT SUMMER is advancing, the extravagant greens that fill my bedroom windows are softened by a lemon-yellow tint: the days are becoming almost imperceptibly shorter and the shadows on the lawn are starting to grow longer. The swords in the irises closest to the wall are scorched. Today a remote presentiment of death clings to everything like a thin film over the season's magnificence: this morning the garden is more like the reflection of a garden in a pond, a shimmering echo of the real thing.

This reflection suddenly breaks up, the victim of a burst of activity and noise: female servants carry suitcases, freshly groomed children cry the way children do before going on a trip, things are forgotten and have to be fetched from the house, the bespectacled husband directs the operation; the whining kids hang on to their mother's hand, but today she's in too much of a rush to soothe them as she usually does. Going away for the summer: so it's not elegant, after all, to spend this season in Madrid, as I had thought at first. Going away to a house near the beach is still the thing: on the ocean, where the air is healthy for children who breathe the capital's smog all year long. Marbella, Ibiza, Cadaqués . . . ? How can anyone know anything besides the information that sometimes appears in *Hola*? Mallorca, a yacht, Puerto de Santa María . . . They've lowered all the blinds. The husband hands a bunch of keys to the man in rubber boots, who's to water the lawn around the swimming pool and the mansion and keep it smooth as velvet. The next minute, they've all disappeared.

For good? No. Only for the summer, leaving the garden empty. She and I don't say goodbye: to show respect for my age and gratitude for my keeping the secret of her embrace, she could have sunbathed yesterday for the last time on the sunny spot where she prepared her aristocratic golden tan for the royal dinner. But I didn't see her all day yesterday: naturally, preparations for the trip. The servants picked up the tricycles from the lawn, the yellow plastic hen, the wicker furniture, and, it seems, even the decorative little clouds in the sky. I won't see her again, because Pancho will already be here when they return and we'll be on our terrace in Sitges, under the clotheslines, with the sea a mere triangle between the sloping roofs.

However, we still have a lot more than a month left here. The pleasure I got out of the garden next door was strictly the result of the blond girl's presence, but right now, with relaxed summer customs, isn't she probably going around the beaches and restaurants of Marbella or Biarritz flaunting her involvement with the "handsome brute"? I have to admit she was the embodiment of pleasure itself. But since the important thing about beautiful things is the pain of the deep wounds they leave, her presence in the garden may have been an obstacle for me; with her now gone, the empty park may be fruitful. Everything is possible in a forbidden and solitary garden. What? . . . I don't know: right now, when I think that I'll never see her again, I'm heartsick with the oldest of all melancholies. In any case, not knowing how I'll fill in that rich green landscape may be an advantage: after all, you don't write in order to say something but to know what you want to say and why and for whom. I read somewhere that Marcelo Chiriboga had said that; it seemed frivolous at a time of hard political struggle, but I understand and admire it now, because I've almost lost the sense of mission I then believed to be the only purpose of literature: the empty garden remains there for instructive contemplation.

I go into the dining room, where I don't touch my papers, and then on to the living room. Katy is taking a nap on one of the sofas with her wooden-soled sandals on. Clutching the telephone, Bijou laughs, talks, makes comments. I listen in through the partly open door for quite a while, because he's talking to Pato and I want to know what they're talking about: nothing special, he doesn't want to go to Marrakesh now, then he mentions a gal, a guy, that Katy is a fantastic woman and he's going to move in with her, that Patrick must come to Madrid and the three of them will live together. The ashtrays on the glass-topped table are dirty, there are beer cans on the white rug, Bijou's Adidases lie on the table like an obscene pop object by Andy Warhol. How long has he been talking? How dare he use Pancho's telephone to call Marrakesh? Doesn't he know what such a call costs? Has he also called Paris or his friends in Sweden? Indignant, I burst into the living room and order him to hang up at once. No, he doesn't know how much the call costs, probably a lot, he says, since Moroccans are idiots and it takes hours to get through and they end up giving you wrong numbers, never the right one. I realize that since he and Katy have been coming here every day, they've probably been using the phone to talk with anyone, anywhere, a kind of pastime that's become a regular habit. I ask him about this, while, stretched out on the sofa, Katy snores.

"She's been smoking," Bijou explains.

"And you also?"

He shrugs. "Yes, but I'm young and I have a better head."

"Where do you get . . . ?"

"What?"

"Kif?"

"Hash."

He lets out a laugh. He says that they sell it all over: in Madrid it's easier to get than beer. While he picks up his shoes, I question, or, actually, interrogate him: who has he talked to, how many times has he used the phone to make calls out of the country? He doesn't lie: one of the most unnerving things about Bijou is that he never feels the need to protect himself with lies, simply because he doesn't feel he needs to justify himself when he has done something wrong.

"Yes, I talk with Patrick in Marrakesh almost every day, when those idiots put me through, that is, and with Giselle in Paris. D'you know, uncle, that by now I may have a son? No: I'm going to have one, but Giselle isn't completely sure it's mine."

"I'm not interested."

"Fine."

"And Katy?"

"What?"

"The telephone."

"She also, her sons, her grandsons . . ."

"But don't you realize that's stealing?"

"Uncle, remember the public phone in Sitges."

"This is something very different."

I know it's not different. I tell him I'd like him and Katy to leave. I'm fed up with them, their hanging on, their daily visits that keep me from concentrating and deprive Gloria of the peace she needs so much and can't possibly have, not with the mess they've made of the apartment: a Thai silk cushion with cigarette burns, cognac stains, cans of tuna, Coca-Cola, *fabada*, and beer all over the place, and filthy plastic bags. Begonia stopped coming a long time ago: she refused to take care of this gypsy filth, she said. Yes, Katy and Bijou have brought in the terrible habit of total neglect that so often goes hand in hand with defeat: they succeeded in bringing it into this apartment belonging to Pancho, who had so efficiently turned his back on it his whole life.

Anyone who suffers from the chronic ill of disillusionment lives like Katy and Bijou, and like us when we live in this apartment that is someone else's. Yes, in Sitges we live a little better, but not very differently from Katy and Bijou, because we too are victims of defeat. I and other exiles as well believe that we're not: it's the result of a conspiracy, and so it has to be temporary. But time is doing its work, the drop of water falling on the rock leaves its mark, and with the years, everything gradually takes on a permanent form. On his feet now, Bijou braces himself on an early-eighteenth-century Venetian bachelor chest, crossing one leg over the other like a heron, to put on his Adidas shoes without untying their laces. While doing this, he stares at a small painting signed by Pancho: against a tinfoil background, it shows a package wrapped in manila paper covered with little specks and tied with string.

"*C'est chouette,*" the boy says.

"And Katy?" I ask.

He shrugs, as if telling me to work things out with her. I

follow him to the foyer, where, after a ceremonious bow to the Etruscan couple, Bijou kisses them goodbye on their nonexistent cheeks. He goes out, pulling the door behind him very slowly, without saying goodbye to me. I need to see him actually leave the house: I step out to the terrace, where the Madrid sun beats down on my white skin, to make sure that he's going. No: he remains downstairs, talking to Beltrán, accepting a cigarette with a laugh because they're friends; right after that the caretaker of the house next door, the guy with the rubber boots, becomes a part of this strange group, smoking and laughing. What are they talking about? I feel like yelling down from the terrace: "Take off, Bijou!"

What would the elegantly uniformed hired help in one of these houses, where you just don't break the rules of discretion even while their masters are away, think of my yowls? Well, he'll go away. The unbearable heat makes me retreat into the house once more. It's six-thirty. Time to work, since Gloria, out in pursuit of culture, has gone for tickets to the outdoor performance of *La vida es sueño* in the Plaza Mayor, and the lines are long. She invited Katy, who answered, "The Plaza Mayor is a wonderful place, but silly theater pieces are for tourists," and instead stayed here smoking marijuana with Bijou.

I keep hanging around the telephone. What right do I have to become furious at Bijou for talking with Paris or Marrakesh on Pancho's phone? Don't I usually do the same to check on my mother's health? Isn't concern about a child's birth, in Bijou's case, as respectable as concern about one's dying mother? My calls to Chile have been so frequent and so long! I make them out of Gloria's hearing, because she'd never let herself be dragged into such a petty conspiracy, just as she'd never be part of a lie.

"George Washington" I call her when she berates me in

public for one of the little white lies I sometimes tell in order to sound clever. "I did it with my little hatchet."

My contempt for her lack of fantasy, however, is mixed with respect for her integrity, which I don't have: I fall into small traps easily, into the insignificant petty crimes of people who no longer have any goals—for instance, the petty crime of making phone calls to Chile. I know that Pancho calls his mother almost every day: he earns so much with his paintings that he can pay for that luxury. So then, phone calls to Chile appear on the bills . . . of course these would be during the time he'd been away from his apartment . . . anyway, why think about it now . . . yes, it's petty thievery, and I don't have any right to throw the first stone at Bijou for calling Pato in Marrakesh and Giselle in Paris. And the same goes for my letting Katy and Bijou open the cans in the pantry and eat anything they feel like—I couldn't stop them when I caught them at it, but I pleaded with them not to let Gloria know, and once I even begged them to let me have, from their plate, some of those very special fat, delicious white asparagus tips that we never dare touch.

After Katy leaves and Gloria comes home, I decide not to call Chile: I'm ashamed to touch the telephone. But kept awake by the noisy jet of water falling into the neighbor's pool—I can't overcome my insomnia with Valium, and no novel seems to hold my interest—I get up at four in the morning, while Gloria sleeps at my side. And staring with wide-open eyes at the phosphorescent garden, I dial my mother's number in Santiago, where it's now ten in the evening.

Sebastian tells me that my mother has just died. She went into a coma this afternoon. We removed her catheters. She died two hours ago. Yes, we're all here, he says.

And to drive the knife in deeper, he adds: only the three of you are missing. Everyone present, the entire house lit up, my mother in the bed she'd always slept in, the women servants who have always waited on her washed her and bound her face so that her jaw wouldn't collapse, and Andrea— Sebastian's oldest daughter, who's married and has children—dabbed a little color, very much against his will, because he's a serious man, on her lips and her cheeks. He hadn't let them turn off a single light in the whole house; no darkness, no sounds of mourning from pious female relatives, no drone of prayers from the servants who were downstairs picking at their worn rosary beads. To forestall gloomy shadows and wailing, he has put a record on—I can recognize it over the phone—Lully's *Requiem Mass on the Death of Louis XIV*, which my father loved so much. Don't I think this is better than ancient rites of darkness and tears? Doesn't it seem to me that Mother deserves this golden, luminous music on her last night in her bed, in her house, surrounded by its silent garden?

"Yes," I say.

Anorexia nervosa. How long had it been since she stopped eating? She weighs less than a newborn baby. She could no longer move about in bed: Andrea shifts her so she won't feel any pain . . . so that she wouldn't feel any pain, I mean, since we must assume that she doesn't feel anything now, and yet when referring to Mother, he, Sebastian, the strong one, can't slip into the use of the present perfect that I've been using for a long time now. But I'm sure of one thing: the survivors were the women, faithful in spite of Allende or Pinochet, the women in town who know that things are better now than before, Sebastian tells me over the telephone. He has an easy life, because he imports radios from Japan and plays golf as he always has, my sweet and easygoing older brother, who has carried the weight of the long suffering of my mother, who died of hunger tonight.

NOW I AM nobody's son: now I am the trunk, I am the root. Now it'll be my turn. Did my brother say they'd sell my parents' home? I can't remember. I hope not, though I don't know what can be done with it: let him wait and not decide till I go back.

"Are you coming home?" Sebastian asks.

"I don't know."

Now that my mother is dead I can return without fear of being trapped by my feelings, and I can live in the real garden next door—not the reflection in the rich artificial water. Patrick, then, would be Pato once more, and Gloria would be able to drink her pisco sours and chat with her friends, giving herself up to a contemporary and, if possible, political version of my mother's work among "her women." No, she'll have to do work that will bring in money, because I've got nothing and the inheritance from my mother will be insignificant.

I can't go back. How? Without a single book published in Spain, with my tail between my legs, without work, unable to get back into the university I was fired from? At least in Spain I can hang around publishing houses begging for work . . . writing jacket blurbs, translating from English, correcting proofs, barely enough to make ends meet. But over there? Nothing. There's nobody I can hang around to ask for work: an exile at home and not abroad. But I have to remind myself that I'm not like Adriazola, that I'm not an "exile" abroad, as he claims to have become: I can go back and turn into an exile at home, if there really is such a thing. But I won't return. Because . . . yes:

because Seix Barral, Alfaguara, Argos Vergara, Bruguera, Plaza & Janés, Planeta are here; fascinating names that might, yes, just might show interest in my novel. Then, of course, I'd never be able to return: the authorities would read my attack on them for throwing me and others into prison. The police would stop us at the airport. Pato, Gloria, and I would be forced to return to Europe on the next plane: complete exiles, this time. Another novel? I don't know.

"I don't know. I don't know anything yet. Goodbye, Sebastian. So long. I'll write to you. . . ." And I hang up.

This novel I'm writing is the only thing that counts. It progresses a little with this August in which my mother has died, after the aristocratic golden presence has left the garden, and it gradually takes on a form I can handle and a language I'm at ease with. Gloria dulls the pain of her grief for my mother by weaving with Katy's group, and Pato stays in Marrakesh at an address Bijou passed on to us through Katy. I call him to tell him about her death. He surprises me by crying at the news. But the tears are his, I realize, not Gloria's and mine; the tears of someone who now has an address of his own, not ours, in a street in Marrakesh. Patrick: never again Pato.

"Why can't we live some other way?" I ask Gloria one evening, as I open a tin of sardines and she gets ready to prepare a *salade niçoise* from a magazine recipe.

"How?"

"I don't know . . . with some other kind of Latin Americans, not these sordid, bitter people."

"Well, we're sordid and bitter too. Anyhow, let me tell you, the women I work with on the looms are wonderful, with strong convictions, and they don't feel that they've failed, like us."

Gloria can be hard, blunt.

"Minelbaum isn't sordid or a failure," I say.

"You're not trying to tell me that the Minelbaums live well."

"No: Carlos gives more than half of what he earns to committees for political aid."

Gloria is sarcastic: "We could do the same with our incomes and quiet our dirty consciences."

"Don't be so hard!"

"Is there any reason why I shouldn't be?"

I think it over a moment and agree: "No. Shall we go back to Chile?"

She's the one who thinks it over now. She answers, "No. Pato wouldn't go."

As she goes past me, sitting at the pantry table, she strokes my hair and my hand touches the hip that is not the neighbor's, who is gone, but Gloria's ample one.

Bursting with conviction, she continues, "Let's stay. Write the great novel about the coup, Julio. If you were committed and convinced, like Carlos, you'd be able to write *the* great Chilean novel."

I stir my soup sadly and answer, "The great novel has never been a novel of convictions; it has always been a novel of the heart."

Gloria stands near the stove, melting something. She turns around: "Then why don't you write it? Don't you have a heart?"

There's despair in her broken voice. But I don't answer, because my answer would be that this feeling of failure on all fronts and, more than anything, my lack of strength to join a collective project—and it's my personal problem, not a general one—have destroyed my heart, melted it like the margarine in the saucepan she's holding over the burner. But one of these days this bitch, my wife, whom I detest, will run into trouble with me! I swallow a spoonful of the most insipid soup I've ever had in my whole life. She comes over. She lays her hand on my shoulder. I circle her hips with the arm that's not busy raising the spoonful of soup to my mouth.

"You have time . . ." Gloria says in a whisper, and goes back to the stove.

"My novel's moving along well now. . . ."

We don't say it but we both feel it's time to change the subject.

"I haven't seen Katy in over a week," I say.

"I see her at the looms. But I'll be going less often. I want to concentrate on this endless translation while you work."

"No, I don't want to deprive you of that pleasure, we'll work out something," I say, afraid that she'll deprive me of my days alone in the apartment.

"Do you know something that's very odd?" she breaks in suddenly. "The other day I saw Bijou walking toward the corner of the next street. . . ."

"What's odd about it?"

"Well, it was one day when he hadn't been here. He hasn't been here in quite a while."

"You must've gotten him mixed up with some other kid. They're all alike and wear the same uniform."

"Yes, but his mincing walk . . ."

"Same thing: Travolta . . ."

"Could be."

This conversation takes place on a dark night: my brother, Sebastian, calls me from Santiago to let me know someone has made an exceptionally high offer for my parents' house, which of course he put up for sale after Mother's death. My father, who lived in a world without risk and had little foresight, had nothing to his name but his retirement pay and that house. They're offering a very substantial amount, Sebastian tells me. I shout no, no, no, no, under no circumstances, he's crazy to sell my parents' house and leave me without a roof. Isn't he the one who's always telling me to return, saying that things are not like before and I won't have any problems, that something can be done about the university? Where does he want me to go back to, if he sells the house? You don't go back to a country, a people, an idea, a city: you—I mean me—go back to a house, a limited space where your heart feels safe.

When I was only a little boy, there were almost no other places in the area besides ours; it was one of the first chalets, as they'd call them then, and the dirt road was surrounded by pastures where cows grazed. People thought Father was crazy to buy a house so far from the center of town. I remember that when I was very very small—one of the first memories that came to light in the short-lived psychotherapy I had in Sitges after my shock at having to leave Chile; I didn't go on with it because I hadn't the time or the money, even though my therapist was a big-hearted Chilean who gave away half of his time attending to others from his country—my mother would carry me in her arms to the corner, where the heaviest traffic goes past now but which was then the spot where the pastures began, to buy milk taken right from the cow; they would fill a big milk can, the kind we had before glass and plastic bottles came in, and would make me drink, because I was frail, not like Sebastian, who was strong and never needed special care.

It's crazy, my brother used to say in his letters, for Mother to go on living in that house: it's old and run-down, it's full of leaks, the roof always has to be repaired before the rainy season, and the work is always expensive; it's almost impossible to heat in winter; it costs a fortune to keep things the way she wants and the servants the way she likes. And all this, of course, comes out of Sebastian's pocket, which fortunately is well lined. But the thought that Sebastian should insist on letting the object-home disappear made me swear at him over the phone, and for the first time in his life, Sebastian, always so patient, lost his head and started shouting that I was irresponsible, a romantic without a sense of reality, and who did I think I was? It was absolutely necessary to sell the house, the sooner the better, and the rest was nonsense . . . and let the garden disappear, so that when I got up in the morning and opened the window, the trees, the lawns, would no longer be there, only emptiness, not even the running stream, or the air, and I have no firm ground to step on, and I drop. I scream:

"*Gloriaaaa!*"

She catches sight of me lying lifeless, drained of color, on the sofa. She panics. I can't breathe or talk, but then, yes, a glass of water, no, cognac to help me recover, no, a Valium, maybe two, I'm about to die, I'm dying, call a doctor, no, it's just anguish, psychosomatic, dear, anguish that they're going to sell my parents' home and I don't want them to. Gloria drops my head, which she was cradling like a good Samaritan.

"How much are they offering?"

I mention the amount. Then she's the one who screams:

"Are you out of your mind? Why shouldn't they sell it? Can't you see what half of that inheritance would mean for us? Economic security. Just imagine, I could open a boutique in Sitges, where, no matter what people say, business is good, a handicrafts shop, for instance, which costs little and pays well, and we'd be rid of the drudgery of translating and proofreading and you could have the peace to write while I ran the shop. I'm good at selling and I have taste, I could go in as partners with Cacho Moyano, who suggested it once. You're completely out of your mind not to sell Rome. . . ."

It's not crazy, I insist, and it's not what she calls petit-bourgeois sentimentality. It's something else. It's deep-seated roots, history, legend, metaphor, one's own ground, a place where the heart lives. Doesn't she understand? Did the Carrera School rob her of all her sensibility? Can't she imagine the outrageous scramble at the closing, the house invaded by a whole bunch of this regime's nouveaux riches, buying and carting away the things we had all our lives? Can she imagine Mother's ugly bed in a room other than hers, occupied by someone else who'll sleep, who'll perhaps die, in Mother's place? Doesn't she care about the sacrilege of the trees being cut down to make room for a respectable building with strangers on the foundations of our family history? Sebastian wants to sell it because he's a fucking huckster, that's all; look at the way he's become a millionaire with this regime. As soon as he's seen there's money in it, he wants to swoop like a vulture onto the remains of our parents!

"You're being unfair," Gloria argues. "Sebastian is an angel and has a head on his shoulders."

"And I'm the family freak?"

"You're acting like it."

I fall asleep to the sound of the stream of water next door. Later on the telephone wakes me and Gloria answers it:

"Chile . . ." she says. "Collect. How strange. Hello, yes, yes. . . . Sebastian Méndez? He wants to know if Julio Méndez will accept the call?"

"Son of a bitch . . . he knows I have to accept his call,

even if I'm broke and he's swimming in Pinochet millions."

I talk with Sebastian. There are three years of medical bills, bills for roof repairs and heating, servants who haven't been paid, years of back taxes, the burial, the tomb, the telephone, everything. We have to ante up. How do I want us to arrange it? We have to split the costs down the middle, since we're brothers. Can I mail him a check right away? The amount is very high, but the house . . . yes, the house; it was once in the open country but now it's right in the heart of Santiago's most expensive business district, with tall buildings all around it, a small green island in the middle of cement: excellent property. They're offering so much for it that we could pay everything off easily, and what's more I'd have a lot left over even after I paid him all the money he's been lending me during my years in exile, and if I invested carefully—in Chile everyone lives off mutual funds, they bring in a good income— that small capital would help me live—

No, no, no: my irrational lips can't say anything but no to my brother's fiendish temptations. No, no; I offer to buy him out with my share. Can we do it? He laughs, not in an ugly way but somewhat sadly or bitterly. With what, he asks, when Gloria's been writing to him saying that sometimes we don't have enough to ride out the month and I can't get anybody to publish the novel I never finish?

"Did you tell him that?" I ask Gloria, who nods. "You've been spying on me, you dirty bitch. Don't you know that's enough to emasculate any man? I'm not signing anything. The house won't be sold and that's that."

Goodbye. I hang up. Gloria is crying. How can I be so unreasonable? Why do I want to keep the house next door now that it's empty? Why, now that nobody wants to live in it, or can? Why do I have to live my entire life suffocated by these metaphors instead of making them real, making them breathe life into my work? We must live the kind of life we have to live abroad, fighting to change the quality of life for everyone and not only a few: that's our sacrifice, and someday they'll acknowledge it. But not me. I'm a do-nothing, impotent, a bad writer, yes, I know, and she knows because she has been secretly reading what I've written during our stay in Madrid, and it reads as if it had been written in limbo: the other version, which Núria Monclús rightfully turned down, was perhaps better. Everyone will go on turning me down. I'm an excellent professor of literature—it shows in your novel, Gloria has said—but she, Núria, is *the* opinion, the "common reader," which is the same thing; she belongs to the group of people Virginia Woolf refers to, the reader with enough sensibility to de-mand that literature be literature and not just a licking of one's own wounds. Or is it something else now? This going back over Chile's tragedy hasn't led me to the struggle, which is somewhere else, or to literature. If I have a mind to join the struggle, why haven't I lent my name—they often ask me for it—or given my contributions to all the exiles' magazines fighting against Pinochet? You don't amount to anything one way or the other, just like in bed, Gloria shouts. I notice she's completely drunk. And vulnerable; I see that she's about to go to pieces. Yet I shout back:

"How the fuck do you know I don't amount to much in bed when you've never fucked anybody but me?"

"Katy, she tells me all about—"

"That old whore. What does she know about making love when she sleeps with that little faggot Bijou? Do you think I haven't noticed him trying to seduce me?"

"You? Who the shit would be after your poor old cock when you haven't even been able to cut off your umbilical cord from your sweet mama? Cute baby, little younger son, but actually a lard-ass who smells like a filthy pig!"

I get up, pour myself a glass of wine in the dining room, and come back to the bedroom all set to show my wife what a good stud is. She's asleep, completely, profoundly, and, I'm afraid, irrevocably dead to the world. She's snoring. I stretch out next to her. I drink my cognac in one gulp, turn off the lamp on her night table first, then the one on mine, and go to sleep.

We wake up with our arms around each other. I don't know how. Or why. Force of habit. Fear. Or whatever. And I don't know what time it is, because the blinds and the drapes are closed. The garden next door no longer exists. They sold it. Liquidated. Nothing: only this embrace that was once a garden but is now something else.

"Let's sell the house on Rome Street." That's the first thing Gloria lovingly murmurs in my ear when she wakes up in my arms.

She rambles on about a trip to Marrakesh she'd like us to take, a surprise visit to Pato so that he wouldn't run off, before we got there, to the Atlas or the Sahara or do something crazy like enlisting in the Foreign Legion.

"Silly," I say. "There's no Foreign Legion anymore."

"Then what are movies about now?"

"I don't know, about being poor, about mismatched married couples, Fassbinder, whom you like so much . . ."

"But I long for a good movie where Gaby Morlay goes along with Jean Gabin when he goes to sign up for the Legion. . . . We could take the plane to Tangier, rent a car, drive to Tetuán, Xauen, Fez, Meknès, Marrakesh, they say that all of Marrakesh is tangerine-colored, and see our son, we haven't seen him in so many months, but he's there, doing what we don't know, but at least he has a fixed address . . . or to Italy, yes, yes, Italy, we haven't gone anywhere since we've been in Europe—a month in Paris, so beautiful but so expensive, then Barcelona and Sitges. We've been too poor to even budge, and now, with this inheritance, a trip, yes, even a short one, a cheap one, your mother would have been happy to give us this chance to enjoy ourselves, maybe Venice, I imagine it iridescent in the fall, I'd love to go to Venice in November, for instance, and Florence or Rome . . . yes, yes, Rome even if Pato isn't there, what does it matter, with the hard time that lousy kid gives us, let's go to Venice and Rome instead of going to see him, to Venice, which they say is going to sink . . ."

Gloria pleads, hugs me, kisses me, but her mouth smells of last night's drinking. She begs me, caresses me, shaking as if she's about to go into hysterics, but I remain stiff, a corpse. Myshkin is asleep at my feet. Gloria begs for a little pleasure. Buried under the weight of worries and work, she has already forgotten what pleasure really is. I see her shutting herself in the prison of depression, where nothing, not even the simplest little positive thing, can appear as anything but a menace, the aggression of others, especially mine, where she is unable to obtain even the most primary pleasure, and she can only see herself walled in and held prisoner by defeat. A prison other than mine, but a prison, after all: both of us incommunicado, here and there.

A little pleasure, she pleads again, rubbing up against my unresponsive body, even though she no longer cares if it doesn't respond. Imagination is all that matters now: for years, this pleasure—called conjugal, after *jugum*, the Latin for "yoke"—has been nothing but a display of other things, like power, fidelity, stability, and serves to prove, to continue, to provide security: anything except what existed when we were a little younger, adventure, danger. It's no longer that. Proof of this is Gloria's attempt to use it to

obtain the surrender of Rome: kissing me, she asks for
Italy, to escape from the approaching storm of her depression toward those ancient stones that still preserve all their
vigor, the opal of Venice that I don't know either and wish
to know, and now she modestly suggests a trip, even if it's
only to Seville or Granada, the Alhambra, it's all so close,
and we don't know it, the *Tales of the Alhambra* when we
were small, in *El Peneca*.★

"Illustrated by Coré."

"Wasn't it Atria?"

"No, I believe it was Coré, he was a brilliant draftsman,
he should have a revival."

"Atria wasn't bad."

"No, but Coré . . ."

If I call Sebastian now, he'll put through the deal right
away and we could even leave tomorrow to go see the
Alhambra or Venice. Gloria, whose words have offered me
so many attractive things, gets out of bed and opens the
curtains. Lifting her lovely mature arms, she raises the
blinds and the lonely magnificence of the garden of my
father's house in midsummer, all mine, stands before my
eyes, all except for a white butterfly, light as a scrap of
onionskin paper, so tenuous and weightless, flying among
the branches of the somber chestnut tree.

"They would cut down the trees . . . no, I couldn't stand
to have them cut them down, the avocado and the orange,
the magnolia, the plum. Where would I land on my return,
when Pinochet topples?"

"Do you honestly believe Pinochet will topple?"

"Of course."

"Then why do you stand there like a faggot without
doing something to help out in the struggle? I help. I sign

★ A Chilean adventure magazine for boys. —TRANS.

letters of protest. I march. I write, and they tell me I do it well, for magazines that support the struggle, with the hope that everything will change. But not you, no . . ."

"In my modest way, with my novel I'm also doing something."

"Don't hand me that line. Don't you remember the way Núria Monclús looked at you in the Rastro? You simply don't exist. Admit it."

"It was Katy's fault."

"It's always someone else's fault. Never yours. You're like the Virgin Mary, an immaculate conception."

"What are you talking about? Do you think we could drag Pato back to Chile now that he's already seventeen? Never. He'll stay in Europe, bumming around, I imagine, slipping into all kinds of petty crime. You won't go to Chile and leave the kid here, even if he won't have anything to do with us. My mother loved him so much . . ."

Standing in front of my bed, Gloria covers her face with her hands, not crying, only to keep from seeing the things before her eyes, the butterfly so light that it can't sink among the trees of the garden in Rome, yes, to keep from seeing the butterfly and not have to admit that she's forever stuck with her unhappiness. What's breaking down inside of her? What has already broken down? Once, Gloria wasn't like this: she was the dance personified, Diana with her graceful walk and daring ways, the huntress, luminous as the moon, with a marvelous natural way of laughing that the years and her life and Pato and I and her father's poor business acumen managed to take from her: Gloria is the butterfly caught in a net, not a spider who, like Núria Monclús, knows how to spin them. Not a net that pins down, like the hostile nets that weigh Gloria down, but a net that Núria wears to look attractive and knows how to use: Núria is free, she's pre-psychological. She chose to eliminate private life: she's not interested in the realm of the lyrical. It's only one more realm, neat and ironed and organized among her dresses, which are all the same, hanging one beside the other in her closet. She's the true-to-life Diana who needs no arrows or quiver other than a string of telephones and computers, a spider who catches valuable writers in her web, symbolized by a fine veil that gives a softness to her face that doesn't fool anyone. It's awful seeing how she makes Gloria suffer. It's Núria's fault, because she keeps me from being successful: she has Gloria trapped in a spiderweb, her prison.

"Don't cry," I tell her.

"I'm not crying."

"Then what?"

"I don't know."

"I only know I can't, my love. . . ."

"Not even for me?"

She takes her hands off her face. Her poor eyes are blurry with tears that dissolve yesterday's makeup: her smeary eyes plead to no avail. And all I can murmur is:

"O, it's only Dedalus whose mother is beastly dead."

Gloria flees to the bathroom and breaks into sobs.

IT'S STRANGE TO see how every human being inevitably repeats his own way of life no matter where he happens to be. He drags his limitations along with him, and with them he once more traces his perimeter, sets the rules of his game, and chooses partners who accept him. It's like a prison sentence in which you can only imagine your right to choose but never actually exert it; a confinement where, I suppose, you pretend freedom and security can coexist. In Sitges, Cacho Moyano would introduce me as "the great Chilean writer." This struck me as funny, because I knew it wasn't true and I could put up with this falsehood, discussing it in private with Gloria so she wouldn't think I was taking it seriously: and yet this lie gave me some ground to stand on, I felt safe up to a certain point in that mediocrity whose standard Cacho set. Safe among Chilean journalists who free-lanced because they could do nothing else; among Uruguayan psychologists who practiced in bars during the season; among Peruvian doctors temporarily taken on by hospitals until they could revalidate their degrees, after much studying and red tape, and be permanently hired; among Bolivian professors of the German flute, Mexican instructors of yoga, Cuban professors of mime, jetsam thrown up on the shore after various wrecks, people who left Paris because they were fed up with being fifth-rate citizens in university circles, discouraged by shortage of money, destroyed families, broken or exchanged married couples, and all the other endemic ills of the people with whom Gloria and I, though we were old enough to be in a different category but lacked the right credentials—how many times was my appointment as interim professor of contemporary English literature at the Autonomous University of Barcelona on the point of becoming real?—were inevitably swept along: nothing we did ever left the slightest mark.

We had hoped that in Madrid everything would be different. We knew that the political groups were active there and were of all shades and colors, not just die-hard Marxists or young hotheads of one brand or another. Literary circles were more open-minded and generous, they felt less threatened than the Barcelonans by the influx of the Latin American phalanx, and there were cafés frequented by writers, soirées and maybe even salons that might be fun. Press agencies, the most important newspapers, the pressures of Spain's internal politics, were all in Madrid. There was direct contact with foreign countries. Moreover, the whole school of Argentine psychoanalysis had been forced to leave the country because the military junta considered psychoanalysis and Marxism to be one and the same: the exodus of these eminent professionals had been a kind of national lobotomy. The most prominent settled in Madrid. I couldn't hide my hope that our social life in Madrid would proceed among these people, who would help me to carry on my uprooted life effectively enough to write and leave a mark, as they were, for they were now regenerating Spanish psychiatry, which everyone knows was still in diapers yesterday.

And yet it didn't turn out that way. With the best intentions in the world, Carlos Minelbaum threw us into the arms of Katy Verini, full of fun, intelligent and charming in measured doses, but also shipwrecked and clinging to anyone—in this case us—to keep afloat. And if we've spent time with anyone, it has been with Katy's friends. It's not that they're not admirable people: the solidarity of Chileans who suffer from separation anxiety, of Argentines who have to hide so that "they" won't come after them, of Uruguayans who sing tangos and lose their jobs because they end up drunk in bars or restaurants, of Peruvians, Mexicans, Salvadorans, Dominicans, and Bolivians, is vital, effective, and not just, as in Sitges, part of the decade's general folklore. A growing number confess that they'll never go back home, even if things change for the better: these are the younger ones, those who have no reason to feel like misfits here, especially those in the film industry or television, who can count on technical material not available in their countries, where they have no deep roots in a city, a neighborhood, or a garden that's about to disappear. But the majority curse their bad luck, they dream, they remember.

One evening we go for a skewered-pork dinner at the home of a Peruvian filmmaker—so to speak, since he has done little in his own country and here he barely manages to survive as a studio assistant—a tall, strong, Indian-looking man with a long shock of graying hair who shows slides he took in the Amazon as part of a project for a movie based on Mario Vargas Llosa's *The Green House*. But the project has fallen through because of the high fee Núria Monclús demanded for the film rights.

Some of the slides are marvelous. Seated on the floor or on the few chairs in the apartment in the Lavapies* neighborhood where the Peruvian lives, the guests watch, asking pertinent and always heartrending questions, comparing the Peruvian, the Bolivian, and the Brazilian jungles. Some specialist comes out with a technical comment from time to time, and on his instrument a quiet Indian flute player comes out with another definition of our native scenery.

Katy cannot concentrate on anything but herself. In the dark she comes over to settle down next to me on the sofa, where I've made myself comfortable. She starts showing intelligent interest in the slides and the project the Peruvian is describing; it's faithful to the poetic élan of the only novel of Vargas Llosa's that has resisted time, in the opinion not only of some younger but also of older writers, like me, those of us who saw our literary careers limited by the saturation of the Boom. My grudge against those writers grows as the screening proceeds, despite Katy's steady whispering in my ear.

Suddenly, while I drink a glass of sangría, I lose the thread of the Peruvian's project, because Katy's words make me sit up. She says she's scared, and this has to be a

---

* A working-class section of Madrid. —TRANS.

secret just between us, they'll come looking for her any day now if they find out that she's let the story out. No, Victor wasn't murdered at a party of drunken truck drivers who took over his apartment and slit his throat after they had sodomized him. The real truth is something else. In the most absolute secrecy, Victor, who was a homosexual but also an excellent lover—he was a young and intelligent doctor with a growing reputation among the best of the upper class, to which he belonged—treated the victims of torture who emerged from the Uruguayan concentration camps. They told him many horrifying stories, facts that he passed on to the resistance. When the Uruguayan government discovered this, they faked an orgy in his apartment and murdered him, then accused him of homosexuality as an excuse not to investigate the crime.

Katy tells me all this in rich detail, in a very low voice, with all her affectations: shyness, giggles, repetitions to get a point across, covering her eyes from time to time with the loose ends of her bangs. As Katy's story goes on, superimposed on the Peruvian's, these affectations gradually disappear and Katy is left like someone stripped naked, troubled, making a passionate, justified attack on the police state her country has become:

"I'm a wreck, that's why I'm in psychoanalysis, don't you think it's weird for a girl like me not to reach an orgasm except with a fairy? That's why I left, I was scared, and I'm terrified that they'll come after me, that's why I move around so much and sometimes sleep at your place or go to France. . . . Now I'm going to Marrakesh with Bijou. There are more Uruguayans scattered around the world than in Uruguay itself, what a country. . . ."

I squeeze her hand. It's easy to understand her, her and everyone else, so easy to forgive. We drink more and more sangría together—what kind of crap have they put in this damn mixture?—watching the jungle scenes, listening to the notes of the flute sprinkling Vargas Llosa's greens.

When we say goodbye, very late, after the usual session of *vidalas* and *chamamés*, *tonadas* and *cuecas*, waltzes and some song or other of Chabuca Granda's or one of Atahualpa Yupanqui's, of course, or the Parras', we're all pretty drunk. Someone offers us a ride home in his car, which is crowded. When we get out I hear more than one cutting remark, especially from my compatriots, about how elegant our place is, but Gloria and I are too drunk to care about one more cutting remark in a world where it's the most popular defensive weapon.

Opening the apartment door and greeting the Etruscans, Gloria and I lean on one another to keep from stumbling and head for our bedroom. But even drunk we can't help smelling the stink of dog and cat shit, dog and cat piss. We haven't taken Myshkin out for his normal walk or changed Irina's litter. And some of the plants in the winter garden are dying and others are drying up, because we've neglected them. I sense that I've stepped on something slippery and smelly: in the bedroom I take my shoes off, while Gloria plops into bed, meaning to sleep with her clothes on, and says, "What a disgusting smell!"

"Naturally. What do you expect when you don't bother to take the dog out and forget to change the cat's litter or leave the window open for her? Look, I've just stepped on a big hunk of shit. . . ."

"And why haven't you taken him out?"

"I'm working."

"Don't make me laugh. Change your disgusting shoes and take Myshkin out. Oh, cutie pie, good old Papa will

take you out for your little walk, even if he drank everything he could grab, including the water in the vases at the
party . . ."

"Your balls is what I'll take out, Myshkin."

I'm changing my shoes, leaving the dirty pair on the
terrace to clean tomorrow. Meanwhile, Gloria sits up in
bed: she makes this effort, I imagine, because she intends
to go out with me. I think that this time there's something
defensive and self-protective about her solidarity; she
doesn't want to stay here alone, she doesn't want to let me
go alone, she's afraid of the solitude and the filth, she needs
to be with me in spite of the mutual resentment brought on
by this degrading situation we're both to blame for. With
Myshkin tugging at the leash, because he knows we're
taking him out, we pass through the living room with the
two windows and the false curtains that Bijou found so
hilarious, through the remains of his and Katy's sloppi-
ness. It's better to go out. We go down to the ground floor
and out into the street. Slowly, saying almost nothing at
first, we start to go around the block, with the dog smelling each tree, pissing a little here and a little there. I tell
Gloria very secretively how impressed I am by what Katy
told me.

"Didn't you know?" she asks in disbelief. "I hadn't
mentioned it, because everybody knows it and I thought
she had told you too. She told me the first time we met in
Sitges, just imagine, and she told me again the first time we
went to the Prado together, and she's told Bijou and everyone else. It's a compulsion, as if she wanted to drop little
pieces of paper so that they'll follow her, like in a treasure
hunt, till two masked men finally catch up with her, bursting into her apartment any day now with their submachine
guns."

We continue our walk. The hot chemical air that burns in the red sky over the center of town scorches our faces like a science-fiction ecological menace, and I imagine that we'll be terribly old when we get back to the house. Few cars go by. From time to time, along Serrano Street, the tiny green light of a taxi, seeing us, its only prospective customers, slows down. We go back into the microworld of parks and deserted gardens in which we live: behind some wrought-iron gate a dog howls and Myshkin answers, as if out of courtesy.

Coming around the other end of our street on our way back to what we're in the habit of calling "our home," we reach the section occupied by the peeling wall of the Duke of Andía's now-empty house.

ROJOS CULIAOS

Enormous red letters. How could anyone possibly have written that? The sight of it is like an electric shock: ROJOS CULIAOS. In this neighborhood it's not unusual for graffiti to remain on the walls for several days, before the authorities have them erased. Who would have gone to the trouble of writing CULIAOS, which nobody but a Chilean would understand? It means somebody who, as Spaniards say, has "taken it up the ass." Only a Chilean could have done it.

Bijou. Of course. Both Gloria and I say it at the same time. Beltrán, the concierge, who is a member of the extreme rightist Fuerza Nueva, has made him do it, perhaps even paid him for it, without specifying a more effective phrase, now that the Duke and Duchess are away. MONARCHY YES JUAN CARLOS NO; LONG LIVE BLAS PIÑAR. We haven't seen such graffiti except in our neighborhood or others nearby. But . . . ROJOS CULIAOS? When it is discovered and deciphered by the police tomorrow, won't the message point to all the Chileans in Madrid?

It's vital for Gloria and me to eliminate it, to save ourselves and all the Chileans who can be smeared by those words. Drunk but galvanized, we rush up to our apartment to get what we need: paint, because the stain can't be washed away. White paint, lots of it. Where? How? We have to do it before daybreak: that reddish glow may be the coming daylight.

Gloria remembers seeing a bunch of keys in a jar on a top shelf in the pantry. Perhaps one of them is the key to Pancho's studio . . . surely we'll find white paint there? Sitting on the floor next to the studio door, her eyes filled with tears, her lips quivering with fear, nerves, and drink, Gloria takes the keys out of the jar, and then I clumsily fumble with the lock.

I don't know how long we remain there, introducing one key after the other, getting them all mixed up, without saying a word, almost forgetting our purpose, until the lock opens at last. We drink our cognacs and enter the holy of holies. We switch the light on.

Inside, the pristine, gratuitous world created by Pancho Salvatierra overwhelms us in the bright light that hits the handful of canvases hanging there, exposing beautiful silver faces, fantasy rescued from its hiding place inside everyday objects, packages, the dried skeleton of a sprig of thyme, a loaf of bread, everything elevated by an accurate eye and unbeatable technique to something more, something other than reality. Side by side with these works of art there are materials, matter that has not been transfigured yet, the working ingredients of the paintings, canvases and boards, sacks, hammers, crates, big pots of paint, sheets of polished aluminum, big and small brushes, colored paper, drawing boards, all the raw material that

Pancho uses to give life to his wild ideas, so true to life and
yet so different. We look in the big jars: sure enough, white
paint, and brushes, the biggest ones.

We turn off the light and lock up, and when we cross the
dining room—our hearts pierced by the insult on the wall,
by Bijou's betrayal, hurt by the spelling mistake that
betrays his hand, unfamiliar with his own language and
showing no respect for it, no respect for anyone, not even
for his countrymen wounded by exile, for his father, his
mother, for us, Uncle Julio and Aunt Gloria—on our way
to face the horror of the painted words again, we each gulp
down a long slug of Courvoisier straight from the crystal
decanter. I see a very strange expression on Gloria's face, as
if, rejecting everything outside, she has suddenly retreated
into herself, into the prison of her suffering, which pro-
vides her with a retreat more acceptable than this: she can't
bear what is happening, the phantasmagoria of idiocy
that's just another form of betrayal and defeat.

We go downstairs. Gloria stumbles and braces herself
against a lamppost whose light is out, while I try to get rid
of the letters with a big brush, CULIAOS. . . . That's the
part we have to erase first, the Chilean, the incriminating
part. But I'm very drunk, because the cognac has gone to
my head, and I trip on the huge jar, spilling a sticky puddle
of white oil paint that slowly spreads on the sidewalk.

"Stupid bastard!" Gloria screams at me.

And we both lunge at the white paint spilled into the
night, trying to recover it with our bare hands, painting
the graffito with our hands full of paint, trying to wipe out
the words on the wall with our soiled hands, without
success, only messing up the wall, and there's nothing we
can do but get out of there, falling all over ourselves and
giving up on the sticky, gooey white mess, carrying our
shoes in our hands so as not to make paint tracks back to

the house. Yes, anyone can blame us for the graffito on the Duke of Andía's wall, because we're the only Chileans in this neighborhood, so elegant that some of our countrymen can't help taking digs at us for living here.

TWO DAYS LATER, Bijou drops in on us, fresh as ever, whistling, as if nothing has happened. We haven't even dared go out, to face Beltrán or the world or the wall smeared with the traces of our failure.

Gloria is lying down, silent, irritable, the victim of a headache that hasn't left her since that night. Lying beside her, I can't look at the empty garden, its wall desecrated by Bijou's graffito. As soon as I open the door for him I shout at him that he's a bastard, a son of a bitch. He closes the door behind him, greets the Etruscans with his usual kiss on their nonexistent cheeks, and follows me to the bedroom, where I lie back down next to Gloria; we're both sick of this young kid, sitting perversely at the foot of our bed and biting his nails, smiling, his only sign of feeling. He'd better not dare show up at this house again! If he does, I'll call the police. It's really the last straw for the son of Hernán and Berta Lagos to let himself get sucked in by the stupidity of a reactionary doorman who's just an ignorant reflection of reactionary employers. The graffito only goes to show what the lack of a civic and political conscience in a moron like Beltrán can do to the hash-softened mind of a kid like Bijou. I'll call Berta and Hernán in Paris this very night.

"If you tell Papa anything," and I notice that I've scared him, because his entire chemistry changes with my threat, "if you accuse me, I'll tell Patrick, who's here in Madrid now, not to come and see you!"

"Don't you threaten me!" I shout.

"Where is he?" Gloria asks, sitting up as if she wished to take a look, for a minute, at the world of reality, of possibility. "How is he?"

"Fine, just fine," Bijou says, smiling once more, at ease now that he knows he's in charge. "But he doesn't feel much like coming here, even though I've told him to come, that the apartment is fantastic. He's with some Moroccans, not bad people, even if they're Moroccans. We're all leaving together for Paris tomorrow."

"I want to see him," Gloria pleads.

"What for?" I break in. "He's going around with Moroccans. God only knows what he's up to."

"Aha! So you're a fascist and a racist too, uncle, and you look down on Moroccans."

"I'm not . . ." I start to defend myself angrily, but I'm so angry at Bijou that I can only shout at him to leave, to go away, I don't want to see Patrick, I don't want to see him, Bijou, ever again, while Gloria begs me to be quiet, to please let Patrick come to see her, she wants to give him a little money she's saved, it's not much but . . .

Bijou answers from our bedroom door:

"Neither Patrick nor I need your money. We're young, and if we need some, we'll manage to get it without having to crawl in front of that Núria that you're so afraid of. Don't worry, you won't see me again . . . and say goodbye to Katy for me, she's old but she's a good gal, even if she's silly, like all you people with your obsessions about saving the world with your liberal or communist or fascist ideas, like that ass Beltrán, I don't even know anymore what you are, or my parents or anybody. . . ."

He walks out. It's almost night. The garden is quiet, and we remain next to each other, without looking at it, feeling it go to sleep before the light goes out completely.

I must have slept. I wake up in the bedroom: a howl from Gloria in the living room.

"Julioooooo . . ."

I leap out of bed and rush out to look for her. I see Gloria, her hands over her face in her usual gesture of pain, a defense and a prison and a rejection, standing in front of the Venetian chest and an empty space on the wall that had been occupied until last night by Pancho's painting, the package mounted on polished aluminum foil. It's not there now. They've stolen it. Bijou. Bijou stole it.

"I'm going to look for it," I say.

"Where . . . how . . . ?"

"I don't know. I'll think of something. Pancho's paintings are worth thousands, hundreds of thousands of dollars. Can you imagine? That shitty little juvenile delinquent. Whatever made us get mixed up with him?"

I start out by taking a cab to Katy's place, but she knows nothing, she's been on the outs with Bijou for weeks, yet she is in touch with all kinds of underworld circles and goes into action; she knows how to share other people's troubles. Her friend Bolados is a forger of famous Latin American painters—Matta, Botero, Cuevas, Antúnez, Conde, Salvatierra—and what's more, he deals in stolen paintings. He's a Spaniard, Katy explains in the cab, but he's the son of Mexicans and is ashamed of it, and yet Mexico, the new Mexico of oil money, is where he finds his most gullible clients; he looks more Madrilenian than all the cats in Madrid. We visit him in his studio over on Onésimo Redondo. It's an enormous greenhouse filled with tropical plants and macaws, and its walls are lined with paintings signed by the biggest names. Down below, not very far off, is the Royal Palace, all lit up and looking like a strange object made of bone, built with leftovers from the Catacombs, surrounded by fountains and trees. From the studio's huge picture window, all of Madrid, all the central part, and the entire reddish sky can be seen glowing.

"No," he says, playing with his Mexican rancher's mustache. "It would be like something out of a movie, having a Salvatierra, especially one from the period that, from your description, the painting you're looking for belongs to. But since you're a friend of Katy's, I promise to help and call you as soon as I have any news. Leave me your phone number."

I give it to him, and he writes it down. He thumbs through a notebook and calls Katy into another room, where they hold a secret conference. Then they come back, and he gives me two or three addresses written on a scrap of paper. He says goodbye very cordially. But none of the addresses are of any use; the person isn't there, or no one there knows him, or else he knows nothing about paintings. Exhausted, way past eleven in the evening, we decide to go to Somosaguas, beyond Madrid's Casa de Campo, well out of the city, to the home of a millionaire who collects Salvatierras and may know something.

"I'll leave you here, my sweet," Katy says to me, stopping a cab. "I'm starting to feel pale with all I've smoked and all this running around, and I'm dead tired. Besides, leaving Madrid . . . well, I'm like Sartre: I hate chlorophyll, you see, even if there isn't much to speak of in Castile. Besides, how do you think they'll receive you in a millionaire's house at this hour? Are you out of your mind? Go home, honey, and look some more tomorrow. In the meantime I'll talk to a couple of people at the guitar concert tonight. Bijou hasn't had time to sell it yet, even if he's crazy enough to trade it for a packet of cocaine or some other shit, and anyway, those things are hard to sell. Besides, you've seen how crazy Bijou is. He may have stolen it just to fuck you up, and he may have thrown it into the river or God knows what."

Slowly, as if I were afraid to, I return to the apartment. The wall of the Duke of Andía's estate is perfectly white, freshly painted; it looks as if they only waited for the owners to leave before repairing the wall, which wasn't in very good shape in the first place. Nothing unpleasant has happened here. It has all been like one of those horror movies they show on television, followed by perfume commercials in which young people are beautiful and happy among tulles and flowers. For a second I cherish the crazy hope that just as nothing seems to have happened outside, where even the paint stain on the ground has disappeared, when I enter Pancho's living room I'll find the painting hanging above the Venetian chest as before. . . . But no: Bolados will find it, yes, yes, I'm sure of it, I tell myself as I go up to the apartment, because Katy told me that their whispering in the next room had been so that Bolados could check in his address book to see if the phone number I had given him as mine was really Pancho's, and she had assured him that I live in his place because I'm such a close friend, and this had impressed him. He hopes that if he does this kind of favor for me I'll introduce him to Pancho, with whom he may wish to make some kind of business deal.

The painting isn't hanging above the Venetian chest, because Bijou stole it that evening, perhaps to sell it, perhaps only to upset us . . . no, to sell it and go to Paris with Pato and some Moroccan friends who deal in kif, but maybe not, I hope, maybe they just deal in round amber stone beads, things from the Atlas or whatever, not drugs. No. Not drugs. Pato would never do that: I feel it in my veins. Anything but that.

Before going into the bedroom, where the light is on, I have to try to calm down. We'll plan an intelligent hunt, we'll recruit friends, people who can help us, who know Bijou's friends in Madrid, the *tout Paris* he mentioned and that seems to have convened here this summer.

When I walk into the bedroom I see Gloria, half dressed, with one limp leg, its stocking rolled down, hanging over the bed. She's snoring in a very odd way: her eyes are closed . . . as if she's dead, but she's not dead. On the floor an empty glass, and on the night table the Baccarat decanter; she has her shoes on, her blouse is open, her skirt above her knees; she's unbelievably drunk, and the whole room reeks of cognac. Terrified, I kneel down next to her.

"Gloria."

Her snoring grows deeper, faster. One of her hands stirs. I try to lift her leg onto the bed, but she's very heavy; she moves her hand again, as if to stroke mine this time, groping for it like someone blind, and then she runs her limp, clumsy fingers over my face as if trying to recognize it.

"Gloria, please . . ."

"Oohhhh . . ." she murmurs, opening her eyes wide and then letting her eyelids fall like someone dropping something too heavy to hold up anymore.

"Gloria, what's wrong?"

"*. . . love me . . . ?*"

"You're drunk, my lovely. I'm going to undress you."

"Don't touch me!"

"Sweetie . . ."

"I'm not drunk . . ."

"Well, okay, you're not drunk."

She lies back lifeless after the strain of saying those few words. I remove her shoes, her skirt that's too tight. She can't sleep comfortably like that, she's on the edge of the bed, if she moves, she'll fall off. I try to shift her. She fends me off with a slap that rises from deep in her sleep.

"Gloria, for God's sake . . ."

She moves, and just as I foresaw, the lower half of her body sags down to the floor, and I try to lift her up on the bed again. But the upper part also falls, as if it belonged to someone else, who's pale, dead, eyes closed.

"Dead! What have you done?" I shout.

"Valium."

"With all that drinking! Are you crazy? How much?"

". . . three . . . five . . ."

I don't know why I try to make her stand, and I don't know what to do. I feel—perhaps from an innate sense of propriety, or simply because of middle-class prejudice— that I should return her to the bed, but the white rug is almost as soft as the bed, and all I'd have to do is slip a pillow under her head. Dangerous but not suicidal, I say to myself. She's heavy, difficult to get her up on her feet, but I manage to lift her body a little, her head, a riot of coppery hair, tipping backward as if her neck were broken. I raise her up some more and start feeling a sense of victory, until I sit her up, leaning on my arm, her head fallen back, her eyes closed. Suddenly, a deep rasping breath makes her stiffen and jerk her head up, and then, letting it fall forward, she throws up all over me, the slimy, fetid stuff soaking my body and my hands; another rasping breath and more hot vomit spills over me, on the white rug, and on her own half-dressed body, now stripped of dignity and humanity. This is followed by a barely audible whisper and a crying jag.

"I want to die . . . I want to die . . . you don't love me. Pato doesn't love me . . . you don't love me . . . to die, to die . . . I want to die . . . I want to die . . . you don't love me . . ."

"Who doesn't love you?"

"You, my love . . . to die, to die . . ."

Horrified, I leave her in her pool of filth in the bedroom,
reeking of stale drink, vomit, cognac, wine, humiliation,
pain. I head for the other telephone, I don't know why,
since I could call from where I am, but I don't want to go
on hearing her cries for death. Who can I turn to? I call
Carlos Minelbaum before anyone else, and tell him what's
happened; no, he doesn't think it was attempted suicide if
she didn't take more than three or four Valiums. I can
check, but it's not important, because she vomited. I ought
to try to get her up, wash her, and then let her sleep all she
wants, I'm not to worry, but I should get someone to help
me, because I won't be able to manage alone. Tomorrow
he'll take the first Barcelona–Madrid flight and will be at
my place around twelve-thirty. Gloria will still be asleep,
of course, but he wants to see her and he wants to see me
before she wakes up. I'm to calm down. The worst part is
the psychological harm, hers, but mine also. I should try
to snap out of it. Get some help.

It doesn't take Katy more than twenty minutes to arrive
after my call. We manage to wash Gloria, put her to bed,
groom her hair, clean the rug, rinse the glasses; Katy's
actions are as precise as a nurse's, as if she were used to such
emergencies. Because, she says, these cases of depression
happen often among our people. She is suddenly transformed from a talkative and useless hippy, incapable of
crossing a street without hanging on to someone else's arm
as if crossing were something terrifying, into a helpful and
practical woman who knows how to share someone else's
troubles because others have shared hers, or as if she had
dredged up from her unconscious the ancient feminine arts
of healing and consolation she's now using to help her
suffering friend and the friend's husband.

She opens the bedroom windows, the blinds, the curtains, to let the real night air, instead of the air conditioner's, circulate: it's as if our bedroom had suddenly vomited all its filth into the garden next to it, to let it dissolve into the empty rustle of its leaves. When everything is spick-and-span, she asks if I'd like her to heat something up for me. Would I like her to make another bed for me, if I'm sleepy? No, she'll sleep on the sofa in the living room or sit up, she's not sure which, she's not sleepy; I should have a good rest in the other bedroom, the living-room sofa is wonderful, she has even made love with Bijou on it, but, of course, she adds, finally laughing again, there's nothing strange about that, because she has made love almost everywhere.

While Katy goes off to prepare beds and food, I stay in the bedroom awhile, watching Gloria's face, white as an unbaked loaf of bread. Age, pain, her darkened, tangled, sticky hair on the pillow: from time to time she moves her head, her lips try to mutter something, one of her hands seems to suggest, with a movement it doesn't complete, that she's trying to brush an imaginary fly from her forehead; she frowns, and then, like the last circles left by a stone dropped in the water, her lips try to speak, and finally the effort dissolves into the deep lake of sleep.

I go over to the window. It's late . . . I mean early, because we've been up all night. A murky dawn is starting to define the contours of the buildings that loom beyond our microworld of trees and private parks where it may seem impossible but all this is happening—the words LONG LIVE FRANCO, GOD, AND FAMILY are there to stop this from happening: to prevent exactly this kind of thing—this small humiliating tragedy that in the end, Carlos is sure, will not even be a tragedy.

As daylight moves in and the sounds of traffic wake up

the tenants in apartments less fortunate than the one in which I live, the garden next door gradually comes to life with slight movements and sounds: birds with unfamiliar names start to stir and chirp in the chestnut's branches, and the branches themselves turn from black to violet and then blue, and then everything is green, until at last shadows are traced on the grass and long yellow ribbons of sunlight unfurl; these are actually green, the sunny green broken up by the pointillism of the full light of day.

Can defeats be so total on a morning like this?

5

AT FIRST CARLOS Minelbaum comes to visit Gloria every other day, and then once a week. He takes the shuttle from Barcelona, spends the day with us, and gets the last plane back. He closes himself in with her for one, two, sometimes three hours to apply an intense supportive psychotherapy and especially to shower her with affection, which she accepts. It's difficult to make her talk—impossible the first week, when he wouldn't let anyone in her room—but later, when Carlos lets me in to see how she'll react, she cries out and tries to scratch me, screaming that I'm to blame for her bungled life, her inability to face any kind of fight or any action or project, because I have devoured her.

So then Carlos once more keeps me from going in, and from outside the door I listen to the harsh sounds of her hysterical voice, cut off now and then by the therapist's. I also hear her sobbing when she's alone. She doesn't talk to Katy, whose good offices she tolerates, or ask her for anything, not even with sign language, and the same goes

for Begonia—she has come back after we begged her to—
who has to guess when Gloria needs anything. Then, with
the passing weeks, when she's shut in with Carlos, I hear
her choppy mumbling turning into a kind of dialogue.
With me, Carlos has anxious conversations that are also a
kind of friendly therapy to help me bear the blame Gloria
heaps on my head, blame for the failure of her life, she calls
it, but I must understand it, Carlos says, as the failure of
something bigger, the failure of an education, a class, a
world, a moment in history, all of which she shoves off on
me. It's not an isolated case. All one has to do is look at the
scars on Katy's wrists.

"Maybe it is partly your fault," Carlos suggests.

"I don't know, I don't think so. . . ."

"In any couple there's not only one executioner and one
victim, both are executioners and victims. To begin healing you must at least acknowledge that. And, most of all,
give more priority to the things that really matter. . . ."

I suppose I'm pretty far from being cured, because I
don't accept the blame as far as Gloria is concerned, and I
can't accept all her accusations. When Carlos leaves and
Katy is asleep, my anger rises and I understand less and
less, because she may feel that I ruined her life with my
mediocrity and lack of spunk, but she has been a drag on
mine with her demands, which have made me feel mediocre. My talks with Carlos are long, they make things
even more confused, sometimes they make me suffer
more, but they're my only comfort. He leaves after having
the dinner Begonia cooks for him because she's very fond
of him: squid stuffed with prosciutto, which Carlos loves.

It's Carlos who puts our affairs in order; I'm not up to it.
He's the one who takes a cab to Getafe, where Begonia
lives, talks it over with her and explains what Gloria's
going through, getting her to rush to our help; and after

much cleaning and straightening up, sending rugs and cushions to the cleaner's, and calling the upholsterer, she succeeds in restoring order to Pancho's apartment. Begonia even has a showdown with Katy, who now lives here, and warns her to cooperate in Gloria's recovery, which won't be easy: she'll have to make sure that both Gloria and I take our respective doses of Deanxit at prescribed hours, vitamins and other medications, and see to it that the patient eats well and at regular hours. But even more important—and Begonia shakes a finger at her—she's to be careful not to mess up the place or leave things lying around. Begonia comes every day to see that everything runs smoothly.

"Quite a gal, *che*! If my mother had only been like Begonia! She's a wonder! I wouldn't have married that idiot, my first husband, at fifteen, and by now I'd have a steady job in some government department, with no economic or political or maybe even sex problems."

As soon as Katy comes to our place, after shaking hands with the Etruscan bigwigs at the entrance, who she says are the real owners of the house, she slips into a fur coat she's found among the ski clothes in the closet in the dressing room and gets down to the business of being nurse and companion.

All she has to do is go to an air-conditioned movie, she says, to have her bones start aching like an old woman's in a rest home.

"What can I do?" she argues with Carlos when they run into each other. "Yes, I know it's psychological: the gal who had me in analysis used to say it was because my mother spent her days playing bridge and the guy who analyzes me now says it's because my father spent his time playing golf. Who can I believe? And aspirins don't work against fathers and mothers. How can anyone change me?

Can't they see I'm a product of history, a sick mixture of Sartre and Marcuse and the flower children and McLuhan and God only knows what other shit? Do you remember when we believed that we'd win our liberty once and for all and came to Europe to smoke marijuana and make believe we were Joan Baez? Darling, I'm only a poor archaeological phenomenon of no importance, a leftover, something the wave cast up on the shore. Or at least that's how the young punks see me now, or the drifters, or the organization men, or the computer experts, which is what everyone who isn't a drifter seems to be."

"Listen, dear Katy," Carlos tries to break in. "There's nothing seriously wrong with Gloria, at least nothing organic, but we've got to pamper her. She's not the only one who's lost her bearings, darling. All, each and every one of us, in our own way . . ."

"But you believe in God, kid, and you're a Marxist—what a big difference, Carlitos."

"A God that's pulling me apart. Even Eurocommunism seems suspect to me, not to mention the extraparliamentarism of our times."

"Well, kid, you're turning into a revisionist, a deserter, a common low-down dissident, and that means a CIA agent. . . . How wonderful! *Dieu est mort, Marx est mort, et moi-même je ne me sens pas très bien!* I can't believe that you too have turned into that cliché."

She jumps on him to kiss him, while I laugh at the ideological excesses of this woman who, as the ladies in Chile would say, has behaved "like a queen" during Gloria's illness. But I realize that both she and Carlos still have a vision of possible solutions, while for me the world has shrunk and my vision has become minimal, very subjective: I see politics, in short, as a private reaction in the face of contingency; the struggle as a subgenus of the lyrical.

I've rejected possible solutions, and at the moment of raising my floodgates the lyrical is precisely what floods my novel, the novel that, during Gloria's captivity, in her stifling depressive state, becomes accessible and progresses while I watch and take care of my wife.

Obstinately silent in the small high-backed chair in front of the window over the garden, like the busy spider she has always wanted to be, she works on an interminable crochet shawl with a stitch that she remembers from the horrid fancy-work class at the Carrera School, something formless I know she'll never finish, because she never finishes anything, but that at this point serves as her only vocabulary: the important thing is to keep her fingers, at least, alive and moving, busy with the everlasting repetition of the same stitch, with identical movements . . . those minuscule finger movements her only link with the world.

Carlos and Katy are young, not quite forty, another mental world, another generation. They were born around the time Gloria and I went to the Amunátegui Vadillo ball in what was then called the Real de Azúa palace, I in tails and she in white tulle; and Hedy Lamarr and Carole Lombard were part of our mythology. Carlos and Katy consider those movies mere nostalgia, ingenuous and absurd. And Deanna Durbin, whom Gloria tried to look like in those days, makes them, and us, laugh now. Katy and Carlos have become committed to systems, but Carlos is painfully critical of his, while Katy is a dropout: they express their disappointment in different ways, but having believed in and been active in collective movements gives them a sense of security and solidity.

Always a little outside of this, I, the son of a skeptical liberal, after all, whom I turned against because he was weak, will end up just like him: a man who toward the end

of his life no longer even read the newspapers, although he
had been a congressman for such a long time. His garden
was his prison, as my novel is mine, as her depressive state
is Gloria's. The secret is that deep down nobody wants to
leave his own prison; that's the real nature of our illnesses.
There are no solutions. How can there be any now that
Pinochet has closed down Congress? And if there are any,
they're partial, contingent. Will I end my days like my
father, sitting on the bench under the avocado tree, watching my grandchildren play with some yellow plastic
object? Torture, injustice, human rights, yes, it's heart-
breaking, and one has to take part in the struggle. But in
my own way, please, in my own way and not now, don't
try to make me think about the things we all talk about—
our record got stuck, Patrick says—leave me alone, at least
until Gloria's madness has succeeded in digging her own
and maybe our ghosts out of this puzzling garden: and
when Gloria's nightmare is over I can begin to prepare
myself for the bliss of nonbeing. Here, Chapete, Tallulah,
Lisca, China, come here, the dogs my father used to call to
keep him company. . . .

"That's your illness, Julito," Katy says, "believing that
the world will be fixed up when you can call your dogs
from a bench under the tree that's been there all your life.
That doesn't exist anymore, man, it's all over, admit it.
Either we all get blown up by a thirty-megaton bomb or
we go on being typical exiled bums who don't have a
fucking idea where all this shit is leading us."

"No," Carlos says, while I leaf through *Time*. "There
are no typical exiles; you, me, Julio, Gloria, Patrick, Bijou
are in no way typical; you can't draw up general rules
starting with us and then fix everything up with a little
rigid system, no . . ."

"You're talking like a bourgeois, darling. I congratulate

you for changing from the KGB to the CIA, the only alternatives that these sons of bitches use to string us along. . . ."

THERE'S NO WAY to find the painting. Katy explores all the underworld circles in any way connected with art, we call Paris, Zurich, New York, all the galleries, but no dice. We phone Patrick in Marrakesh, in case he's there instead of in Paris, and he is there and answers rudely: he wasn't in Madrid this summer, it's one of Bijou's lies, he's always butting in, could we stop bothering him. We call Berta and Hernán Lagos, who believe that Bijou is staying with us. They're about to break up; Hernán's going back to Chile, Berta will stay on in Paris studying psychology. Carlos thinks there's no point in making them worry by telling them about Bijou's theft. We ought to wait. We'll soon have news. Then, too, Pancho is such a good friend, and if we tell him what happened, he'll understand, he'll forgive . . . it's not as serious, not as important, as our state of mind has made us blow it up to be.

Carlos kisses Gloria on the gray part in the middle of her hair, where there's no tint left. He tells her that he won't be able to see her as frequently anymore. There's little time left before Pancho comes back and we return to Sitges. Carlos assures me that now it's no longer urgent for him to see Gloria so often. It's a little hard for him to come, because it's on his only day off from his work at the hospital. So we say goodbye till sometime soon: he tells me I'm doing fine, making progress with my work, looking for new approaches in my novel. And convalescing is, after all, one of the most pleasant activities anyone can think of.

As the season mellows, people disperse: a few days later, Katy announces that she has to go to Paris to help out a daughter who has just had another baby—when will they stop busting my balls, making me a grandmother, what do I know about raising kids, my mother raised mine, and I don't like them a bit! She says goodbye with kisses and tears, promising to visit us in Sitges, where I'm sure she'll be lost forever. Kissing the Etruscan figures with feeling and Begonia with tears, reminding her to take care of us— needlessly, because Begonia does everything to perfection and with a reserve incredible in an Andalusian—Katy leaves Gloria and me in the huge silent apartment, to wait for Pancho's return and the moment for rendering accounts.

Everything is empty now. The house in order, the garden next door deserted, like a stage set filled with shadows that now, at the beginning of September, start to grow longer on the grass. Each blade of grass, each little flower, casts on the lawn the minuscule sign of its particular shadow, inalienably its own—even if you don't see, unless you're very careful, anything but a velvet lawn—until a few days from now, when the man with the rubber boots, Beltrán and Bijou's friend, mows them and restores the smooth surface of the green carpet streaked by the long golden light of September. The days grow shorter. Her brow no longer frowning, just tense, Gloria watches these days from her small chair, without uttering a single word for so long now. Well, at least she no longer bristles up when I enter her room, where I'm starting to spend a good part of the day, looking at her, when I'm not working. Withdrawn into herself, all she tolerates is her condition as prisoner of her illness. I think of my six days in the Santiago prison, about how different and yet how much like this illness they were and how much they also are like this thing my novel is turning into.

But something curious is happening. Irina, Pancho's

Siamese, blue-eyed and with a fine smoky finish on her beige fur, has been shy, selfish, except with Myshkin, to whom she's bound in a passionate friendship. And yet one day, while Gloria goes on, obsessed, with her crocheting, Irina leaps up into her lap and settles there, while a jealous Myshkin lies down at her feet. At first Gloria doesn't seem to notice these two warm lives that decide to nuzzle up to her body. But I soon notice that once in a great while she lets her fingers rest from her crochet and strokes Irina's back or bends over to scratch Myshkin's head while he lifts it to answer Gloria's look with the dark metal of his own. From the bed, where I usually lie down to keep her company, I sense that I must not tamper with this relationship. I hear Gloria sometimes making sounds of affection in answer to the purring or the moans of love the two animals address to her, and, surprisingly, even bits of words. At one point I watch her stand up, letting her shawl slide off her knees, take Irina in her arms, and show her the garden next door: its greenness is reflected in the blue eyes of the Siamese. Seeing this, Myshkin starts whining with envy. Gloria says to him:

"Silly . . ."

And sets down Irina to show him also the Duke's deserted garden. It's the first word I hear from her. She knits less now. Irina is no longer the only occupant in her lap, purring and warming her; Myshkin is also weighing it down, and Gloria talks to them both, especially when the cat rubs its velvety nose against her chin, making her smile with pleasure.

Meanwhile, in the solitude that has settled over the apartment, I go on with the novel that, good or bad, I must finish. From the dining room, where I work, I follow the conversations Gloria keeps up with the two animals that warm her lap, but she doesn't speak to Begonia or me, only points to anything she needs. Once, when I try to kiss her cheek, she shies away. But she knows when I'm lying on the bed. One afternoon while I'm in the room, she laughs, inviting me with her eyes to join her laughter at the antics of the two animals playing together at her feet. The next day, I mention this to Begonia, who approves of it with a nod of her head only, happy but also miserly with words.

One day Begonia comes into the room, and from her chair next to the window Gloria says to her:

"Please . . . food . . . water . . . here, on a piece of plastic so as not to mess up . . ."

Almost on the verge of tears, Begonia runs out to let me know. I fly to her side to say to her, Gloria, Gloria, talk, say something, my love, don't stay there like that. She just smiles at Irina, who strokes her chin with her soft dark nose, her eyes riveted on the garden spread out in front of her. She doesn't see me, doesn't say anything to me. Begonia gently pulls me away. I watch Gloria pick up Myshkin in one arm, Irina in the other, and show them the garden, so green, so empty, where suddenly three dogs appear, happily romping and playing. She starts pointing them out in front of me:

"An Afghan . . . a wirehair . . . an old and ugly but nice dog . . ."

She sets the animals on the floor. She concentrates on her crocheting again, and after I wait for five minutes beside her to see if she'll say something to me, I get ready to go back to my work, and then she says:

"They'll be back."

"Who?"

"The people next door."

"How do you know?"

"The dogs are already here."

"Ah, yes . . ."

"Did you take him out today?"

"Who?"

"Myshkin."

"No."

"Don't forget to."

I phone Carlos Minelbaum to give him the news about this dialogue. He's pleased: I'm not to force her, I'm to leave her be, it's the beginning of a recovery. But it's a strange recovery: she refuses to talk about anything that doesn't have to do with the animals, Myshkin and Irina, and the three dogs that romp with the gardener in front of her window, waiting for their master's return. She talks about their cute tricks, not to me, she recites, says it to the air, but she reminds me to buy Friskies, two kinds, for cats and for dogs, and then the meat and liver kind for Myshkin so that he'll have variety. She appears to be completely absorbed in the animal world, as if their needs were the only demands she can put up with.

Like a convalescent, I'm also gradually coming to the end of my novel. I don't know what I've written or what's been happening to me while I've been writing. I can't see myself or "see it." I only know that I'm left with the sores from a long illness and that coming to the end doesn't mean that I'm healed. But one thing—I feel as if I've rooted out something malignant that had to come out and that the pain I had before, from my illness, has only taken on another dimension now that I've taken it out. What does it mean? What is it? How important is it? What will they say about it? And yes, even the shameful and shaming question: will they like it? Who will like it and who won't? Is it my salvation or my doom? Núria Monclús—or her phantom team, the readers who will weigh and evaluate this work that is part of my being and who will pass judgment on it—has my fate in her bloodstained finger-tips.

There's one thing I realize when I finish the novel: Gloria has to read it before Núria Monclús, because, as I finished it, she occupied the first place in my imagination. Would I have been able to finish it without the silence of her illness, without the peace her pain and her imprisonment have given me? I doubt it. But I know that the novel is for her, I've written it for her, and her opinion, her vision of it, is the most important, really the only one I care about.

A few days go by, during which I listen to her talking to the animals or to Begonia about the most elementary things, without my finding a way to tell her I've finished: your *Hopscotch* is ready. Finally, one day I simply go over to her with the manuscript in my hand and place it in her lap next to Irina, who's on her other knee: at her feet, Myshkin looks on at this intrusion. Gloria doesn't stop crocheting and doesn't look at this animal I've set down next to the other one. She doesn't touch it. Doesn't open it. She keeps on staring at the garden, and her fingers remain busy at their work. But when it's time to help her into bed and Begonia tries to take the heavy manuscript from her knee, she snatches it away angrily, and Begonia has to help her undress and climb into bed without breaking her hold on it. She puts it next to her lamp on the night table. She turns off the light and goes to sleep. I go to bed, as I always do now, in the other room so that she may rest undisturbed.

On the following morning I find her already dressed, crocheting by the window, with the cat and the dog, and the manuscript like a third animal, bunched in her lap. But she never touches its pages, though I see her do it once as if she were touching Irina or Myshkin. For several days she sleeps with the manuscript on the night table, next to her head. She lets me kiss her cheek before I retire to my room.

Then one morning I find her by the window with the shawl dropped at her feet and the animals lying on it, while she has my typescript in her lap, opened past the middle, and is reading it.

"Why are you starting there?" I ask.

"I'm not starting."

"Then, how . . . ?"

"At night."

"You shouldn't."

"Why not?"

"You have to rest."

"I rest."

"And why are you reading in daylight now?"

"Because I know you'll be happy to know I'm reading it."

"And do you like it?"

"I don't know yet."

"Doesn't reading tire you?"

"Yes."

"Do you want me to read it aloud for you?"

"Okay."

"But not too much."

"Yes, so I won't get tired."

And I sit at her side, reading her passages every day, while she, with her eyes riveted on the neighboring garden and her hands busy with her crocheting, doesn't say a word, and in her face I can't discover any reflection of my reading: as if she couldn't hear, as if I, my voice, and my novel didn't exist. But I gradually feel that some strength is growing behind the facade of that impassive face, once as variable as the sea, and that something is taking root in it.

Caught off guard by very excited barking in the garden one morning, I almost drop the manuscript: children invade the garden, followed by servants, young people, the blond girl, her bespectacled husband, porters carrying luggage—and the lawn begins to stir with life once more, and to lose its identity as a blank space for our ghosts. We must leave! I can't stand this invasion of my territory! Luckily, I explain to Gloria, I've been able to finish the novel before these people could interrupt. I get up and go to the dining room. I raise the blinds, and for the first time I see that the villa's windows are all open: women servants draw curtains, the jet of water comes to life again, and people lounge on the chaises and the wicker armchairs beside the swimming pool; there are people I've never seen before, intruders drinking, some in swimsuits, all with deep tans, some in the water, served by servants who bring trays and then disappear behind the cypress, whose distinguished figure I had forgotten.

"Go on," Gloria says when I come back to our room, where she's still crocheting as if nothing has changed.

"Okay."

And I go on reading, pausing every now and then to get my breath or jot down something or look out the window: she goes past, draped in her ample Klimt tunic. She's cut her hair. She no longer has the golden bell but one of those short formless bobs women have done when they want to "feel comfortable" or go through a neurotic stage whose first victim is their hair. She's a different person. Too many things have happened. I don't need her love to finish my novel: the space usurped by her presence and that of her family is my biggest loss. I go on reading to the end, without looking again at the house next door during the two days of reading left. I turn the last page.

"What do you think of it?" I ask, hesitating.

"I'm not Núria Monclús or her readers or informants," she says, flinching.

"What do you mean by that?"

The cat strokes her chin, as if interceding for me. From her lack of expression I'm afraid that she hasn't liked it, but the cat makes her feel sorry for me. And then, with a tremendous effort that restores all her faculties and gives them structure, Gloria comes out of her torpor and talks to me at length about my novel, displaying shrewd critical appreciation: I see that this effort has finished rescuing her from the darkness and set her feet on firm ground. Of course, I know that she hasn't liked it as much as she says she does, but I can also see that she has liked it enough not to think it impertinent of me to send it to Núria Monclús: she's once more able to feel sorry for and be aware of others, and also to use her judgment. She returns slowly, but whole, from the shadows.

"The merit of going back over your memory and your personal history so as to make it so much ours . . . but also . . ."

"What?"

She's no longer as rigid as her chair, and when she took a deep breath to speak, her body regained a certain vitality, a slight but exciting mobility.

"Also its risk: it's possible that no one, besides Chileans, will understand anything, and that no one, outside of our generation, will be interested. We're not all Pablo Neruda, who made our conger eel stew famous. But tell me, who besides those who lived in our world and are our own age, even in Chile, will remember who Blanca Fredes was, or the Trullenque brothers, or Anita Lizana? Or Eglantina Sour or Juan Carlos Croharé, or La Nena del Banjo and Rosa Valenzuela? Or what the sandwiches at La Novia were like, or who Capulín and Charles were, or the Ahumada Promenade or the hairstyling at Gath & Chávez? You make it come alive for me because I recognize the ciphers used and can break the code: you fill them with a

life that is my life. But what about those who don't share
that code with us? I can't pass judgment, I'm too close to
all this. If you have enough art, if you handle words and
images and the stage set as subtly as the great artists, and
that's something I can't judge, these things get under your
skin before you know it, and a comma in the right place, a
plural instead of a singular, is enough to light up a street in
Kiev, as in Chekhov; or animate the soul of a cat, as Colette
does. I don't know. I can't make out its tone because it's
mine. It has changed completely: this is something 'big,'
and you've known how to introduce, with the same tone,
an authentic political fervor. Your novel has all these elements, but I can't judge it because it's mine as much as
yours and because I love you. . . . Let's send it to her. Now.
You can make your changes in the galleys. Let's send it to
her right now. There's brown paper and string in the pantry. Bring them, I'll wrap the package for you here on the
bed while you write the letter. . . ."

THE NOVEL IS in the hands of Núria Monclús. Perhaps
she's already reading it or having it read.

The morning mail brings a thick envelope from Chile,
from Sebastian. Gloria, who generally has an early lunch
served in bed by Begonia before she leaves, so that I won't
have to wash the dishes, is already having her siesta. The
letter is unusual because of its weight and thickness, which
scares me right away. I sit down in the living room with
my back to the empty space where the painting of the
package hung, before Bijou stole it.

But it's not a letter: it's an incredible number of photocopies of expenses, receipts, bills. And with them a very
short note from Sebastian: "They are offering 300,000
dollars. Keep the house if you like. But you have to pay me

half its price plus half the total of the enclosed bills. Sebastian."

Not even a greeting. Nor even a reference to Gloria or Pato. He's fed up. He thinks I'm an idiot, a fool, and I am. Sebastian has been carrying my mother's house alone for the past seven years: servants' and gardener's wages, grocery and other food bills, back taxes accumulated over the years. Doctors, X rays, biopsies, nurses, burial, tombstone . . . everything, in short. He has sent me all this to make me feel guilty for being a stubborn idiot, for refusing to sell the house at this exceptional price. Adding it all up and splitting it in half, it comes to a considerable amount of money, without throwing in the cash advances out of his own pocket that I have to return in full.

I'm sure that Sebastian, who is rich and generous, would not have charged me anything or sent me any bills if I had returned to Chile with Gloria and Pato in answer to Mother's call and had devoutly closed her eyes. No, there would have been no bills, nor this feeling of empty rage in the pit of my stomach, rage that's nothing but guilt. Had I answered that call, we'd be like this family that's just come back from a trip, loaded down like them with luggage and surrounded by dogs and servants and greenery: a normal family is what interests Sebastian.

But there are no normal families anymore. They're finished. That world no longer exists. Congress is closed, painted and well kept, to be sure, but closed: nothing happens inside it, and my father's image, which stood for a proud tradition, has been wiped out. What color were my father's eyes? I don't remember. It's a detail I never noticed: eyes, that's all, and lovely or not, they were there to do their work, to see. His eyes are closed like those of the Congress where he served all his life. But I'm here and I don't want to stay shut away there, if I return, when there's

still so much to see in Europe: Hilaria del Carretto resting
with her dog at her feet on her tomb in Lucca . . . Stone-
henge . . . the garden in Giverny where Monet painted
those water lilies that can take away all the cares in the
world . . . to have ice cream at Florian's café in Venice,
surrounded by the ghosts of Byron and Teresa Guiccioli, of
Baron Corvo and Henry James. . . . The defeat of going
back without having even one book brought out by any
Spanish publisher. How can I go back before Núria Monclús tells me I can go back? It's a matter of days.

And since I refused to go see my dying mother, since I
now refuse to do something reasonable like selling the
house, Sebastian, rightfully fed up, sends me this tough
little note dictated to his secretary, along with photocopies
of everything that has to be paid . . . including the pain of
having to let the servants of a lifetime go, giving them
money to retire to their native darkness in the provinces.
Now he is not about to keep on playing blind with a
brother who has been such a bad brother, such a bad son
not to go back when . . . and they even say I'm turning into
a communist here in Europe, I who was so moderate in
comparison to Gloria: that's the reason for the affront of
these disgraceful photocopies, the humiliation of the final
defeat at my older brother's hands, and this pain in the pit
of my stomach, almost keeping me from breathing, and
the tears that burn my eyes but won't come. . . .

What can I do?

Selling Rome is out. Not only because I can't let Sebastian twist my arm, but because our neighbor's family has
come back to take over and dismiss me from their garden.
Pancho will be here in ten days. We must leave before then.
Carlos Minelbaum says that Gloria can now travel to
Sitges. Practical and affectionate, Ana María is taking care
of putting our apartment back in shape, because our ten-

ants left it a mess. It will be ready shortly. I can almost see her: Ana María will buy flowers for our bedroom and new plants to replace those that summer neglect let burn up. Return to our apartment in Sitges? There's no view from our bedroom there: a brick wall in a run-down courtyard; from our living room, the dining room of the apartment across from ours, where the television is never turned off; from the terrace, zinc roofs and a tile roof on some exceptional house, or else a rooftop strung with lines full of wash, half of one scrawny palm tree and a distant promise of depths in the pubis of sea between two sloping roofs. Go back to that as a final step? Knowing that Patrick will not return? And that if he does return our fights with him will be so loud that the neighbors will stick their heads out to shout at us to stop shouting so much? Sell Rome so that I'll never have a place to land on, not even a tree branch? How can Sebastian ask me to do that? Naturally, he doesn't know what poverty is, or what it's like to roam the world without solid ground under your feet, with no air to breathe except the neighbor's empty air or Sitges's foul air, smelly with chicken on the spit and fried potatoes.

Gloria calls me from the bedroom. I stick the bills under the cushions of the armchair I'm sitting on.

"I want to get up. Was there anything in the mail?"

"No, nothing. *Time* magazine, things for Pancho, nothing. Get a little more sleep, dear."

"A little, but I don't want to sleep too much now because then I won't sleep tonight and will have to take a Valium."

"*Verboten*, Carlos told you."

"You shouldn't take any either."

"No. Me neither. Now sleep a little more."

"Wake me up in an hour."

"Yes. Sleep."

I close the door. There's no sense in wandering around

the apartment in search of solutions, or in watching the girls dive into the Duke's pool, or in carefully studying the false curtains, which remind me of the false package whose absence I'll have to justify as urgently as I have to pay those bills. I'd better forget them. Get rid of them. It's important not to add this concern to Gloria's fragile condition: it could destroy her. And if I ask Carlos for advice, like anybody else, of course, he'll tell me to sell. It may not be much, but that money will help you to live with fewer cares: you're just the right age for a stroke, you know that, and if you don't take care of yourself, something bad can happen to you; sell, and it will take a load off you. But he doesn't know the house on Rome Street, and so he has no right to advise me. On the contrary, it would be the worry of not having a house to settle down in that would give me a stroke. Let them put Sebastian in jail if he doesn't pay up; they can't seize anything of mine, because I have nothing.

I take the photocopies from under the cushion and throw them into the incinerator. I open *Time*. Later, Gloria wakes up. For supper we have something cold that Begonia left for us. After the silence during supper, Gloria says:

"Shall we take Myshkin out for a walk around the block?"

It's the first time she's shown interest in going out, and I'm so delighted at this new sign of life that I forget everything else. I say fine. She goes into the bathroom and comes out with makeup on and her hair groomed. She hadn't done this for a long time.

"I'm a mess. I'll dye my hair tomorrow."

"Good," I answer, as we go down in the elevator.

The street isn't quite dark yet, and slowly, unsteadily, as if I too were recovering from an illness, or like a pair of old people walking arm in arm to help each other, we follow Myshkin through the semidarkness of nine o'clock. The

windows and the sky are lit up at this Magritte hour,
happy, alive with the laughter or crying of children, with
maids busy on the terraces and tenants arriving in their
cars: this Magritte is not terrifying, because I'm familiar
with it. Gardeners are watering the lawns with their hoses,
and the fragrance of the wet grass, of the terebinth tree, the
honeysuckle, the jasmine, comes together with the renewed freshness of the water on the leaves and the grass:
that fragrance is the perfect madeleine of the neighborhood
where I was born and my mother has just died, and where
my brother sensibly wants to pull up my roots and leave
them exposed to Madrid's polluted air.

Walking around the block very slowly, to pull her out of
her prison with a little entertainment I recite these lines I
know she likes so much:

> *"So, we'll go no more a roving*
> *So late into the night,*
> *Though the heart be still as loving*
> *And the moon be still as bright.*
>
> *For the sword outwears its sheath,*
> *And the soul wears out the breast,*
> *And the heart must pause to breathe,*
> *And Love itself have rest."*

When, I ask myself, when will the heart pause to catch
its breath? Never, I guess, since breathing is what makes
the heart go. But it's a comfort to know that someone, at
one time, should have believed it and transformed its fal-
lacy into such moving and straightforward verses. In any
case, I explain to Gloria, as I explained it in class so many
times, Byron suffered from the romantic ill of optimism:
that's why he was naive enough to believe that the sword
survives its sheath, which is false. All we have to do is look

around us at all the Chileans, Argentines, Uruguayans, Cubans, Bolivians like sheaths without swords, surviving even after being stripped of our swords. As for my mother, she was the sword, but her sheath survives, it's the house on Rome Street, which must be protected against everything, especially against Sebastian, so that something of hers will remain. When we get back to the apartment, Gloria says that the walk has exhausted her, and she falls asleep right away. To go on forgetting, I also fall asleep beside her.

I wake up at seven in the morning. I stay in bed, tossing: more than enough time for Núria Monclús to answer has gone by. She's had my novel for two weeks, and everything depends on her answer. I make up my mind to call her at nine—or better yet, at ten minutes past—I know that at this hour, when she's in Barcelona, she's normally behind her desk with her little veil wrapped around her eyes, watching, giving orders, promoting, condemning, inventing, cutting heads off.

Her answer is that she's very sorry. As soon as my manuscript arrived, along with such a gloomy letter, she had three photocopies of my novel made. She's kept the original in her safe, as she always does. She has sent out the photocopies to her three most trusted publishers, for the very special attention of readers who are good friends. She already has negative answers from two publishers. Do I want her to call the third one?

I almost tell her that it doesn't matter: I try to act as if I don't care. But she asks for my phone number and says she'll call back in ten minutes: the longest ten minutes in my life, which will end—why doubt it?—in a negative answer.

"No," Núria Monclús says. "None of the three publishers is interested. Even less than in the previous version.

They say it's pure rhetoric, an imitation of what's fashionable among Latin American writers today. You have no vocation for the lyric. And all those adjectives, much too rich, it sounds false. The structure, derivative of Vargas Llosa's *Conversation in the Cathedral*, and the disquisitions and the humor, which is very forced, seem to be pulled out of *Hopscotch*. No, I have to be frank and tell you that they all thought it was an error of perspective and taste. It seems to me that the other, the first version was better; this one is like it, but hypertrophied, sick, declamatory, shrill. If you like, I can try other publishers, but it will take much longer and be more difficult. Perhaps some Mexican or Argentine publisher would be interested . . . well, I'd have to see. Anyway, here in Spain only those three houses I've approached handle Latin American literature and would risk publishing an unknown if they thought he showed great promise. . . ."

An unknown. Defeat. "If he showed great promise." After this illness, an illness parallel with that of my wife, who is coming out of her prison while I go back into one that's different and worse. The door closes. Now it would only be a joke, showing Núria Monclús the book with my clippings, where Gloria and I, when the sentence didn't seem so final to either of us, would paste everything they said about me: "a very fine vision, rich in nuances," "the decadence of the middle class," "nice touches of imagination," "ample cultural references," "we expect a lot from his pen." A lot, yes, but not failure. Emulation is not imitation, it's giving something more vigor, perhaps simplifying and reducing, not the hypertrophy I've come up with, according to Monclús. In sum, it's being yourself: limitation as essence of the writer's personality, that's what I teach my students, and also that the whole must be stripped down and refracted by this "limitation," which is the writer's I. Why, why wasn't I capable of it? Is not being capable my true prison, not the six days in jail I thought would be the key to help me get out of the prison to which I was condemned by Chilean critics? Listening to words from Núria Monclús that I no longer hear or understand, I have the presence of mind before hanging up to send greetings to Marcelo Chiriboga, because the most important thing is not to let Núria Monclús know that she's had the power to destroy me completely. She hangs up: closes the door and puts the key away forever.

This is important: Gloria must not know that Núria has ripped me to shreds and that every entry has been barred; I must not tell her that her final opinions about my novel were wrong. That precisely the things she pointed out as merits are its defects, errors, and vulgarities. It's to protect her and so protect the little that's left to protect in me. The day's first bather dives into the pool. The cypress is white with sunlight, has no shadow, like a fine cardboard cutout made by a child and placed next to his childish concept of a mansion. It's too late to turn around and live a different way, one that won't end in disaster. Something's very certain: Gloria must not find out about this defeat. Yes, other publishers. What's wrong, let's say, with a Mexican publisher? Núria Monclús will handle it, yes, she won't drop me. . . . I have to do something constructive to let me forget, let me hope, let me keep the knowledge of this defeat from Gloria, it could kill her. It's true that she had almost the same reservations as the publishers: she and Núria are both my executioners. But it would kill her to find out she was right, she who is so fond of being right and has to be told again and again that she has a good eye, yes, she guessed that painting so unlike a Rothko is indeed a Rothko as she claims, that her cooking is good, that she's a good mother, a good critic, that she's still beautiful despite her age, and elegant despite her poverty, and desirable and amusing: "Say it, say that you love me, say it, you must say it," Gudrun insists hungrily, in a novel we both admire.

I roam around the house. Gloria won't wake up till eleven, when Begonia comes in; she hasn't thrown out the pile of invitations that have come in the mail for Pancho, no, she'd better not throw them out, she'd better leave them where they are, in a kind of silver tray . . . but they're not all for Pancho. There's one for me. I open it. *Patrick Mendez. Les plus beaux culs de Marrakesh. Photos. Vernissage. Lundi le vingt-huit septembre 1980. Trattoria Luigi. Marrakesh.* Well, well, something very off-off-Broadway in Marrakesh, I imagine, for the idiotic little theme my idiot of a son has come up with. Still, at least he's doing something. . . . But why Marrakesh? Why not Madrid or Sitges so that Gloria won't feel that he's so far away? When Patrick finds out about my failure he'll laugh at me, and he'll be glad. . . .

"Whose turn is it to cry now?" he'll ask.

He's the big bully, not me. I want to knock down the door, to break out of this real prison. The bad thing is that what I like least about this whole apartment are the doors, I don't know why. This one, for instance, has something about it, I don't know, something pretentious that the rest of the apartment doesn't have. I open it. The huge window in Pancho's studio reveals a Madrid sky that's starting to grow weary of fall, to be no longer the lowering, sifted skies by Velázquez, with one particular cloud that promises an incendiary twilight. A blue very different, for example, from that of this painting, which has a phosphorescent, electric-blue background. It's the only one I see, because it catches my eye the minute I walk in: a nude woman's lovely body, seated, but invaded by hundreds of meticulously painted insects, like jewels covering the cool lovely flesh, cochineal bugs, dragonflies, bluebottles, beetles, crickets, grasshoppers, spiders. The seated figure has a toad on one knee, arranged to cover her sex: the animal has penetrating eyes, and its moist, livid mouth is open. The frame is a silver strip that decapitates the figure, whose head is left out of the painting. It's not large, but it's beautiful, voluptuous, a barbaric metaphor of all the fears that, as an adolescent, I observed in Pancho but never mentioned, though we were such close friends. It's not a large painting, maybe seventy-five by fifty centimeters. Its title must be written on the back: *Portrait of Countess Leonor de Teck*. Carlota's sister, I suppose. Pancho never stops talking about "the Teck women," just as he used to talk about "the Vergara women" in Santiago.

It's not a heavy painting. There's paper on a table: I wrap it up. What am I doing? No, I unwrap it: I block out *Portrait of Countess Leonor de Teck* with black paint and write: *Portrait of Señora Gloria Echeverría de Méndez*. I wrap it up again, because I know very well what I'm doing. Right there on the drawing board, I take a pencil and a sheet of paper and write: "Darling: I didn't want to wake you but I had to run over to the bank. Good news: Núria says yes, Bruguera's accepted me, and I'm going to open an account at the Bank of London so that they can make me an immediate transfer of part of the advance fee. Kisses. I'll be right back. Julio." Yes, it's the only way out.

I give the cab driver the address of the Mexican on Onésimo Redondo Street. On the way there I blow on the new title so that the paint will dry: I've used a lot of turpentine and I have to air the cab out thoroughly. The Mexican looks at me curiously. I'm not too nervous to see that this man, accustomed as he is to dealing with occasional delinquents, has noticed something. He must have made too many deals with lost and weak and cornered people like me not to recognize me as a member of that sect. Still, he knows I'm a very close friend of Pancho's: how many months have we been living in his house? Four, one more than we originally planned. As luck would have it, I add, Pancho had to leave for a show of his in New York, just when my wife fell ill, and it turned out best for us not to go back to Sitges. This dealer has heard too many stories about a sick wife, a crippled son, the need for a checkup because I'm going blind, an urgent trip to Norway to visit my sick son, they treat exiles very well there but it's very cold and they have different food and different eating hours, that's why we have to go and comfort him: yes, he has heard this too often to give any importance to Gloria's pain. He says that this painting is worth a lot of money, he can give me the equivalent of five thousand dollars as advance and we can write up a paper agreeing to round out the fifteen thousand within a month.

"Why, this portrait of my wife is worth a lot more!"

He shrugs, looking helpless at my fit of anger, and says: *"Anah mezquin."*

"What?"

"I'm poor."

"In what language?"

"Arabic."

"I thought you were Mexican," I say, in a final attempt to force this schemer to change his mind, while he, indifferent to me, strokes a white parrot; feeling this caress, it obscenely unfolds the fan of its yellow crest as if it had a sudden erection.

"No, Moroccan, from Tangier."

"My son," I immediately puff up, "is a photographer and is about to open an exhibition of his photographs in Marrakesh."

"Where? At the Hotel La Mammounia?"

"No, at Trattoria Luigi."

"Ah!"

That discouraging "Ah!" confirms everything I guessed about where Pato's show will take place. We close the deal, sign and exchange papers, he hands me the money, and I leave.

I walk to the Plaza de España. Then along the Gran Vía, bustling with nearly Catalanlike activity at this hour in comparison with those evenings when Gloria and I would occasionally come to see a movie in this area. Has an hour gone by? Maybe not. Begonia hasn't come in. Gloria isn't up yet. Air Maroc. Tangier. Yes, yes, Tangier, to escape to Tangier, no, to Marrakesh, where I'll suffer the humiliation of the success—only relative, it's true, because it will take place at Trattoria Luigi and not at La Mammounia—of the exhibition of photographs by Pato: Patrick Méndez. Tangier: "Come with me to the Kasbah," Charles Boyer said to Hedy Lamarr, it wasn't in Tangier, it was in Algiers, but the geographical difference is only a technical detail, it's not worth quibbling about after so many years. Tangier: Barbara Hutton's palace, Paul Bowles trapped and destroyed by the place, the palm tree Matisse painted from the balcony of the Hotel de France.

I have plenty of ready cash, and that's the way to have it, ready in my pocket. Two to Tangier for tomorrow. And I hire an Avis car for fifteen days—will I be able to keep up the comedy of thorough enjoyment for fifteen days, till pleasure restores Gloria's vigor and I feel up to telling her the truth without dying of shame?—to travel to the interior, no, not to the Atlas Mountains or the Sahara, only as far as Marrakesh: there we'll rearrange our plans to fit our son's and I'll contact your representatives there, I tell the travel agent. R. D. Laing, whom Gloria read with such pleasure a few years ago but has forgotten completely, as has almost everyone else, because he "went out of fashion," just like so many convulsions we were once victims of, yes, after coming back from living in Ceylon for a year—Laing said: "One should change cultural context from time to time in order to renew oneself." Yes, Tangier and then on to Tetuán, Xauen, Fez, Meknès, till we come to Marrakesh, with snake charmers and the exhibition of Moroccan buttocks signed by my son. Settle there? Why not live in Marrakesh, which is much cheaper than Sitges?

I get back home at eleven with my pockets stuffed with airplane tickets and paper currency. Naked in bed, smiling after just taking a bath, her body perfumed, Gloria is reading *Sophie's Choice* in the ample morning light, with the many-colored towel wrapped around her head like a turban, waiting for me, once more the Odalisque I love so much: I am the victor and I must be given pleasure.

I look at her from the doorway. Still frail, she turns her face: her half-profile and her back, her long back and her long legs, her endearing buttocks, the long eye under the turban like those we'll find in Morocco, watching me, and outside the green of the garden of our youth, recently married and we were . . . ah, we were all we no longer are and will never be again. What a pity youth is wasted on the young. I turn the key in the door so that discreet Begonia may not take it into her head to interrupt us. I go over: the false victor, the fake macho, the thief, the delinquent, the liar who tells himself he's lying to protect her, and not the real truth, to protect myself. I take her, then, with the pleasure of broad daylight, as I haven't done in years because I'm afraid of the imperfect reality of each of us and of everything. *Est-ce que je suis toujours ta belle grappe de glycine?* No, unfortunately: and neither am I nor have I been its masculine counterpart for a long time now. What does it matter? Now I'm sure of my triumph, it will last at least those lying fifteen days of vacation on our Moroccan trip. That will put off everything. It will be the last present I'll give myself before accepting the end.

I CIRCLE HER throat with the very dark, almost black amber necklace of fine quality, whose beads, slightly worn from handling, are set in filigree work of Berber silver: it gives a warm harmony of burned tones to her dull complexion and her reddish hair in this bazaar cluttered with dusty, dented, much-fingered, tarnished objects that look amazingly genuine and precisely because of this are probably false. So I was warned by Bolados, the man from Tangier who passes himself off as a Madrilenian and whose clientele murmur that he's a Mexican born in New York, because he does business with Mexico and speaks English with an American accent.

R. D. Laing's recommendation has its effect: after landing in Tangier, we drop our bags at the Hotel El Minzah— let's live high off the hog for once and enjoy this famous hotel instead of staying in something second-class—and we go out into the street immediately, eager to see, to smell things.

"This necklace is too expensive," Gloria says.

"Try to haggle."

"All right. Listen, sir . . ."

How long will I be able to stand putting it off? Today, here, at this neutral hour between day and night, I find Gloria beautiful; this makes me want to be near her. And also because she's happy, happiness I have to break up if I really want to get close to her: acknowledging Núria Monclús's rejection—daring to destroy her once more—the theft, the mountain of debts incinerated but not canceled, and yet for now I'm getting away with this subterfuge.

Gloria will throw me over when she knows the source of the "small fortune" that lets me buy her a necklace that's not cheap, she who seldom asks for anything and whose elegance is the result of pure inventiveness. And then our stay at that strange place, the Hotel El Minzah: a fountain flows in the middle of the courtyard, and, wearing fezzes and a kind of red gaucho's costume, the help run around serving English officers in civilian clothes, with blond mustaches and blue eyes, who have come over from Gibraltar to spend a weekend in Tangier, "living their own life."

"But the bedrooms aren't much," Gloria says.

"What difference does it make?"

"None."

Outside they're about to close the shops they never finish closing; they just skimp a little on the lights, now burning timidly. Under medieval hooded cloaks and protective veils, the eyes on the faces of those passing by light up. The eyes, transfigured by kohl in the hidden faces of women and the eyes of slim boys excited by the prospect of the night ahead of them, who smile, openly inviting. In these countries the young are highly considered merchandise, I explain to Gloria, justifying glances and insolent gestures that she doesn't miss: in Madrid no boy would bother to look at me, but here my respectable, intellectual look, the remains of my class superiority, which is the little that one doesn't lose with age and failure, are regarded by them as power, strength, authority, experience, wisdom: that's why they're attracted to me.

"And you to them?"

"I don't know. 'I'll think about it tomorrow in Tara.' Right now my mind is on other things."

"Then they don't upset you."

"I don't think so."

Gloria strokes the amber beads at her throat and asks me, "Isn't there anything that ever upsets you?"

I immediately put on my mask: "Patrick . . ."

Gloria squeezes the arm I've got hooked into hers. "We'll only be with him a short while. Why would he send us the invitation if he doesn't want anything to do with us? Doesn't it show that there's something ambivalent, a positive side to his rejection? Isn't it his need to have us admire him? I'm sure he'd love to see us. We'll invite him to eat in a good restaurant, and then, if we see that he wants to get rid of us, we'll go on with our short tourist visit without getting in his way before going to Rabat. So what are you worrying about?"

"What can this place have turned him into?"

Gloria is not satisfied with this peripheral conversation. Neither am I: I have to ask her if there's something about this world in which the night is submerging us that upsets her . . . but not now; as if any other form of contact would cause me too much pain, I prefer to remain on this periphery that cheats us both. Why is it that we're only happy devouring each other, forever probing inside each other until there's no troubled or dark or private corner left, not a single fantasy we can personally hold back without exposing it?

That need is less urgent here: the noisy crowded street hems us in with faces covered by the shadows of hoods like cowls and sweeps us along at a rhythm that may be fast or may be normal. They sell cascades of tangerines, heaps of fruit I don't have a chance to identify, and the store windows display sweets that look repulsive and delicious at the same time: tasting them, tasting anything here, would be an adventure. I make an effort to change the drift of Gloria's thoughts, collaborating with Tangier to distract her: a free port twenty years ago, with hundreds of international banks, a headquarters for the traffic of foreign money and sex and drugs, it was overrun by sophisticated millionaires in search of pleasure, hidden away in the Zoco in palaces camouflaged by walls that looked run-down. Only the vestiges remain now. What could André Gide and Oscar Wilde have talked about during their famous encounter in a café at the top of the city as they watched the Atlantic and the Mediterranean embracing down below? The Zoco can be dangerous at this hour; it's full of people in rags. But poverty disguised as another culture doesn't shock with the sudden pain of poverty in Chile, where you see only a kind of discouraging attempt to give it a dignified front. Here one cruelly tints poverty with other colors. Everything, including us, changes its badge of identity. Our faces and other faces are transfigured and can't be distinguished from one another: the aggressive greed of the merchants who call out from behind a pile of babouches, the slavish dancelike movements of children making lace inside the tiniest workshops, the languages, the laughter, everything answers to a code it's impossible to make out, everything's hermetic, terrible, filthy, cruel, but for them it's natural, clean, benign.

"What a pity that idiot Charles Martel had to win the Battle of Poitiers!" Gloria says. "If he hadn't, we'd all go around dressed like that, I'd live comfortably in a nice harem, and besides, we'd belong to the OPEC countries and have no gasoline problems."

"Morocco doesn't belong to OPEC."

"Anyway, at least we'd walk around with veils over our faces."

Veils to cover up our shame? Is that what Gloria is hinting? Here no one can read the shame in our expressions, but in Santiago they'd be able to read it in Providencia as easily as in the La Vega neighborhood. Here, how

can you guess who is what, what the looks behind those
hooded cloaks mean, what form they have and to what
economic or cultural class those bodies hidden behind the
coarse wool of their *cache-misère* belong to? It's easy to get
lost forever here: what a tempting idea, because, in this
crowd tinted a golden color by the flickering electricity of
the bazaars, it would mean taking on a different moral
code, a code that wouldn't make me confess my humiliations to Gloria. The detritus of what Katy would call my
Western middle-class morality forces me to confess everything to my wife. Otherwise, I'd be deceiving her, and in
the first place, we're not allowed to deceive. But in this
smelly poverty in the Zoco, in its shops with leather goods
and cloth and spices, and souvenirs and Pond and Nivea
creams for tourists, in these heaps of rotting trash, in this
disorder that may be another form of order, couldn't we
imagine that deceiving is *not* against the rules? Gloria in-
spects some horrid caftans hanging at a shop's entrance. . . . What if I should use her inattention to plunge
into this gloomy, sloping, narrow, twisted little street and
disappear forever in the giddy night of the bazaars to be
reborn at the other end of it with a reversed kind of morality? Yes, hidden among this herd of people, all I have to do
is take one step to stop being who I am. Guilt has completely taken over my conscience, and as we walk along I
try to drive it out by recalling, for Gloria's benefit, the
presence in these same streets of Diaghilev, de Falla,
Tiffany, Ravel, Belmondo, each of whom came here to get
lost in his own way, and to acquire a personality other than
the one forced on us in the West: here Núria Monclús and
Marcelo Chiriboga would have the same power as I, and
we'd have the same right to disappear through secret doors
that save us from unpleasant things at the Rastro.

What did Pato come to look for in this world, and, even

more, what is keeping him here? Perhaps that: changing the identity imposed on him by a domineering father and a political situation. Gloria and I agree, however, that on our first night on the edge of this abyss we're still too new to it to draw a conclusion about Pato. But I can't help feeling the pull of these repulsive streets, and it fills me with anxiety that I'm being turned inside out: it's the same anxiety, but reversed, that I felt at a green window, so remote now, above the swimming pool of a town mansion, where girls and boys designed by Brancusi—especially one, her hair styled to look like a golden bell—danced beside the water, under the cypress tree, one night. Those pleasures were as out of reach, as "strange," as all this I have around me now, and I believed I knew the symbols of that code, but I may have been wrong: the full measure of that pleasure may only have existed in my own mind. Still, one thing is true: facing both situations, I've felt a dizzying urge to stop being who I am and plunge into the abyss.

Now—and why not then also?—my wild hunger to be "them" is only a way of putting things off: one day or fifteen mean nothing, because the airplane this afternoon is separated from this medieval night not by hours but by the centuries with which I long to weigh the values of good and evil: I must not be horrified, as no one in this crowd is horrified, when a dog in this medieval world digs something greenish-white that looks like a fetus from a pile of garbage and devours it.

The crush of people is overpowering now that the shops are starting to close. To catch our breath, we go into a narrow little street that's dark but doesn't look so frightening, less crowded but not empty. Farther on, a light is shining above a Moorish arch, and in front of it, a short distance up ahead, a tiny shop throws its shaft of waxen light across the alleyway before it disappears into the

blurred outline of some steps going up. Veiled women and
hooded men go through the arch: inside, they take off their
shoes and babouches. The small swarm of beggars hanging around the entrance is strangely sure of itself, as if it
were only performing its role in the social scale, occupying
the place destiny has assigned them. The street is narrow,
and we can't step back to appreciate this mosque's archi-
tecture. The group of beggars grows noisy, buzzing as we
pass: they're not much interested in begging for alms.

A little apart from the group, near the wall lit by the
yellowish oil lamp in the shop, which sells Chesterfields
and amulets against the evil eye, I notice the figure of
someone lying there. A dead body? It wouldn't be impossible; but as we go by him, he lifts a discouraged hand, the
mere sketch of a begging gesture never quite rounded out
before the hand falls back: he's not dead. A child not much
more than a year old, with bare buttocks, crawls like a
louse over the body lying there and stuffs its mouth with
something he fished out of the garbage pile.

This lasts only a second. We pass on: I don't know if
Gloria has noticed this. And yet, I remember that second in
detail because my vision's intensity makes up for the moment's brevity. It's as if I had spent hours studying him.

Like all the others he wears a brown djellaba—the *cache-
misère* that doesn't hide anything—and the hood over his
head evokes a multitude of shadows: from among them,
however, my eyes pick out a very fine profile, a thin
growth of beard, two eyes with the faint gleam of sensual,
golden weariness you sometimes find in the people of the
Rif as well as in Klimt's inventions under the myrtles in a
certain garden as out of bounds as this little street. But
those eyes whose light is about to go out can see: as we
went past, the beggar—the sick boy?—raised his hand to

beg. I don't give him anything, because nothing can change the despair into which he has somehow settled. The child . . . his child? Why does it feed him garbage, opening his mouth to show exceptionally excellent, moist teeth? Why shouldn't he be the son of this man who is not much more than an adolescent? Bijou, and the baby Giselle will soon be having. He has lost everything or has never had anything and doesn't expect ever to have anything: his fate is to lie next to a pile of garbage, close to a group of beggars superior to him, until typhus kills him and he himself turns into garbage again.

Envy: I would like to be that man, to crawl into his sickly skin and into his hunger, to hope for nothing or fear nothing, and most of all to get rid of this fear that my background and my culture will make me confess tonight—or sometime during the next fifteen days—the complex story of my defeat: a garden lost, a demanding brother, a successful—successful?—son, a wife frustrated by the damned hope of a place in life inferior to what she had, my justification for my life, painful roots in another hemisphere, desertion of the collective project. So many things that would have so little meaning here! The pity full of envy I feel for this human ruin, my fleeting impulse to save him, cure him, nourish him, comfort him, means that I also need to be saved, cured, have someone put his arms around me: to have someone convince me that confession, contrition and atonement, truthfulness, are not necessary and there's no need even for restitution when you're transformed into this beautiful sick beggar who has never known hope and is lying here next to a mosque in Tangier.

Who is Núria Monclús here? Who is Marcelo Chiriboga? Who are those who stripped our country of its meaning? They don't exist here. I don't have to fight them, because those fights are only other versions of the scuffle breaking out at the moment here among the beggars at the mosque's entrance and dying down just as fast without leaving a trace, as we once more reach the street where the crowd flows: but the injustice that sparked off the scuffle goes on, unresolved.

We walk toward the Zoco's exit, because we're afraid— she is; I'm not: the beggar is my guiding star—of getting lost. I want to go somewhere less crowded, quieter, to examine the fire burning inside me.

"Shall we go back to the hotel?" I suggest.

"Why?"

"I'm a little tired. Airplanes always tire me. We'll be able to see all this more slowly tomorrow."

We have dinner at the hotel. The excellent food is rotted garbage I put into my mouth without disgust. The man lying back there has no enemies like my wife, this monster who demands certain behavior of me to make me be clean again. She doesn't know that I'm strong now because the option of misery and despair, the most seductive and terrible of all, is open to me now.

"Are we going to the Jatifa tomorrow?" Gloria asks.

"What is it?"

"Gide and Wilde, the café you told me about."

"Why do you want to go?"

"I wonder what they could have been talking about. . . ."

"There's no record of their talk."

That's what I need, I tell myself, as I ask for the key and go up to our room on the second floor arm in arm with my wife. To rub out my tracks, to turn into somebody else and not be afraid of the woman whose arm I've taken and who is my conscience. I go to the bathroom: cockroaches in

Tangier's best hotel. Does it matter? Not now, because this night that belongs to others stretches my nerves. Is she humming *Death and the Maiden* very low, happily, while she sets out on the chair the things she intends to wear tomorrow? I can't even do that, hum Schubert, whom I like so much, and much less write a novel. Gloria, who does well anything she sets out to do—her feminist articles, for instance—could write the story of all this better than I. With my mouth full of toothpaste foam, I suggest it to her.

"Do you think I can do it?"

I spit out the toothpaste:

"I think you can do anything."

"What if my experience is different from yours?"

"I'm sure you saw the same things I did in the Zoco."

"It's possible."

She no longer torments me, humming *Death and the Maiden*: I've defeated her, offering her hope, the greatest of all evils. Washing my hands, I'm about to ask Gloria if she brought along some soap that's not as fetid as what the El Minzah has provided, but I tell myself that its bad smell is probably a delicious fragrance in this world that's so different, and I resolutely wash my hands to join the ranks of the hooded creatures that walk along the streets below: outside, others devour the night, because I can't cross into the looking glass and live on the other side, like them, perhaps like Patrick.

As I wash my hands, my heart suddenly jumps with joy: and what if, when I confessed them, my actions—the theft and deceit and my stubborn decision not to sell Rome, and my personal and collective failure—seemed such a great crime to Gloria that she left me? When we were younger, she almost did, for smaller offenses. Isn't this my chance to make her turn against a criminal like me, the way she turned against Bijou? Where is Bijou, I ask myself, my ally in abjection, the perfect Virgil for the hell of these evil narrow streets where everything is possible? He would not be afraid of them like me, or of the cockroaches and the filth. Bijou is strong: he's comfortable in his own skin wherever he goes. I'm not strong. I have too many things that break down easily. One is Gloria, her searching look, her quiet contempt because I can't hum *Death and the Maiden*; you should be like this, you ought to be like that, something bigger, nobody can be a colorless liberal like you, you must enter the political struggle, commit yourself, sign open letters, join the action, be a good father, good son, good brother, good husband, you have to bring money home . . . everything, in fact: obligations.

When I finish in the bathroom, I come back to the bedroom without my shirt on: she looks at me smiling, even happy, despite my gut, yes, of course, because I've carried out all my obligations; my contract with Núria Monclús makes that clear. The nightmare is over, Gloria thinks, because my man will defeat them all, Vargas Llosa, García Márquez, Sábato, Cortázar, Fuentes, Chiriboga, especially him, so conceited, so wrapped up in the false refinement of the demands he's recently become entitled to, will beat them with a single novel, the one Gloria believes they'll publish but never will be published. My novel is pure shit. Chiriboga's prose, on the other hand, has a deceptive simplicity that melts under your tongue, filling your lungs and your whole being with an aroma that the rough surface of his prose didn't lead you to expect. I can't: that explains everything. I'd like to write like Chiriboga. But I can't.

If I can't write, I must wipe away my crimes: all I have to do is send a telex to my lawyer in Chile and he'll sell the house on Rome Street right away. They'll destroy the pointillist greens and violets, the Bakelite hens—no, plastic; they were made of Bakelite when I was a small boy—the shadows whispering in the garden, where they'll cut down avocado trees, chestnuts, lindens, araucarias, cypresses, the plum tree—she was under it when they came to get her, but they let her go because she scared them when she asked: "What do you have for my dinner tonight?"—and they'll destroy Brancusi's smooth-skinned golden bird dancing next to the water, which also reflects a cypress.

Gloria takes off her clothes. She turns her back to me, an unusual touch of modesty, as she bends over, on the other side of the bed, to pick up her nightshirt and start putting it on. Her flesh looks creased, greenish in this weird Moroccan electricity. How the years have destroyed her magnificent buttocks! The thighs, not at all like a Brancusi . . . I don't want to look at her, because the only real danger would be for her not to be like this: for the perfect Odalisque to come back to life in Tangier's tenuous light. What for? Isn't the street full of young mysterious glances, bodies moving sinuously under tunics that hide them, bodies that are keys to open my way into the night? The night is opening like a flower and gives off a perfume that may seem nauseating at first but, like the soap, ends up intoxicating us. Yes, I'm ready to slip out of my Western clothes and leave them here with my wife and my failure. Bijou will guide me through the narrow streets he knows as well as those in Sitges and all other labyrinths—the two of us like silhouettes of monks hiding race, age, condition, and taste under the brown djellaba—and he'll take me to look for something I crave, I don't know what it is, but today of course it's not the backside of a fifty-odd-year-old woman I've always seen going through the same routine: she lifts one arm to put on her nightgown and the nightgown slips down around her body, hiding it. I don't pick up my pajamas but my shirt. Gloria notices me putting it on. She smiles, she doesn't frown:

"What are you doing?"

"I'll have to go back down again. I forgot to tell the concierge something about the rental car. God knows how long these idiots will take to have it ready for me."

"Why don't you phone him from here?"

"No, if I go downstairs I can take care of anything I may have to sign."

"I don't see why you should have to bother."

She still hasn't frowned: any signs of uneasiness she may have she covers with her mask of cream. Then she lies down in bed to read Styron: I remember that we've also stolen this book from Pancho's place. But what importance can that theft have in the limitless night outside? Voices talking a strange gibberish go by under our window. On the corner, in the dark little café that smells of mint and is full of staring eyes—they're the only thing alive in that den under a heavy stillness it's hard to explain—Bijou, my accomplice, is waiting to lead me around: under his monk's cloak I see his blue eyes wink at me to follow him. Gloria smiles at me over the top of her open book, with the light dimmed, her body veiled by her nightgown. I must hurry or Bijou will go away. Buttoning my shirt, I explain:

"We have to leave day after tomorrow. I don't want to stay in Tangier forever."

"Why not?"

"Would you like to?"

"I don't know."

"So then?"

"All this moving around . . . if it weren't for Patrick's show . . ."

Hateful, glandular women whose natural instinct is to think first of all about their sons! It's all that counts for them. In the end, man's only function is to make them feel, from time to time, that their bodies—the only thing they possess, since a medieval synod deprived them forever of their right to a soul—are still desirable.

"Who cares about Patrick! Tangier is horrible!" I break in.

Over the top of her book, she looks at me, penetrating all the way through those amber eyes I stole from the beggar: she knows everything, there's no need to confess now. I mustn't fool myself: Gloria is the demanding embodiment of everything she pretends to reject about the bland middle class in which she was born and which she can't leave behind. No political worries, no cliché about the "psychoanalyzed and liberated woman" she offers as an image of herself can shake her out of her actual being.

"Why is it so horrible?" she asks me, closing her book to start a conversation and hold me back. "We might feel freer here. It's such a strange and cosmopolitan city! And since neither Sitges nor Tangier is Chile, and we can't live in Rome or Paris or London, we might as well live here. We'll always be out of the struggle. Patrick may be right and it's all the same. We could take up Islam, go native, and I'd wear a veil . . ."

"Don't make me laugh . . . from the Carrera School to Islam. . . ."

Gloria laughs and goes back to her book while I stuff my shirt into my trousers. Why doesn't she stop me? Why is she even suggesting, in a way, that she could do the same thing I'm about to do now and also lose her identity? Let her try to get in my way, to stop me and not let me leave, not let me go downstairs, lose myself, head for the place where the beggar is waiting and sink into his yellow eyes, as I once desired to sink into other golden eyes, into other arms hidden in a djellaba that was more sophisticated than this one because it was invented by Klimt! Gloria doesn't know how carefully I checked our way back here so I'd be able to return to the mosque's door. I'll find the beggar I'm going to be from now on because I'll stick a knife into him to let his soul escape. I'll be dispossessed, free of all its guilts: I the humiliated, the victim of injustice, not its agent. I'll be the one for whom revolutions will catch fire, yet not the one who commits himself to fight or defend the rights of others with his blood. No: I'll remain outside the struggle and outside history.

"I'll be back in ten minutes, dear."

"Okay, I won't turn the light out yet."

"Yes, don't, we have to trace the route on the map and figure out how many kilometers we'll be putting on the car."

"They say it's not worth spending a day in Tetuán."

"That's what I'm going to find out downstairs. . . . If it's not worth it, we'll drive straight to Xauen; they say the whole town is blue."

"Well, I hope so."

I'm all set to say goodbye, but it would sound too final and she'd suspect something. I watch the Odalisque, so calmly bent over her book, so confident that she doesn't even bother to raise her eyes to see me leave the room, she's so sure I'll be coming back in ten minutes.

6

NONE OF THE terrible stories going around about her are true: she is charming, generous, sensitive. But she's also shrewd and domineering despite her love of privacy. And she has read everything.

I've just come from lunch with Núria Monclús, just the two of us, in a restaurant as elegant as those I frequented as a teenager, traveling with my parents in Europe: in this one even the maître d' is courteous with Núria, who knows the waiters by name. We had some tiny frog's legs and for me an *endive braisée* a little less exquisite than those I can remember.

Núria is sharp and to the point, but only her bearing is majestic, for professional reasons, I suppose, to keep the importunate in line. This is what has set the rumor going that she's a despot. Not only was she excited about my novel, but, on a personal level, I believe that in her subtle way of handling things with great care she has made my novel a private bridge between us, something that almost seems a luxury I don't deserve. Will this friendship with

Núria perhaps be the first step toward other people who
live outside the world of failure?

She admired my novel, which she considers a tour de
force because I succeeded in working my way into the skin
of a character so different from myself, but confessed that
she felt there was something missing at the end. She asked
me to reread it once in order to "see it"—a phrase that
sounds so brilliant when Núria puts it between quotes
with her rather blunt diction—and notice that the threads
of the story were there but weren't all tied up . . . to add
something or cut something, it made no difference which:
like everything, it was only a question of proportion. We
talked about her, about me, about her old love for Marcelo
Chiriboga, which everyone knows about, but that flame
went out years, alas, so many years ago, leaving a friendship as consuming as the love. She advised me to turn in
the unfinished translation of *Middlemarch*—she'd arrange it
so the publisher would forget the advance, since it was the
same house interested in my book, presented by her as the
season's great new attraction—and to start work on another novel soon.

"We need novelists like you," she said. "This novel is
extraordinary, but the second one is always the ordeal by
fire."

What she liked most, what she found really incredible,
was this: in the end my narrator was not a shoddy but a
lost, trapped character; and as corollary to this compassion
for him, my stark treatment of the writer's wife, my not
trying to make her beautiful. But there was something
missing at the end; editors, who in general are not very
perceptive, would not notice this, she said, but she would,
she and the handful of people for whom literature was
written.

I'm writing this many kilometers and many months

away from that night in the Hotel El Minzah; everything has changed since then—has turned around, as it were.

Our return from Tangier was followed by a long lonely autumn in Sitges when a kind of order started to replace the Sargasso of frustrations suffered toward the end of our stay in Madrid. I avoided any compromising relationship, except with a skinny, scruffy black cat—the kind that bring bad luck—I had found in the street and taken home; I nursed and fed her until she turned into a lustrous mink, and then, as a gift, I bought her a rhinestone collar that makes her look like a queen: I baptized her Clotilde.

That fall was mellow, endless, and warm; with it the Mediterranean became itself again, with the sun stretched out like an animal sleeping on the empty beach and the blessing of those short days when I felt as safe as if I were in a little nest. When it's sunny and not windy, which has been the case almost every day this fall, I take a long slow walk on the Paseo Marítimo, wrapped in the shawl I wove during my depression in Pancho's apartment, as if I had known I was going to need it. The waves wash up quietly on the sand, the doors and windows of the summer houses are closed, and sounds come in very clearly from far off, because during this lonely season they travel long distances with nothing to dampen them. You see few people on the street during the week, and as soon as the sun hides itself I come back to our apartment, I snuggle up near the fire, and Clotilde curls up warmly in my lap while I write these pages and wait for Julio's return. With his absence because of his work—he's so taken up with it; he says Spaniards have no idea about English literature and there's a whole world he can open up for his students—he grants me the great gift of solitude.

During the off-season in Sitges no one has to put on a cheerful or sociable front and everybody accepts me as I am now: a tall woman with graying hair, neither short nor long, a little shy perhaps, but not hostile. Seeing me snap a breadstick over the endive, Núria observed that not only does she like the way my nails look without polish, because they bring out the slenderness of my hands, but also that my graying hair, shorter and more in place, makes me look younger.

"It's only a question of proportion and precision," she says.

Some Sunday mornings when I wander as far as Las Gaviotas, past the boats drawn up and overturned for repairs on the beach, and past acquaintances who seem slight now but who will eventually turn into lifelong friends, I feel everything becoming more peaceful, taking its place in this perspective that may be false or poetic but that I now have the courage to accept as my own. Pato used to shout, his face flushed, bursting with rage, that Julio wasn't an artist, that he was dogmatic and cruel. Julio isn't cruel, but I think that Pato's anger was partly justified when he described my husband as someone who only knows how to live within structures imposed on him from outside and can't create for himself the imaginary world that answers only to its own laws, the artist's world. That's why he's such a good professor: this interim one-year stint at the Autonomous University of Barcelona has made him be himself again, and his being away all day has given me back time to look after myself, an unexpected gift, a present just for me, to let me think of myself in a clear way, without the confusing fears I had in Madrid, and to "see myself" as someone apart from the family, because Julio needs me less and Pato not at all now that he's living with a French girl, who's really not much but is likable, in a house they themselves painted red like all the houses in Marrakesh.

Yes, every day was an autumnal gift, a small gift to do with as I pleased, like a jewel that was all mine, a brief, clear space between my late rising and the early close of day, when I stay home and wear something comfortable and long and warm and read and write until Julio comes home . . . a peaceful time for me, when I can "see myself," as Núria Monclús would say, between quotes. And while I read and write he gives his translation of *The Spoils of Poynton* its final touches. Is there something in common between it and the house on Rome Street—whose sale allows us to live a little better—between it and the sale and dispersion of its furniture that could be the furniture in Poynton? I've read Julio's translation: it's daring, creative, a masterpiece.

As I write this, I see that he's completely absorbed in revising, on this sunny Sunday in winter. I watch him and I feel the pinprick of something I don't know, something I never want to ask him about, because I want to respect that blank space that's his alone, that time unapproachably his, and it makes me think of Tangier with longing in spite of the new beautiful look of our terrace dressed up with plants the way Pancho Salvatierra showed us; he turned up here one fine day with a van full of furniture, decorative objects, tapestries, paintings—among them the triumphant *Portrait of Gloria Echeverría de Méndez*, which he brought me as a gift, after recovering it quite easily.

"Bolados is a good guy," he said. "He gave Julio the money because he saw how desperate he looked, and he kept the painting for the time being, on deposit. It would pay off; he knew that with the painting he would get through to me. And he called me to tell me he had it, the day after I returned to Madrid; I don't know how he found out, because I came back incognito, the way people do now. He thinks he's on the trail of the painting Bijou stole.

We do good business together. . . . Take that away from
there, Gloria, you don't know a thing about this, you put
too much frilly stuff on top of everything, darling. You
dress beautifully, but you shouldn't mix one thing with
another, you have no idea how to decorate a house. . . ."

All this, of course, after what seemed to me hundreds of
collect calls to and from Madrid, of accusations, insults,
threats of lawsuits, words in our behalf from Katy and
Carlos Minelbaum and Begonia, tears and vows of eternal
friendship. In the meantime, I think back with some relief
of what Pancho told me about my lack of taste in decorat-
ing a house: I am not always right, something I'd never
have admitted before that night in Tangier, though I believe it had been hatching during my near-dementia in
Pancho's house, where I filled the green light of the garden
next door with fantasies of a complete peace dangerously
beyond reach, peace in which my sick mind took refuge so
that it could go on being sick.

Pancho referred to the unaccountable suicide of the poor
young blonde, and I think that perhaps she was never more
than a fantasy whose clue can be found in Klimt's *Embrace*
and in a pair of golden eyes wide open behind clusters of
myrtle: Pancho, who insists that poor Monika Pinell de
Bray was just a run-of-the-mill American, says that she
had washed-out blue eyes. No, Monika Pinell de Bray was
not omnipotent, as I believed her to be.

When we came back here, I started filling notebooks
with my laments and conjectures built up around that
phantom. And when Julio would leave me to go to work, I
would realize that I could not exact everything from him
or from myself. I wrote down my complaints in my diary,
so heartrending that I can't draw up the courage to reread
it now; but rereading it then to stir up my resentment and
writing and rewriting those pages, going back over them

again and again, I was eventually able to sort out everything during the long spell the seasons next to the Mediterranean have conceded me, sorting out my real image,
Julio's, the image of our marriage, until I found out that if
this scrutiny was ever to take on the force of reality, I
would have to create something outside myself that
would, however, also include me so that I could "see"
myself: a mirror where others could also "see" themselves,
an object that I and others could contemplate outside of
ourselves, even if my share is now in a minor tone.

That night at the Hotel El Minzah, I didn't have to take
my eyes off my book to see him leave the room, but I was
dead certain—with a kind of wishful thinking thrown
in?—that Julio would never come back. Dry-eyed, under
my breath, I said: "Goodbye."

And overcome by my furious wish that this would come
true, I hurled my book at the other bed. Let him go to hell.
Let him get lost for good. Let him kill himself. Let him
leave me in peace with his lies about Núria Monclús's
enthusiasm and his sudden windfall. Let him no longer
stop me from having a few stiff drinks whenever I felt like
it, no longer spy on me or get so nervous whenever he saw
I felt like getting drunk, one of my few pleasures—or so I
felt then—that he doesn't ration. Let him stop accusing me
of not bringing in money and making Patrick run away
from our apartment in Sitges because I always kept it such
a mess. Yes, I confess that I even let out a sigh of relief,
thinking he might commit suicide and that I'd be free.

Then I remembered, anxiously, the classic case of the
husband who tells his wife he's going down to the bar to
buy cigarettes and never comes back. I had noticed that he
was all keyed up during our walk through the Zoco, telling me too many stories about people whose identity I
wasn't always sure of, too often drawing my attention to

just anything, to the way the tangerines in the stores were arranged in mounds, to some Berber boy whose slender figure he pointed out, to the tunics on sale, to the provocative walk of some of the veiled women. I know that after twenty-odd years of marriage for us, no image is ever complete until we have shared it: that may have been one of the many errors in our union. But there's usually a separation in time between the act of perceiving and the act of telling and comparing and sharing that generally follows later on.

On our short tour of the Zoco he seemed to be overacting, almost vulgar, as if he were determined to grip my attention and keep me from thinking about what perhaps he imagined I might think or feel. Julio didn't know that the contrition and the confession tormenting him weren't necessary; as soon as I heard the telephone ringing in Madrid and he went out to answer it in the living room "so as not to wake me," I used a typically feminine ruse and did what any woman would who has no other weapon for survival except these ruses: I picked up the bedroom phone on my night table and listened to his entire conversation with Núria, in which she condemned his novel and closed all doors to him. I must confess that I did it, because bogged down in the Sargasso of my mind and vaguely and grudgingly filled with fear, I suspected other things, I saw phantoms, fancies that replaced reality completely: a call from Monika Pinell de Bray—whose name I didn't know then—to meet him and invite him, a potbellied Bacchus, to take part in an orgy with young people by the pool, from which I'd be left out; or a blinding crush on Bijou, who is intelligent but doesn't have a heart or any feeling, a fling that wouldn't have upset me in the least; or a secret love affair with Katy, which, on the other hand, would have upset me very much: anyway, from my sick woman's stubborn silence next to the window, I saw only fictive images, a flotsam and jetsam, everything in turmoil, a prey of the terrifying actuality of my Sargasso Sea. And I saw him—I know now that both my illness and his death at the hands of Núria Monclús accounted for this—growing more tense each day, as things came to a head.

It was plain that his great excitement in the Zoco was only an offshoot of this mental state and the beginning of his effort to confess, with no need for it, since I knew everything. I had talked to Sebastian a thousand times and had told him I couldn't take the chance of trying to make Julio sell the house, a decision he had to make himself; if I did, I'd have to bear his resentment for his loss the rest of my life, and I'd had my share of resentments. But it was my cruel idea to send Julio the photocopies of all the bills and outstanding debts to force a decision he'd eventually have to make; Julio may be unreasonable under emotional pressures, but he's not crazy, and I had always been sure that the house would be sold. I had imagined that the money for our trip was a top-secret loan from Carlos Minelbaum, with whom he has one of those longstanding relationships between men that no woman can ever fathom.

I want to make this very clear: when I found out that Núria Monclús had turned down his novel, I felt compassion and sorrow for Julio along with a good dose of vengeful pleasure at the failure of the male in the family, whose duty it is to succeed and save its members from poverty and obscurity; this is a mission before society that we both despise but still have to depend on. This final defeat of Julio's helped me more than anything to come out of my depression: I needed to see him less strong. Wasn't Julio paying with his failure for my father's mistake in taking me out of the nuns' school in my fourth year, when I was the

first in class and dreamed of becoming a doctor? Didn't
this serve to placate my grudge against him for not sending
me to Harvard as he would have sent my brother, if I'd had
one, and as he didn't send any of my sisters, whose intel-
ligence was promptly buried under the dust of conventional husbands and consumer lives? Instead of educating
us he showed us off in the ephemeral salons of Europe that
we were steered into by his diplomat's life. My envy of
Julio's thinking, formed by his education, and of his capacity to "do" things, no matter what they were or how they
turned out, died there: in my disgusting, spiteful, resentful
joy at his failure—that was sinking us all—at the hands of a
woman whose fingertips were stained with the blood of
failures like my husband and who thus avenged all women
like me. Yes, that's the way it was, or at least that's how it
was seen by my understandably envious imagination,
which went back a long way and was now asking amends
for many things.

And yet my anger died down the minute Julio closed the
door: all I had needed was the impulse to throw my book
at the other bed. I remained lying there for a long time
without stirring, nailed to the bed by my delight, but it
soon started turning into fear.

What was I to do if Julio didn't come back? Return to
Chile? No. That was out of the question. Pato wouldn't
want to go back to a reality we hadn't been able to pass on
to him, and for me returning meant dependence on my
three sisters and my brothers-in-law, who were partial to
the regime. No. Not Chile. There was a barrier around the
country, and it could be knocked down only with a deter-
mination to fight that I didn't have. I wouldn't have known
where to start doing something about it. No, Chile without Pato, without Julio, was now out. A fifty-year-old
woman alone, without money or a profession, no longer

good-looking but still able-bodied, is one of the most obsessively pathetic and ridiculous sights I can think of.

Sitges? In the fall, I remembered, it was a gentle sea resort, solitary and peaceful, and winter was timorous, insinuating, full of light and sea gulls. Perhaps I could organize something to help exiles with less experience and means than I? Translations? A small income that Sebastian, when he heard about Julio's desertion, would send me every month, the product of investments made with our portion of the sale of the house on Rome Street? Peace. To be myself, at last, not just an incomplete part of what Lawrence Durrell wrongly calls "that wonderful two-headed animal that is a good marriage," an ideal that served me for such a long time to support my marriage. The freedom that results from being a victim and being deserted, not to be responsible for my actions to anyone but myself. Not to have to account for anything.

"And why didn't you leave Julio instead of waiting for him to leave you, since solitude appealed to you so much?" Núria asked me sharply, tearing apart a frog's fragile structure with her carnivorous teeth.

I thought it over for a while, yet it's possible that it was nothing but a collage of impressions and memories run together in just one second full of emotions, before I said one word:

"Odalisque."

Núria asked me to explain. Simple:

"The Odalisque I'm so proud of doesn't exist except in Julio's memory and imagination; even now, he sometimes succeeds in bringing back to life that Odalisque of long ago, with his embrace that evokes her waist, his caresses of not this but the other satinlike skin and the curves of her thigh once modulated with the eloquence of a sure line but somewhat blurred now. Who else, except Julio, can restore the body I had then and make that Odalisque of the past real? A kiss, a towel wrapped around my head, is enough."

"What did you do then?" Núria asked.

"When?"

"After he left the bedroom."

"I turned out the light. Down below, outside the hotel, I could hear car horns howling in Moroccan, and once in a while voices I couldn't understand would lash out with what I made out to be swear words. A mixture of aromas from the Zoco floated up even into that sheltered room: cumin, orange blossom. What had Julio gone out for? He had left to disappear forever, or perhaps not forever, in the Kasbah; a good reason for his nervous excitement during our tour. And in the dark, I couldn't help seeing how hard it must seem to him to have me face the truth and confess to me what I already knew, your verdict on his novel about those six days in prison, and for him to realize that in his weak writer's hands those days had left nothing but a hazy record of injustice."

"Oblivion . . ." Núria murmured. "When the dust settles on the recent ruins of great collective tragedies, it covers them with a gray layer of oblivion. Governments are then free to act as they please, protected by the forgetfulness of the great powers that are openly critical of those governments but are also implicated in the tragedy. Other tragedies continue after that, other revolutions in other places, other wars that gradually take over the front pages of newspapers and banish those tragedies we call 'ours' to the last pages, where nobody reads about them. So naturally no publishing house wants to buy a mediocre novel describing part of the tragedy that has gone out of fashion, except for a handful of people. . . ."

"Julio hit somebody once for saying that. That was when my depression started: I couldn't pack or unpack a suitcase, or get up in the morning; any act that had to do with me became, in a paranoid way, an offense or a theft or a failure to appreciate my value or a betrayal. Lassitude, sadness, a sadness that turned to mutism, almost insanity, in Madrid. . . ."

"And what brought you out of it?"

"A cat rubbing up against my chin. And the fact that among all the greenery falling like rain over the brilliant lawn of the Duke's garden I was able to pick out someone as dazzling as a Brancusi: I owe a lot to poor Monika Pinell de Bray. Her death probably makes me suffer more than it does the 'handsome brute,' who'll soon forget her; but I never will: this is, after all, her novel, the novel of the phantom suggested to me when I saw her in the garden, which perhaps if I saw it now wouldn't seem so unforgettable. All of you—you, she, Julio—are only reflections in me, in our changing subjective visions. I can't help suffering because of Monika Pinell's suicide, the real and the imagined girl: Brancusi's perfections should be eternal and joyful."

Núria, who is common sense itself, didn't ask me what I thought Julio had gone out to do, disappearing into the Kasbah in Tangier, wandering about in those fetid yet fragrant Moorish streets that can destroy you. This is the last effort I must make for my peace of mind: to stop that stretch of silence in Julio's life from hurting me, to accept its obscurity, its secret, its turbidity, to live together without tormenting each other or myself, as I still do, without wanting to.

One thing troubled me more than anything else that evening in the Zoco: as we walked along the narrow streets, Julio mentioned Bijou almost obsessively. "If Bijou were here he'd tell us . . ." "Bijou is a delinquent who believes all other delinquents are as naive as little kids . . ."

"I'm sure Bijou could show us the way. . . ." And I'm sure he doesn't know how many times he repeated Bijou's name. Perhaps that image of Bijou, blond, unscrupulous, tough, much tougher at his age than Julio and I now, his ambiguous adolescent figure pointing to the infinite possibilities open to a human being, was what tempted Julio to go in search of that chimera or some dangerous substitute that would help him to vanish into any one or several of the labyrinthine possibilities that exist in each of us.

In the minutes after he disappeared from the hotel, I was sure that I would never see Julio again. With my arms behind my head, in the dark, left to myself, I felt the tears welling in my eyes. What would Julio turn into? Into the beggar, who I'm not even sure he saw, lying at the door of the mosque, while I'd turn into a lonely, mature Latin American woman who has taken up translating or the craft of weaving in Sitges? I tried to sleep and not go on torturing myself thinking about such horrible possibilities. But I spent hours tossing in bed, once more on the brink of the sick fancy that replaces reality in an absolute way, thinking of the unknown torments that were making Julio pay for his weakness, for not being man enough to accept and acknowledge his defeat.

"And for not having any talent," Núria added.

I had to think it over before accepting this hard verdict:

"And for not having any talent," I finally mustered the courage to agree, adding: "Of course, one can very well live on as a writer who is a failure."

"Don't fool yourself: I know them too well. It's hell."

"I don't agree. It was only that night, when I saw that you can also live as the wife of a writer who has failed, only then was I able to understand and accept Julio's desire to lose himself, it didn't matter where, that night or even longer. That's why suddenly, very late, at the first light of dawn, I made up my mind what to do."

"What did you do?"

"I dressed quickly, but not to go looking for him. Or lose myself in the Kasbah too. No, I went down to see the concierge, who was asleep with his head on the glass counter. I asked him for an envelope. I stuck his passport in it, Julio's I mean, with a very large sum of money and his return airplane ticket. I added a note: 'I'll wait for you in Sitges. Gloria.' I asked the concierge to call the travel agency as soon as it opened and change my return flight to Spain for the following day at noon. And to leave my husband's ticket open and give it to him when he came back in a few days, or if he hadn't claimed it within a week, to give it to the Spanish consul, whom I'd inform about it. He was to wake me the next morning at ten so I could catch the return flight at noon.

" 'Nothing else, madame?' the concierge asked me.

" 'Nothing,' I answered.

"I went up to my room and packed my suitcase as well as his, leaving his ready to take down next morning and give to the concierge."

"And were you able to sleep?" Núria asked me.

"I took ten milligrams of Valium; it was strictly forbidden, but I had managed to hide a little bottle of it, and I was soon dead asleep. Telling it now, all this seems very rational, something that had nothing to do with the despair I was then feeling as an aftereffect of my breakdown in Madrid. It's not easy to find yourself forced to face a whole new way of living, when you're a woman who's alone and isn't quite sure what or who she is."

"Of course, in Sitges, with the help of your obsessive notebooks, you were able to find a solution."

"It's not a solution, but it helps me to go on and not think constantly about how destructive it is to be useless. That in itself is plenty."

"I envy you."

Not ready for this, I looked at Núria.

"Are you laughing at me?"

She actually laughed then: "Bijou was right: the headless Etruscans are not statues, they're still alive, and they like, even need, people to greet them when they come in and to say goodbye with respect. I'd like to take a look at your notebooks, the diary you were writing in Sitges."

I shook my head.

"We all have a right to our secrets, and mine are there. No, you can't look at them. I myself don't even dare open and reread them, not even to learn how to write my second novel. . . . I don't want to know the elements that made me drop my political fervor and accept my 'minor tone' that might then turn out to be a mere imitation of the 'major tone,' like Julio's in the last version of his novel. It's not that I'm no longer politically restless, especially about Chile. I'd do anything to change the situation in my country. But I know this has nothing to do with literature, at least with my literature, I mean. I assumed this ambivalence, studying my illness in Madrid with my notebooks in Sitges, and I discovered that it had been my prison. And assuming a 'minor tone' may have been my salvation. As later on, after the Zoco, Julio assumed his own tone, that of a professor of literature, after his disaster with his bad novel, which had been his prison or his illness, and was in a way parallel to mine. Yes, the second novel is the important one."

"I agree that you shouldn't show me your notebooks, but you haven't finished telling me . . ."

"Wait . . . I'll tell you what I can, I mean, everything I know. When the phone rang in the morning and woke me,

I discovered that I couldn't sit up in bed, I seemed to be weighed down, physically tied to the bed. The weight I felt was Julio's arms around me; I could feel his familiar breathing on my neck, behind my left ear. I freed myself from his arms to reach for the telephone. The concierge told me that the gentleman had arrived at six in the morning but he had thought it better not to hand him the envelope.

" 'Was I right, madame?' he asked.

" 'Quite right,' I answered."

"An excellent concierge," Núria remarked. "Good enough to hire for my agency."

" 'Does madame still want me to confirm the flight at noon on Air Maroc?'

" 'No, no, thank you, leave it open, and please check with Avis, yes, the car for today at four instead of tomorrow.'

" 'Very well, madame!' "

"Everything perfect," Núria exclaimed, fascinated, especially at the concierge's efficiency.

"And I hung up," I continued. "And like every woman whose husband comes to bed after a night on the town, I smelled his breath, his face, to see if there was any sign of alcohol, kif, or perfume that wasn't mine: nothing. Besides, what would be the good of knowing? I tiptoed out of bed, opened our bedroom door, and put up the 'Please do not disturb' sign for the maid's benefit. I went back to bed, pressing up very close to his body, with my back to him, he behind, I in front, in parallel semifetal positions, and I wrapped his arms, heavy with sleep, around me. I fell asleep at once."

Núria laughed, I'd say it was almost a horselaugh if it hadn't been so well controlled; it was certainly her equivalent of a horselaugh. She was enjoying herself very much.

"*Please do not disturb!* What an ironical happy ending for such a bitter novel!"

"What?"

"Well, isn't this the missing chapter, the one you haven't written?" Núria Monclús asked.

About the Author

Born in 1924, José Donoso is recognized as one of the greatest writers of the South American Boom generation. His first novel translated into English, *Coronation*, won the William Faulkner Foundation Prize in 1962. Donoso lived eighteen years out of Chile, first in the United States, then in Spain; he has since returned. He is the author of short stories, essays, and novels, including the highly praised *The Obscene Bird of the Night* (1973), *A House in the Country* (1983), and *Curfew* (1988).